Inseparable

Also by Dora Heldt:
Life after Forty
Vacation with Dad (forthcoming)
Aunt Inge's Secret Escape (forthcoming)

Inseparable

DORA HELDT

TRANSLATED BY Jamie Lee Searle

PUBLISHED BY
amazoncrossing

Text copyright © 2006 Deutscher Taschenbuch Verlag GmbH & Co. KG
English translation copyright © 2011 Amazon Content Services
All rights reserved.
Printed in the United States of America.

Inseparable was first published in 2008 by Deutscher Taschenbuch Verlag GmbH & Co. KG as *Unzertrennlich*. Translated from German by Jamie Lee Searle. Published in English by AmazonCrossing in 2011.

Published by AmazonCrossing
P.O. Box 400818
Las Vegas, NV 89140

ISBN-13: 978-1611090222
ISBN-10: 1611090229
Library of Congress Control Number: 2010919356

For Rainer, and not just for the editing;
for those who are far away; and for my Sylt "family,"
without whom I wouldn't have so much faith in myself.

Prologue

November 10, Hamburg

Forty-four years old. It had to be a joke. Christine leaned in closer to the mirror and stared at her eyes. They were still blue. Still the same eyes she'd had at age six, age twelve, twenty, thirty. She scrunched them up slightly. That was the difference. Lines. That half circle stretching from one corner of the eye to the other, radial and unrelenting. Christine raised her eyebrows. The lines were still there. Forty-four. She took a deep breath, reached for her eye shadow, and used a makeup brush to glide silvery-gray powder over her eyelids. Silver-gray shadow gave you a luminous look. At least, that's what the brand promised. Allegedly, it drew attention above the eyes so you didn't notice the lines under them. After the powder came eyeliner. At least her hands hadn't started shaking yet. Christine had been putting eyeliner on every morning for the last twenty-four years. She imagined it all forming one continuous line, and wondered whether she had drawn a line all the way around the world by now. It was more than likely. The last step was to put mascara on her lashes, two coats on each side. Most women opened their mouths while putting mascara on, which looked totally dumb, and there was no obvious reason to do so. Christine always forced herself to keep her lips closed, even when no one was watching. It was a matter of discipline. She stepped back from the mirror and looked herself over. Her hair was dyed a little too dark, which made her look pale but also made her eyes look bluer, which hopefully detracted from the lines. She couldn't help but laugh; how silly was she? It wasn't as if it mattered that much.

When her mother was forty-four, Christine was twenty-one; her brother Georg, eighteen; and Ines, her sister, fourteen. For her mother Charlotte's forty-fourth birthday, her kids had given her an electric knife as a present. With three blades. Not perfume, not underwear, but a kitchen appliance. Christine silently asked for her forgiveness. Although…had it actually been such a bad choice? She would have to ask her. If she was miffed at the time, she certainly hadn't shown it. Perhaps that's how you get when you're a mother. Thankful and uncritical.

That would never happen to Christine now. That ship had sailed. Forty-four, divorced, no children, no pets. Successful in her career, but privately, her life was pretty average.

After her divorce she had thrown herself into her work. She worked for a big publishing house, started at eight in the morning, left at seven in the evening, went to yoga once a week, sometimes went out to dinner with colleagues, and in her free time wrote a column for a city magazine. Everything was planned, organized, and above all, peaceful. Although sometimes it was admittedly a little dull, too. But she didn't really mind that; she wasn't keen on surprises. Her brother Georg said she was a control freak, and he was right: she liked to keep her life in order. She'd had

enough experience of having to dance to someone el.
tune. Today was her forty-fourth birthday. By now she knew
what she *didn't* want.

The doorbell rang, interrupting her thoughts. At the
very same moment, the door was flung open and Dorothea
called her name. They had been close friends for years and
now lived in apartments opposite one another. Each of them
had the key to the other's. Ringing the bell before coming
in was an unwritten agreement. A sign of respect for each
other's private space, no more than that. Recently, however,
the time span between ringing and coming in had become
so brief that Christine wouldn't have had time to hide away
anything private. Whatever that might have been.

"I'm almost ready, Dorothea, pour yourself a glass of
champagne while you wait. It's in the fridge."

Christine applied her lipstick then put it in her purse.
Dorothea was standing in the hallway in her coat and looking at her expectantly. She'd already wished her a happy
birthday when they'd had a quick coffee together here earlier that morning. A table was booked for ten people at the
Italian restaurant around the corner in half an hour's time.
Christine's brother and sister, a few colleagues and friends:
the usual crowd.

Christine's enthusiasm for birthdays was limited, at least
when it came to her own. Dorothea was wearing a new skirt
under her coat, green, velvet; a low-cut top to go with it; and
heels to top it all off. Christine's look was just as surprised
as the one Dorothea was giving her. Dorothea reacted more
quickly.

"Come on, it's your birthday, do you really have to wear
jeans and a gray roll-neck sweater?"

"Firstly, I'm cold. Secondly, the pullover is new and was expensive; thirdly, we're only going to the Italian place; and fourthly, I don't understand why you're so dolled up. But if it makes you feel better I'll put a blouse on and freeze my butt off for you."

Dorothea rolled her eyes. "So, first of all, it's cold in here because you've got all the windows open; secondly, you can't tell the pullover's new because it looks exactly like the other three you already have; thirdly, we have a small change of plans when it comes to the Italian place; and fourthly, I'm dolled up because it's your birthday, sweetie."

Christine stared at Dorothea. "What do you mean, a small change of plans?"

Dorothea ran her hands through her dark locks in front of the big mirror.

"I mean, we're not going to the Italian place anymore. Now don't get all worked up, just relax."

She looked at Christine, who was looking bewildered, in the mirror. There was a good chance she would get worked up. And she did.

"Have you gone mad? I've booked the table, preordered the food, everyone will be there at eight, and you want me to just blow that all off? Are you crazy?"

Dorothea looked at herself in the mirror, calm as a cucumber, and wiped a little smudge of mascara away from the corner of her eye.

"It's fine," she said. "I canceled the reservation already and planned something even better. So put something chic on and let's get going. I'm driving."

Christine was lost for words. She couldn't stand birthdays, and she hated surprises just as much as she did people changing existing plans. Dorothea knew that. And despite that she was doing something like this on the spur of the moment. Christine tried to stop herself from getting annoyed and took a deep breath.

"OK, fine, I'll go and put a blouse on. But you know I find this kind of thing silly."

She disappeared into the bedroom. Dorothea watched her go, feeling a prick of doubt. *It'll be fun*, she told herself.

Ten minutes later they were sitting in Dorothea's Mini. Christine had changed her sweater for a black blouse and had a black blazer on over the top. She tried to get Dorothea to spill the beans on where they were driving to and what was going on, asking whether she had managed to get in touch with everyone about the change of plans.

Dorothea just smiled, waving her questions aside.

"Just wait and see. Everything will be great. And besides, it's boring going to the same old Italian restaurant all the time."

Christine concentrated on the street signs and tried to figure out where Dorothea was driving them. After a while, she gave up. Her imagination ran wild. She had images of those awful, cringe-worthy male strip shows, so popular for girls' nights out, particularly where bachelorette parties were concerned. But she wasn't getting married the next day, it was her forty-fourth birthday; surely that couldn't be reason to go? Or could it? Please God, no.

"Just tell me this. We're not going to one of those weird girls' shows with the 'California Dreamboys' or something, are we?"

Dorothea looked at her, amazed, and laughed loudly.

"Oh God, that wasn't what you really wanted was it? Well, you should've told me—I could have organized it." She kept on laughing. "What a shame you didn't say something sooner."

Christine was relieved and tried to dig deeper: "Come on, Dorothea, just give me a hint."

"No, we're almost there. And it's nothing bad. Completely the opposite, in fact, so just chill out."

The word *surprise* was lingering in Christine's mind, bold and italicized. Dorothea worked in television. A thought suddenly came into her head. And a name along with it: Kai Pflaume. One of those do-gooders who bring quarrelling couples and long-lost friends back together. In front of millions of viewers. Oh God. The faces of her ex-boyfriends came into her mind in slow motion. First Bernd, her exhusband, followed closely by Holger, Denis, and oh God, Michael. An appalling thought. Christine shook herself and looked at Dorothea. She wouldn't do that to her, not ever. Would she? She took a deep breath but didn't dare ask.

Dorothea turned off toward the harbor. Christine felt herself start to relax a little. It was one of her favorite parts of Hamburg. In the last few years, lots of great restaurants and clubs had opened up here. Perhaps Dorothea really had just wanted to find a different venue. But she could have just said that, if that were the case. No, there must be something else.

Dorothea drove into the restaurant parking lot of Indochine.

From outside it looked very nice, and the parking lot was full. Dorothea turned the ignition off and beamed at Christine.

"So, here we are. Good luck!"

When she saw Christine's shocked face, she laughed and nudged her with her elbow. "Happy birthday, we're going to have a great evening."

Christine followed her up the stairs. As they neared the entrance, Dorothea let Christine go in front. A handsome waiter met them at the door and led them to a side room. Then, suddenly, a chorus of twenty people started singing "Happy Birthday." Christine stood speechless before them, looking at all the faces in bewilderment, and didn't know whether to laugh or scream.

Seven months earlier: April, Hamburg

Each year, in springtime, there's a day when you suddenly notice that winter has gone. Christine had already felt it that morning when she rode off to the publishing house on her bike. The air was different, hardly anyone was wearing a hat, and the faces of the people she passed by looked cheerful. There was a springlike mood at work, too; even the eternally grumpy Mr. Schlüter seemed to give Christine a smile as she came in. The window was wide open in her office, and a bunch of tulips stood on Gabi's desk.

Christine had been working for the publishing house for almost three years now, the same one she had previously worked for as a traveling rep. Gabi had told her back then that there was a vacancy in-house. Christine, who had had enough of the endless journeys and all the nights in hotel rooms, had applied immediately. She got the job, not least because Gabi, who had been there for ten years, knew the personnel manager well and had given Christine a glowing recommendation.

They had shared an office ever since. Gabi was a great colleague. They had similar working habits: both drank coffee, kept private chatter down to a minimum, and had settled into a friendly way of sharing the space.

Gabi looked up as Christine came in the door.

"Good morning! Well, we did it! This horrible winter is finally over. Or what did the groundhog say?"

"What are you implying: that I can feel the seasons turning in my old bones or something?"

Gabi laughed. "Well, my granddad could; he could even predict the wind speed."

"Charming, thanks." Christine sat down at her desk and started to look through the mail. On top was a note: *Call Ruth!*

Ruth was the editor of the city magazine *Kult*, which was published by the imprint Christine worked for. Ruth was as loud and in-your-face as Gabi was reserved and quiet. The two of them had done an apprenticeship together in the publishing house and had been friends ever since—despite being like apples and oranges.

Two years ago Ruth and Christine had had a debate at the Christmas party about whether there was any point to regular columns. Christine liked them; she always bought *Zeit* just to read Harald Martenstein. But Ruth thought they were unnecessary and outdated. So they had made a bet. Christine would write a column about single women over New Year's, and Ruth would print it in *Kult*. If there were more than five letters sent in by readers about it, Ruth would have to make stuffed cabbage roulade for Christine. It seemed there were masses of single women who were at a loss over New Year's, or in any case, a large number of them had written in. So Ruth had to keep her side of the bet.

Christine referred to it as the biggest mess that was ever made in her kitchen. But she polished off three roulades with schnapps to wash it all down and had been writing a monthly column ever since. Ruth set the subject matter. And never made roulade again.

Christine dialed and heard Ruth's voice after two rings.

"Hi, Ruth, I had a message to call you."

"Oh, Christine, wonderful. So, I've decided on the topic for the May edition. Not a very original one, perhaps, but it's all about the target audience at the end of the day. I'd like you to write something about first love. After all, it's spring now. And on the topic of spring, given the weather today I think we should kick off the Alster season tonight. Five o'clock at Prüsse? It is Friday after all."

"That sounds good. I'll ask Gabi if she wants to come. Gabi? Prüsse? OK, she's nodding energetically and working quicker already. See you later!"

• ● •

The café on the Außenalster Lake was one of the most popular meeting places in the area for after-work drinks. Luckily though, it wasn't such a cult destination that it got too packed with people.

Ruth was already sat at a table on the small wooden terrace as Christine and Gabi walked over the footbridge. She looked up as she heard their steps, pushed her reading glasses up into her hair, and laid her notes aside. Then she stood up and flung her arms out theatrically to distribute the obligatory girlish kisses. Her voice jumped an octave higher.

"Hello, darlings! How wonderful to see you."

Christine cringed inwardly. She really liked Ruth and found her really funny, at least when they were alone. But when she was in company, she fulfilled all the clichés it was possible to have about women. She was in her early thirties, somewhere between slim and skinny; her shoulder-length hair was highlighted with blond streaks and usually held in place by sunglasses. Since last winter she'd needed reading glasses, but Christine suspected they weren't actually prescription but just plain glass, their main function being to keep her hair in place until sunglasses season came around again. As Ruth hugged and kissed Gabi, Christine quickly sat down, managing to skip the heartrending greeting.

That's just how girls are, she thought, making an effort to smile at Ruth. After all, she was delightful really.

After their orders had been taken, Ruth settled back down and pulled notes back toward her. She looked at the others.

"I'm in the midst of hectic planning. My best friend is getting married next month, I'm maid of honor, of course, and I want to organize something really special for her. So I'm wracking my brains trying to think of ideas. Any thoughts?"

Christine's response didn't exactly answer her question. "You don't even need a maid of honor nowadays."

"Yes, but it's symbolic. You bring your best friend to the altar. After sharing so much, it's about being there on the most wonderful day of her life."

Christine wrinkled her forehead. "You can't be serious! You read too many glossy magazines. The most wonderful day in a woman's..."

She was interrupted by her cell phone ringing. As she pulled it out of her jacket pocket, she tried to finish off her sentence.

"...in a woman's life, that's nonsense. Yes, hello? Luise, you can come join us. I'm with Ruth and Gabi; we're talking about weddings, and I'm explaining to Ruth how you make paper flowers for the door wreaths."

While Ruth looked on, baffled, Gabi started to laugh.

"That's right; Christine got married in the countryside. Ruth, you'll be able to get loads of tips on traditions and customs."

Christine finished talking to Luise. She put her phone back in her pocket and said: "She's coming."

Luise worked for the same publishing house, but as a rep. She handled the bookstores between Flensburg and Göttingen, promoting new titles to them.

She had known Christine for a long time as a colleague. After Christine moved to Hamburg to get over her divorce, Luise had provided emotional first aid. Once Christine was through the worst, Luise separated from her boyfriend. By that time, they were well rehearsed in tackling the problem, and they'd been close ever since.

Ruth piped up again: "What is it that you find so silly about it? I mean, you got married once, too! Didn't you celebrate and have a good time?"

Pictures ran through Christine's mind. Her ex-husband, Bernd; Antje and Adrian, the witnesses; her in-laws; neighbors with schnapps glasses in front of the wreath-covered front door; the expensive jazz band, which had finally consented to play the old German folk song "Das alte Försterhaus" for the guests. She shrugged her shoulders.

"Sure we did, for three whole days even. We had a big party in the country. But it didn't do much good."

Gabi waved her comment away. "Whether a marriage goes down the tubes or not has nothing to do with the party. I'm sure it was really fun, the celebration I mean. What did the guests organize for you? Go on, just give Ruth a few ideas."

"Yes, please do." Ruth picked up her pen and looked at Christine expectantly. "For example, what did your best friend do?"

"Well, on that particular day, she hadn't done anything yet."

Christine swatted away an invisible fly and wondered if she should continue. Gabi made the decision for her.

"Doves," she said dreamily. "Why don't you arrange to have some white doves and release them in front of the church?"

"I don't know, isn't that a bit much? It's not like she's getting married in front of the paparazzi from *People* magazine."

Christine laughed. "And there's always the danger that the damn things will shit all over her bridal gown."

Gabi shook her head. "You're not taking it seriously, Christine. And besides, that would be good luck anyway."

"And give you stains you'll never be able to get out. Not that it really matters, because no one ever wears the dress again anyway."

"Ladies, please, can I get one real idea from you? Christine, tell me what yours was like. You've done it all. And I'm sure you enjoyed the surprises your friends arranged for you. Did you have a wedding newsletter?"

Christine saw Antje in front of her. Antje in a lime-green outfit, the skirt a little too tight over the hips, a stack of wedding newsletters under her arm. That "I'm-your-best-friend" smile on her face.

"For God's sake," she said quickly. "They're always full of silly recipes and botched crosswords. They're not even funny anymore." She thought for a moment. "At ours we had a song, they changed the lyrics of 'On the North Sea Coast' to 'When Tina and Bernd kissed.' That was the kind of thing our friends went in for. If you like your friend, then spare her anything like that. She'll be eternally grateful."

"Who will be grateful to whom?"

Luise had come up to the table without the others noticing, and was standing behind Christine's chair. Ruth jumped up immediately to start the kissing campaign all over again. Even Gabi couldn't restrain herself from joining in. Christine could, and watched with a rather mocking expression. One minute and six kisses later, all three of them were back in their seats. Luise put her hand on Christine's arm briefly. She knew her well.

Ruth brought Luise up to speed on their conversation.

"My best friend Hanna is getting married; I'm the maid of honor and want to think of something fun to arrange for the wedding day. And our friend here, Christine, who had a three-day-long party out in the country and presumably a great deal of fuss, is just ridiculing everything instead of giving me some great ideas."

Luise looked bemused. "But Christine's been divorced for five years."

Gabi rolled her eyes in mock despair.

"Yes, but to get divorced you have to have gotten married at some point. My dear, it's not about the marriage, it's about the wedding. The party."

Luise still looked so confused that Christine had to laugh. "Come on, we'd need to explain the whole concept of country weddings to Luise before anything else. So where were you today?"

Luise pulled her cigarettes out of her enormous purse. "In Bremen, but I only had three appointments. It was good."

She winked at Christine. Christine felt herself blush. Richard lived in Bremen. Luise was one of the very few who knew she was having an affair.

"What? What's in Bremen?" Ruth rarely missed a trick. She looked at Christine curiously.

"Oh, nothing. It's just that Bremen used to be my favorite when I was a rep. That's all."

She reached for her coffee cup, took a sip, put it down again, and managed to compose herself in the meantime. "So, back to this wedding. I don't have anything against getting married in itself. But these made-up songs, sanctimonious speeches, and the games, it all seems, well...a little pathetic. And hardly any of it feels genuine."

"But I mean it genuinely. I've known Hanna my whole life, I know everything about her; we're soul mates. So, everything about it is genuine."

Christine noticed Luise looking at her. She cleared her throat. "Then I'm sure it will be. Maybe my wedding was just organized by the wrong people. I'm sure you'll do a great job. I really mean that, in all honesty." She looked at her watch. "Right, I'll have to make a move now, I have a hair appointment. Ruth, if I think of something, I'll give you a call. And I'll start on the column tonight." She stood up and put a few bills on the table. "Don't get up. See you on Monday, Gabi, and, Luise, I'll see you soon."

"Wait, Christine." Ruth stood up anyway, suddenly seeming agitated. "About the column, I'd like to change the topic. For Hanna. Could you please write about 'my best friend'? I think that'd be a good one."

Christine wrinkled her forehead. Luise noticed that her shoulders had tensed up. She could imagine what Christine was thinking and tried to salvage the situation.

"Why, what was the first topic?"

Ruth waved her hand dismissively. "Oh, well first I was thinking about 'first love' because of it being spring and all, but somehow that seems boring. Most of our readers are women, and they can relate more to the best friend topic. After all, everyone has one."

Christine looked unsure. "Well, I actually preferred the first love idea."

Gabi looked at the others, noticing that Christine seemed to be struggling, and tried to suggest a compromise. "Then write about 'my first friend' rather than the best. That's a nice idea, too."

Ruth beamed. "That's even better. Hanna was my first friend, too. Super idea, Gabi. So, Christine, what do you think?"

Christine nodded slowly. "OK, I'll give it a go. I'll mail it to you over the weekend, then we can talk about it. So, girls, I have to shoot off now, but have fun, and I'll see you soon."

Ruth watched Christine as she unlocked her bike, waved at them, and then pushed it over the footbridge. She turned back to the others. "Is she really so scarred by her divorce that she can't even talk about her wedding day?"

Luise shook her head. "No, it's not about the wedding, but the whole topic of best friends and honesty was a real faux pas."

"But why? She doesn't even know Hanna."

"Her bridesmaid Antje was her best friend her whole life; she planned a lot of fun things for the wedding day, and then, four years later, she starting fucking Christine's husband. And carried on for years before Christine realized."

Gabi scrunched up her face. "That's awful. And then what happened?"

"Well, it seems that Antje realized she'd rather have him to herself officially than keep her best friend, and pretty much put a gun to Bernd's head. Either he had to separate from Christine or she would tell her dearest friend a few home truths. So, Bernd separated from Christine, using some pathetic explanation; she moved to Hamburg and he kept their house. Unfortunately the whole thing came out a few months later; too many people knew about it. Since then she's had no contact with either of them."

Ruth had been listening with a shocked expression. "Oh God, and I've been running off at the mouth about weddings and all that. And coming up with the idea for the best friend column. How awful."

Gabi gave her arm a reassuring pat. "How could you know? I didn't either, by the way. Only that she used to be married. And the fact that it fell apart because of another woman. Although I always got the impression Christine felt it was the best thing that could have happened to her. What an idiot he must have been. Did you know them?"

Luise shook her head. "No, we only got to know each other better after she moved to Hamburg. She sometimes talks about her ex-husband, but never about Antje. To start with I often wondered why Christine always seemed to be quite reserved. She never comes by without checking first and can be very distant at times; I always thought it was because of me. Until her sister Ines told me about Antje and Christine. For Christine, Antje was really her rock for thirty years. I think her betrayal hurt more than the end of her marriage."

Gabi nodded in agreement. "That's true, Christine can often be like that. For years a few of us from work have been going away in September for a long weekend in Nordeney. A real girl's weekend. We've never been able to convince her to join us."

Ruth had been listening silently and drawing stick men on her notepad. She looked up.

"But you can't lose your faith in all future friendships just because of one bad experience. Nor your belief in female friendship in general!'"

Luise shook her head. "It's not that extreme. She's friends with Dorothea, after all; they live next to each other now. And then there's Marleen, she lives in Christine's old village and helped her a lot through the move and the divorce; she visits a lot. And I meet up with her quite often, too."

Ruth interrupted her. "I met Dorothea once, she's the costume designer who used to go out with Christine's brother, right?"

Luise nodded.

"So she's almost family. But doesn't she have any friendships that go way back? Girlfriends she's known since school?"

"We spoke about it once," said Gabi thoughtfully. "Christine thought it would only make her realize how much older she was. She kept thinking about people she hadn't heard from in years; they would just suddenly come into her mind."

'So why didn't she keep in touch?" Ruth looked curious.

Luise answered, "If you divorce after ten years of marriage, you end up breaking ties with your circle of friends as well. Lots of people don't know how to handle that. Besides that, Christine was an army child; her father was in the Bundeswehr and so they moved around a lot. That made holding on to friendships hard for her. It must have been difficult: she also said once that she had to leave almost all her friendships behind every time they moved. So it wouldn't have done her any good to dwell on lost friends and memories. It must have been really tough."

Ruth was thinking. "How old is she now, Luise?"

"She'll be forty-four in November."

"That's nothing." Ruth looked lost in thought. "It just seems so sad to me. Apart from Hanna I have three other girlfriends I've known for over twenty years. It's wonderful. Why don't we try to find Christine's old friends, then invite them to her birthday as a surprise?"

Luise looked skeptical. "I don't know. For one thing she doesn't like surprises, and for another I have no idea how we would go about finding old friends that even she hasn't heard from in years. I mean, maybe she doesn't even want to see them anymore."

Gabi, on the other hand, was quite intrigued by the idea. "Well, you know her sister really well, and she's sure to have known them. Or we could ask her parents or her brother."

Luise was still unsure. "I'm really not sure. It could backfire, and then she might break off contact with us, too."

"Nonsense." Ruth was in her element now. "I think it's a wonderful idea. She said herself that she'd been thinking of old friends recently. It's just that it's hard to make the first move. Everyone knows that. After a while you feel like you've lost your chance; it gets harder and harder to reestablish links with people from your past. So *we'll* do it for her."

Luise gave in. "OK, fine, I'll speak to Ines about it. We can see what she thinks of the idea."

Ruth smiled contentedly. "Wonderful! I love this kind of thing. I think Christine will be pleased, and so will many of her old friends, wherever they are. We'll send them an invitation and put a questionnaire in with it. We can ask when they met Christine, what their best memories of her are, what they like most about her, a few things like that to get people in the mood. I'll put something together. It'll be great." She raised her coffee cup. "Cheers, girls, together we'll make the world a better place. To us, and to female friendship."

Luise's expression was hesitant. Gabi smiled.

• ● •

"My First Friend"

Nineteen sixty-eight was the year my life changed. It had nothing to do with all the attention on student-activist Rudi Dutschke, nothing to do with the Olympic Games in Mexico, and nothing to do with the fact that the FC Nuremberg became Football Champions in Germany or that eleven-year-old pop sensation Heintje released his first album. No, to me the most important thing that happened that year was something else entirely: I started school and three of my greatest wishes came true.

The first was to own a pair of red patent leather shoes, with little cutout patterns at the front and bows at the back. From the moment I saw them in a shoe shop I knew I couldn't live without them. My mother didn't agree. She placed a great deal of importance on sensible footwear: closed toes with a sensible sole. She had seen photos of children with deformed feet, and probably had nightmares about them. Her suggestion for a compromise was a pair of bright red lace-up buckskin Hush Puppies. I refused to try them on and started crying. She marched me from the shop, irritated.

My second wish was for a little sister. I already had a little brother, who unfortunately hadn't lived up to the promises that had been made to me three years before. I found him unbearably boring and couldn't do much with him. So I placed all my hopes on a sister. The odds stood at 50:50, because my mother was already pregnant.

I've never told anyone about the third wish. I wanted a friend, a friend I could call my own. My mother had one. She called her Inge Joan Garden Gnome, even though Aunt Inge was grown up now. There was a picture of them on her first day at school, in which they looked identical and were holding hands. I wanted that, too.

My first day was on the eighth of August, and three weeks before that the mood at home was reaching boiling point. I had a white pleated skirt and a dark blue blazer. They were beautiful, but I only wanted to put them on if I could do it with the red patent leather shoes. Especially since I had to miss out on getting a red satchel; mine was brown. My grandma said I couldn't see it anyway when it was slung across my back. I could see her point, but the shoes were still an issue; after all, I could see my feet.

And so my pregnant mother marched her stubborn child into the Flensburg city center. There were six shoe shops, and the afore-mentioned patent leather ones were in the second. In the third and fourth shops I refused to try on a single pair, in the fifth I started to cry, and by the sixth I didn't even want to start school anymore. Shortly before the shops closed we were back in the second shop, and with a tear-streaked face, I finally tried on the most beautiful shoes in the world. When asked if they fitted me properly, I lied: they rubbed like crazy, but I got them. I was on cloud nine.

The evening before school started I was horribly ill. Whether it was down to the excitement or the Hawaiian pizza, I have no idea, just that I was sick all through the night. In the morning I was exhausted, bad-tempered, and my shoes were hurting me. Once we were standing on the school playground and I saw all the other children, I felt even worse. Then my mother let go of my hand and pushed me forward. All the children had to stand in a row. I stared at the floor so no one could see my tears and noticed that all the other girls were wearing black or dark-brown shoes, with closed toes and normal leather. Scrunching up my toes so that mine didn't rub so much, I felt distraught. After that we were separated off into our class groups. A small altercation on the steps unsettled the order we were standing in. My gaze was still fixed on the floor, when, suddenly, I saw them. Another pair of red patent leather shoes, just like mine. My heart started to beat faster. Above the shoes were white knee-high socks, then a white pleated skirt and a dark blue blazer. We looked identical! The girl looked at me, smiled, then waited for me.

Once we were standing next to each other, I noticed she was half a head shorter than me, and her hair was blond. But apart from that I felt we looked identical. In the classroom we sat down in the third row together. She said her name was Linda Love. I had never met someone with such a beautiful name. I was very happy.

Linda's father was a butcher, she said. She came from the Rhineland and spoke differently to me; her accent sounded lovely. My route to school went past their shop, and every morning Linda would sit on the steps and wait for me. We told each other everything. She had a big sister who was really mean, and had to wear her hand-me-downs, which she hated. I gave her my yellow pull-over. She had to roll the arms up because I was bigger than her, but in spite of that she looked very lovely in it. During school vacation I went to stay with my grandma while Linda stayed at home, and I thought I would die. By the time school was about to start again, I was beside myself with excitement. I had my first Barbie doll, and showed her proudly. But suddenly, Linda seemed to be different. She thought Barbies were silly and had a doll called Klaus, which I found a little strange. Klaus had pigtails.

In spite of that, she was still my best friend. We still walked to school together every day, sometimes hand in hand. But after a while Linda started shoving her hands in her jacket pockets, saying that we weren't babies who couldn't walk by ourselves anymore. I was a little sad, but admitted she was right.

We didn't play with our dolls anymore either. Klaus was too good for Barbie. So instead, we jumped rope and played cootie catch-er. But sometimes Linda still seemed very different.

She suddenly seemed to think her big sister was great. She was helping Linda with her homework every day; her parents were too busy in the shop.

Six months later my father was transferred and we had to move from Flensburg to Hamburg. I was very sad and didn't know how to tell Linda. In the end, my mother came with me to her house. Our mothers sat in the kitchen and drank coffee with cream, while Linda and I sat on the steps in front of the shop door. Devastated, I tried to find the words to tell her, and then started to cry. Linda looked at me, curious. After a while I managed to get out the words mov-ing, Hamburg, and another school. My heart broke, and Linda picked at the scab on her knee. After a while our mothers came back outside. My mother gave me a tissue and stroked my back. While she said good-bye to Mrs. Love, Linda ran into the shop.

I slowly started to make my way home with my mother, and then suddenly Linda was stood in front of me again. She was holding a hotdog in her hand. "Here," she said, holding it out to me. "And when I'm in the second grade, I'll write to you." I ate the hotdog on the way home. It comforted me.

My third wish came true, too, by the way. Two months later, my mother had a baby girl. Ines. My little sister.

I never did get a letter from Linda Love. But every time I eat a hotdog, I still think of my red patent leather shoes. And of my first ever friend.

May, Hamburg

"Linda Love!" George shook his head, laughing. "That really is a beautiful name."

He was sitting in Ines's kitchen and eating cheesecake. His little sister found that baking marathons helped her relax after a stressful day at work. The previous day, she had helped twenty students through their care-of-the-elderly, exams, and the result was three cheesecakes. She had ended up calling her brother. Luckily, he liked cheesecake.

While he was eating, Ines read the column from the May edition of *Kult* out to him. She had to clear her throat several times in the process; stories about childhood always choked her up a little.

"It seems really sad to me that Christine never got a letter from Linda. Can you remember her?"

Georg thought about it. "Only very vaguely, I was only four at the time. I think she was very small, had yellowy hair, and always smelled a little like sausages. Let me look at the magazine will you?"

His hand reached out for it, but Ines pulled it away.

"You've got really sticky fingers; I'll end up with marks all over it."

She smoothed it flat, tore the page out carefully, then straightened off the rough edge with scissors and stood up. From the cabinet she took out a clear plastic cover, slipped the article into it, and smoothed it flat once again, then handed it to Georg.

"Just make sure you don't bend it."

Her brother looked at her, amazed. "But I used a cake fork to eat with. Do you always do that with columns?"

Ines pulled the binder out of the cabinet and put it on the table. "Only Christine's. I've saved them all."

"And always in plastic?"

"Of course. Otherwise they'll go yellow and look bad."

Georg shook her head. "You're such a typical civil servant's daughter." He scanned through the text then handed the page back to her with mock, exaggerated caution. "Here, you'd better put it away quick in case it gets ruined."

Ignoring him, Ines filed the article away in the binder, then put it back in the cabinet. She sat down at the table and pushed the cake plate back toward her brother.

"Another slice?"

Georg laid a hand on his stomach. "I've had three already; I can't manage any more. Doesn't Christine have to help?"

"I phoned her, but she's busy. She has an appointment but didn't want to tell me what for. She might come by later. Luise is coming in a minute though."

"Luise? Why? Has she decided to throw in the towel at the publishing house and take up caring for the elderly?"

Ines laughed while she covered the cake with foil. "I highly doubt that. No, she called last week. She wants to talk to me about something. Christine's colleagues are trying to arrange a surprise for her birthday, so I guess we'll find out." She looked at her watch. "She should be here by now actually."

And, with that, the doorbell rang. Ines opened it, and Luise, a bunch of tulips in one hand and an edition of *Kult* in the other, came into the hallway.

"Hi, Ines, it smells great in here; is that cake? It's great that you're free today. These are for you."

She pressed the flowers into Ines's hands and followed her into kitchen. Georg had stood up.

"Luise, lovely to see you, it's been a long time."

"That's true; the last time must have been Christine's birthday meal at the Italian place." They hugged. "It's good that you're here, too, actually."

She sat down at the kitchen table and put the magazine down in the middle. "Have you already read your sister's enchanting 'Linda Love' column?"

Georg nodded. "Of course, and it's already been preserved in plastic for an eternity."

Luise looked at him, confused. Ines explained.

"I save the columns in plastic sleeves. Georg thinks that's a little too much."

"Why?" Luise looked at Georg. "That's a good thing; otherwise they'll go yellow and look bad."

Georg rolled his eyes. Ines took the cover off the cheesecake and put a plate in front of Luise. As she ate, she told them both about the conversation at Prüsse, of Christine's seeming restraint when it came to female friendships, and of Ruth's idea of trying to find Christine's old friends in time for her birthday.

"Ruth was over the moon when Christine sent the column to her. She's looking for Linda Love already."

Georg looked skeptical. "First you'd need to find out who you're really looking for. Perhaps Linda Love is now called Linda Müller. And if she is, it'd be like finding a needle in a haystack. And who and where are the others?"

Luise looked at him. "That's exactly what we want to find out from you. Who was Christine friends with? Twenty years ago, ten years ago?"

"Antje, but you can forget that," said Ines and scrunched up her face.

"I know." Luise swept the name away with a wave of her hand. "I know the story, but that's exactly what this is all about. You can't distrust others just because one friend let you down. Antje was an exception; it's not always like that."

"One was called Frauke. They were both in love with David Cassidy. They used to sit around on Christine's bed and giggle like fools." Georg was making an effort to remember. "Christine must have been about twelve, an awful age. I was nine and hugely embarrassed by her at the time. Then there was Gudrun, around the same time. Christine used to go riding with her. And, oh yes, Dani, she lived with her when she was in her mid-twenties."

"Christine played volleyball for years." Ines was searching her memory, too. "For a while she coached a team together with a girlfriend. What was her name again…oh, that's right, Lena. She did her training exam on my eighteenth birthday, which means she was twenty-five at the time. And Lena was one or two years older."

Luise took a notebook from her bag. "I knew you guys would remember." She sounded excited.

Ines rested her chin in her hand. "Hold on, Luise, I don't know a single surname. Do you, Georg?"

Her brother shook his head slowly. "Frauke…Schröder or Schneider? And they were all from all over the place. Flensburg, Hamburg, Bonn, Cuxhaven. Dani lived in Vienna for a while, she came to Christine's wedding. She had really long hair. And Gudrun had a horse. Well, of course she did; they're kind of essential for riding. I can't think of anything else. I'm sorry."

Luise sighed. "That can't be it. Come on, Ines, Georg, think harder."

"Lena was really tall and scored the most baskets. She moved away from Cuxhaven at some point. Christine was already married to Bernd at the time. I don't know where she moved to. I didn't used to see Christine that much back then. Hmm…"

The three of them looked at each other, at a loss for ideas.

"I'll call Mom. She's got a memory like an elephant; perhaps she'll be able to remember some surnames."

• ● •

At that very moment, a few streets away, Christine sat in the editorial office of the women's magazine *Femme*. The confident bleach blond receptionist had led her into a small waiting room, given her an espresso and an ashtray, and asked her to wait for a few minutes. Christine flicked through a few editions of the magazine that were arranged on the glass table.

It was a typical women's magazine and didn't claim to be anything other than that. Fashion photos, makeup tips, how to find the love of your life, horoscopes, recipes, book of the month—which always seemed to be about the same thing—and a column, "Marion's View of the World." Christine had read two of the columns, finding them amusing, by the time the door opened and a red-haired, freckled woman in her mid forties came into the room and walked up to her with her hand stretched out.

"Frau Schmidt? I'm Ellen Wagner, pleased to meet you. Shall we go into my office?" As she spoke two dimples danced around on her cheeks. Christine liked her instantly.

The office suited her; it was spacious and sunny, with a glass writing desk and a few chairs in the corner. There were also two large bouquets of flowers, piles of books and papers, and photos and children's drawings on the walls.

They sat down opposite one another in two wicker chairs. On the table in front of them were fresh cups, along with the latest edition of *Kult*.

Ellen Wagner noticed Christine's glance at once. "Exactly, that's what we're here to discuss. May I call you Christine?' She didn't wait for an answer. "So, Christine, we've had 'Marion's View of the World' as our column for the last four years. The magazine comes out every two weeks, as you probably already know. Now, this is the situation: Marion Korn has been approached by a publishing house that wants her to write a novel. That's great for Marion but bad for me, because I want to keep the column. Marion won't be able to handle both the novel and the column. Now, have a guess which publishing house we're talking about." She didn't wait for an answer this time either. "Exactly, the one you work for."

She smiled at Christine triumphantly. Christine smiled back and waited. But she didn't have to wait for long.

"I was at the Literatur Haus recently with a few friends of mine for an event. I ran into Mathias, your director, in the cloakroom. 'Mathias,' I said, 'you've stolen Marion Korn away from me, so you're going to have to write me a column.' He used to do that, you know, write columns for a college magazine back when we were students together. He's embarrassed about that now, though—they were pretty awful."

Christine suppressed a laugh. She had an idea of what was coming, and really hoped she was right.

"So, to cut a long story short, Mathias sent me the last three editions of *Kult* so I could take a look at your column. My favorite was the 'Linda Love' one. Would you be interested in writing a twice-monthly column for us as well?'

Christine thought quickly. She would have to speak to Ruth first. Ellen seemed to read her thoughts.

"Oh, I forgot to say: I spoke to Ruth Johannis on the phone this morning; we've known each other for a long time. She said I should ask you whether you feel you can take it on, and if so, it's fine with her."

A jubilant chant started whirling around in Christine's head: "I'm gonna be published in *Femme*, I'm gonna be published in *Femme*, I'm gonna be publishcd in *Femme*."

"Christine? What do you think?"

Christine shook the melody from her head and pulled herself together. "Of course, I mean, it would be an honor. I hope that…"

What was she saying?

"I mean, I'd love to do it. I just don't know…" At the last moment she stopped herself from saying it. That she didn't know whether she could. She cleared her throat.

"Well, I mean...yes. I'd love to."

Ellen laughed. "I caught you off guard there, didn't I? Could you bring me your portfolio of columns by Wednesday? I'd like to read a few more of them."

The horrified inner cry at hearing the word *portfolio* was resolved by the comforting thought *Ines!* When she saw Ines's folder of her collected columns for the first time, she had collapsed into laughter, despite feeling somewhat touched. Now she gave inner thanks to her sister and her obsessive compulsion to file things away in plastic sheets. She was so organized. The world's best little sister.

"Sure, that's no problem. I can bring it by tomorrow."

They discussed formalities like contracts and invoices; then Christine left the editorial office. She felt unbelievably important.

• ● •

Ruth sat at her desk, talking on the phone. Seeing Gabi standing in the doorway, she gestured at the chair opposite her and put her finger to her lips.

"I think it's great, Christine." She winked at Gabi. "This is a huge opportunity for you...of course you can do it. Just imagine, a column published nationwide every two weeks... oh come on, you can put it together in one evening a week. Did she read 'Linda Love'? She did and she liked it? Of course she did. Then just do more columns about your old girlfriends."

She gave Gabi a conspiratorial look. Gabi rolled her eyes and signaled to her to cut the conversation, at which Ruth looked disappointed.

"You think that's boring? Oh, I don't think so. But fine, OK, Christine, I have to go now, I've got an appointment. Have a lovely afternoon off, see you soon."

"'My God, Ruth, it doesn't get much more obvious than that, more columns about her friends. Great. Why don't you just ask her for their names while you're at it? I mean, seriously!" She looked at Ruth reproachfully. "I've already heard about *Femme*; Mathias told me about it in the canteen. That's great news."

"I think so, too." Ruth shoved piles of papers into her bag. "What about you?" She looked at Gabi. "Have you found anything?"

Gabi shook her head. "Nothing, the Internet search was fruitless, no Linda Love, no Love Butchers. Luise was planning to see Ines today, so maybe she'll be able to get some leads from her."

"Hopefully. After all, we don't have much time left until November. OK, I have to make a move, see you soon."

Ruth rushed past Gabi, who watched her go, irritated. She only hoped Madame Ruth would pitch in on the search, too, and not just get her coworkers to slog away on it.

● ● ●

Meanwhile, Ines was dialing her parents' number and looking back and forth from Luise to Georg as she listened to the dial tone.

"Schmidt."

Ines put the telephone on loudspeaker so the others could listen, too.

"Hi, Mom, it's me. Listen, you've got such a great memory, do you remember what Frauke's surname was?"

"Frauke who?"

Georg sighed loudly and mimed having a breakdown. "Well, that's a good start."

"Ines, was that my son? If it is, tell him he left a shirt behind here and I can't get the stains out."

Georg looked up and spoke loudly toward the phone.

"There weren't any stains."

"Oh, Then I must have dyed it accidentally. Was it expensive?"

Ines gestured to Georg to stay quiet. "Mom, listen, we're trying to find Christine's old friends, and one of them was called Frauke; she had long curly hair, it was back when they were in love with David Cassidy. You must remember her."

"David Cassidy. Yes, that's right, he was in that TV show with the Partridge Family. Shirley Jones played his mother. I liked her, she had such lovely blond hair."

Georg pitched in again. "Yes, but it's not about them, Mom; we want to find out Frauke's surname. And the shirt was from Hugo Boss."

"Really? You buy expensive shirts like that? Well, I guess you're right, they fit better. Why are you shouting? Wait... Frauke, her mother was a bit strange I think, I can't quite remember. What was her name? Erdmann or Erdemann, no, hang on, that was Marie."

Luise sat up straight. "Marie who?"

"Who's that there with you?"

"It's Luise. Hello, Mrs. Schmidt."

"Luise, how are you? Marie was one of Christine's friends; they used to go to dance lessons together. She was such a sweet girl. She was actually called Annemarie, but everyone called her Marie. Her parents come to Sylt on vacation now, and I see them now and then, but I haven't seen the girls in a long time. Why do you want to know? Has Christine gone missing or been kidnapped or something?" She giggled. "If so, I very much doubt that Christine is hiding away at Frauke's. Is that what you think?"

Ines's voice sounded reprimanding. "'Mom, be serious, will you? We want to find all of her old friends so we can arrange a surprise birthday party."

"But that's the kind of thing you do for someone's seventieth, don't you think?"

"Mom!" Georg called out impatiently. "Just have a think about your daughter's childhood friends. OK? Look through some old pictures; I'm sure a few names will come to mind."

"Of course. Georg, you sound on edge. Are you working too much?"

Georg sighed and laid his head down on the table.

Perhaps Charlotte heard the sigh, for she started to speak more seriously. "Something's just come to mind, but I'll have to give it some more thought. I can't this evening though; we're playing bowls at seven. I'll call again tomorrow. OK then, my dears, until then, *Tschüss.*"

Ines put the phone down and looked at the other two with raised eyebrows. "Our mother!"

Luise smiled. "Come on, we have Marie Erdmann; that's a start. We forgot to ask for her parents' address though; perhaps your parents will know. And we didn't ask about Linda Love, but Gabi wanted to have a look online first. We'll find them somehow, and I'm liking the idea more and more. What is it, Georg? What's with the funny look on your face?"

Georg gave a strained smile. "My best shirt's ruined."

• • •

"Tidying Up for Mom"

My friend Karola has canceled our sauna trip. We normally go every week. She didn't cancel because she's sick or has to work; no, she said she has to clean her house, including all the windows and cupboards, inside out. Now, Karola doesn't live in a pigsty, nor is she messy. She lives in a small house in Hamburg, together with her husband, who works in Munich during the week. They have enough money to live comfortably, beautiful furniture, and a cleaning lady who comes every two weeks. No, Karola has to clean because her mother is coming to visit. And I completely understand.

As a daughter you learn everything that you'll need for an independent life after you leave the parental nest, and you usually learn it from your mother. The education starts with emptying the trash, then washing the dishes ("Just be careful with those glasses, they were expensive") and drying up ("The pots last, don't forget"). If the crockery casualties are kept to a minimum, then you can progress to more meaningful tasks, like peeling potatoes ("Don't carve out figures, now, just peel them"), picking herbs, cleaning vegetables, and then the lesson to end all lessons: the Sunday roast. Of course, you can't do that alone, especially given how much the meat costs, but the time span from making a start until the mother pushes the child aside in order to finish the roast herself gradually gets longer and longer. There are also courses in making the bed ("Make sure you do up all the buttons now"), ironing, cleaning the windows ("Use newspaper; cloths don't do a darn thing") and other comments that should always be instantly fixed to memory because they could be called upon at any time: "To tackle burned lids, boil dishwasher tablets. Put sunflower stems in boiling water, hang up curtains while they're still wet, and, and, and..."

Eventually, once you've learned all these lessons, you move out. Then it's a whole new ball game. When I invited my parents for dinner in my very first apartment, I cooked smoked pork with sauerkraut and potatoes. My mother came into my kitchen and lowered the temperature on the oven, something for which I'm sure there was no good reason. Then she asked if I'd salted the potatoes, too, and when she tried the sauerkraut she said: "Shame, it tastes better with stock cubes." And by the way, I had done everything just as she had shown me to.

If you survive the first year after moving out, the mother's attempts at influencing the daughter's running of her new home become less extreme. Instead, there are other minefields to tackle.

"What do you weigh at the moment? Those pants are really too tight on you" is a frequently uttered sentence, generally in the presence of the wonderful man you've only known for two days and who happened to be there at the same time your mother dropped by unannounced.

Or: "Did you cut your own hair or something? It looks strange." That was the first time I'd been to an expensive hairdresser, who had recommended I go for layers and highlights. My skirts were too short, my heels too high, and my favorite black clothes made my mother feel depressed. "Especially because yellow suits you so much."

A child's social environment is placed under the microscope, especially—up to a certain age—with regard to male companions. All mothers have an internal scanner tucked away somewhere that can run a son-in-law test in mere seconds. Although, when it came to my mother, the results were seldom comprehensible. Not that I'm blaming her for the failure of my marriage, of course; perhaps her scanner had a loose wire back then.

For years, the daughter's friends are welcomed but rarely paid much attention to. That changes in a flash if those girls then have babies. It only takes a birth notice in the paper or, even better, a phone call from the new mother for the mother to burst enthusiastically into stories of how sweet the baby is, how much she always liked the friend, how she's done so well for herself, it's simply wonderful. At times I think I only missed having an adopted sister by a hairsbreadth.

As a daughter, you just have to sit these phases out. At some point they'll be over. Even the most ambitious of mothers will eventually realize that her child has become resistant to advice in some areas. That happens once the daughter is truly grown up. After that it will be possible to spend a carefree weekend with together at the spa, or go on shopping trips. By then, you can talk from woman to woman. Then, mothers and daughters can become good friends.

Karola told me, by the way, that her mother was only there for coffee. Karola was exhausted and had pulled her shoulder cleaning the window, which hindered her a little when cutting the cake. With the words "Why are you making such a big fuss of it?" her mother took the knife from her hand. "You have to cut equal portions; otherwise how will it look?"

Karola had bought the wrong apples for the cake, but apart from that it tasted really good. And the long-life whipping cream didn't help either; it doesn't whip properly. But apart from that the afternoon was very pleasant. Up until when they said their goodbyes, and Karola's mother hugged her and said: "Chin up, my child, in six months your husband will be working in Hamburg again, and then you won't be so sad. I can understand that you're letting the housework slip a little at the moment, but just make sure you don't let things go too much."

After that, Karola was done with trying to impress her.

I have to go to the station now; my mother is arriving by train to go shopping with me. I've cleaned everything, gotten rid of the empty wine bottles, and hidden my cigarettes. But I hope she doesn't come upstairs. My windows aren't as shiny as they could be...

June, Hamburg

Christine stretched and looked at the clock. "OK, it's time for me to pack up now and head off on vacation." Gabi looked up briefly before continuing to flick through the pile of client lists. "You lucky thing. I just can't find that damn advertising invoice, and the company's already complained. The thing has just vanished into thin air. Oh, I hate this, I want a vacation, too...oh, there it is!" She waved the sheet of paper triumphantly. "And we've already paid it, too; everything's in order. So, are you going to Sylt today, or are you here for the weekend still?"

Christine rummaged around in her bag, lowering her gaze. "I'm going this afternoon and staying until next Friday. You can reach me on my mobile if you need to."

"Who's watering the plants on your balcony?"

Christine looked up, baffled. "Dorothea. She lives opposite me. Since when were you worried about my plants?"

Gabi shrugged her shoulders. "I just wondered, I mean, all the flowers are blooming so beautifully at the moment."

Christine shook her head. "You really do need a vacation. You haven't been over to my place since March, and nothing was blooming then, but feel free to worry about them if you want to. So, I hope you have a peaceful week— see you the Monday after next."

"Have a wonderful vacation; say hi to the island for me and have fun."

They smiled at each other; then Christine disappeared out the door. Gabi waited a few minutes, then grabbed the phone and called Ruth.

"She's gone. She's going to her parents' place this afternoon. Dorothea's watering the plants, so she'll have the key."

"Great! Do you know where the photo albums are?"

"Hopefully Luise will; she should ask Ines."

Ruth's voice sounded hesitant. "Perhaps Ines should go there herself; if we do it, it's like prying. I think it's better if her sister does it."

Gabi laughed. "That's what I've been saying to you from the start. Do you want to phone Ines? Or Luise?"

"Oh, Gabi, I've only met Ines once; could you call her for me please? I've already put together the text for the invitation and the questionnaire though; I'll e-mail it to you now. You can show the others. I have to go now, I've got an editorial meeting, but we'll speak soon. Ciao."

Gabi clicked on her mailbox and printed out Ruth's documents.

● ● ●

Just a few hours later, Dorothea stood in front of Christine's apartment door as Ines and Gabi came up the steps. She hugged Ines and shook Gabi's hand.

"I think we've met before. You're Christine's colleague and were at her last birthday party, right?"

"Yes, exactly. Have you heard about the plan?" asked Gabi.

Dorothea nodded and turned to the door to unlock it.

"Yes, Ines told me on the phone. So who's Ruth Johannis? According to Luise it was all her idea."

Gabi followed Dorothea into Christine's apartment. The hallway was filled with the aroma of Christine's perfume.

"Yes, that's right, Ruth is really excited about it all. It was her idea, but she generally leaves the hard work to the rest of us. That's how it always is: she gets everyone enthused then puts the pressure on."

"Hmm, am I sensing a catfight coming on?" Dorothea looked at Gabi curiously. She quickly shook her head.

"No, nonsense, we're good friends. We did our training together ten years ago, and we've been working for the same firm every since. She's in the magazine section and I'm in the publishing house. We play tennis together, too. Oh, and she's already put an invitation together, along with a questionnaire."

"Then that all sounds good." Dorothea sank down into the red chair and looked at Ines. "Go on, you're the sister. Grab the photo albums; maybe we'll find traces from the old life of Christine S."

"I'd like to see the questionnaire first." Ines stretched her hand out toward Gabi.

Questionnaire

Name, age, and place of residence?

When and where did you meet Christine?

What was your best experience together?

What made your friendship stand out? And what sets Christine apart as a friend?

What's your motto in life?

A friend is…?

What was your first reaction to this invitation?

One hour and three albums later, Dorothea went to fetch some champagne from her apartment. Ines had stared, frustrated, at every photo in which Christine appeared together with other children and teenagers. She rubbed her eyes.

"It's impossible, not a single written note under the pictures; my sister just hurls the pictures into the album without organizing them. How can someone be that sloppy? Apart from my cousins, I don't recognize anyone."

Dorothea, who was coming back in with the opened champagne, laughed. "That must be really annoying to a fan of plastic folders and ring binders." She poured the champagne into three glasses and sat back down. "I don't even put my photos in albums, I just throw them in boxes."

Gabi sat up. "Me too. Perhaps she has boxes somewhere, too. Ines, go have another look."

Sighing, Ines stood up and went back into her sister's study. Ten minutes later she came back, drank a sip of champagne, then went into the bedroom. After another five minutes she reappeared, standing in front of them with two boxes.

"There are loads of pictures in here. But it's a total mess."

She put the boxes on the table and lifted up the lid of the first. At that moment the telephone rang. They all jumped and looked at it. After the third ring, the answering machine kicked in. "Christine Schmidt is not in at the moment; please leave your message after the beep." After the beep there was a brief pause; then they heard a male voice. "Christine, it's me; I just wanted to check when you'll be here. Since you're not picking up, I guess you've already left, so I'll try you on your cell."

Dorothea looked stunned, almost aghast. Ines looked at her curiously.

"Who was that?"

Dorothea quickly pushed her hair back from her face, then shrugged her shoulders. "No idea, he didn't say his name."

She avoided Ines's searching gaze, looked into one of the boxes, and pulled out a stack of pictures, notes, and old tickets. She spread them out in front of her.

"My God, what a hoarder Christine is. Look, cinema tickets for *Dirty Dancing*—that's certainly going back a few years!" She rummaged around in the photos and pulled one out. "Hey, isn't that Marleen's house? I went there once."

Ines looked at her questioningly and took the picture from her hand. "Yes, that's Marleen. God, what does she look like? She must have been at least ten kilos heavier back then. It must have been at Christine's wedding. Yes, that's right, and there's Dani; she stayed with Marleen."

Gabi looked over Ines's shoulder. "Who's Dani? Oh, and is that the Marleen from Cuxhaven who has a pub?"

"That's the one. Dani and Christine lived together before Christine met Bernd. Then Dani moved out and Bernd moved in. I don't think they've seen each other since then. We *have* to find her."

Dorothea poured more champagne. "If I remember correctly, they didn't exactly part on good terms."

Gabi looked at the photo more closely. "That's why we have to find her. Maybe Marleen has her address."

Dorothea was skeptical. "After fifteen years? Give me the phone; I'll call her if Christine has the number saved."

Halfway through she paused and then started to laugh. "I don't even know Marleen's surname. Do you, Ines?"

Ines thought with great effort and then shook her head. "That's embarrassing, I don't know either, and I've known her for a long time. But try looking under M for Marleen."

Christine really had saved the number under M. Thankfully, Dorothea pressed the speed dial. Marleen answered after the third ring.

"Hi, it's Dorothea here."

"Dorothea! Is something wrong with Christine?"

"No, no, she's on her way to Sylt for a week's vacation."

"I know, we spoke last night on the phone. I thought something must have happened because you were calling."

"No reason to worry. But we're planning something… that is to say, two of Christine's colleagues had an idea and have talked us all into it. Listen, it's like this…"

Dorothea explained about Ruth and Gabi and their plan, and about Linda Love and the so-far unsuccessful investigations.

"And now we're in Christine's apartment, rooting through her photo albums. So far we haven't found a thing, no notes with the photos, no addresses. But there's a photo of you and Dani at Christine's wedding. Do you remember her?"

Marleen answered at once. "Daniela, her roommate, yes of course; she stayed with us for the wedding. I think I even still have her parents' address. Dani lived in Bremen back then and left her house key here, so I took it to her parents' place in Cuxhaven. I'll see if I can get in touch with them."

Dorothea nodded at the others and gave a thumbs-up.

"Oh, Marleen, you're our first breakthrough! This is great. I'm really starting to enjoy this detective work."

"Well, I just hope Christine enjoys it, too; she's not exactly a big fan of surprises."

Ines took the phone from Dorothea. "Marleen, it's Ines, I was listening in. You know, I was skeptical at first, too, but Christine's been getting quite sentimental recently and keeps talking about the old days. Luise told us; she's helping us with the search. Can you think of anyone else?"

Marleen was still a little doubtful. "OK, then I hope that's the case. Let me think…Have you already thought of Lena?"

"Yes, the volleyball player. But we can't find even a trace of her. Oh, tell me you know where she is!"

"There are a few of the old ladies that help us in the pub. They bake our cakes and help make the meatballs when I'm preparing casseroles for wedding parties. Lena's mother is one of them, and I'll be seeing her tomorrow."

"Marleen, I could kiss you! Are you in?"

Marleen laughed. "For the kiss or the search? OK, I'll see what I can find out. I'll call you. Give my love to the rest of the detectives. Bye."

Gabi and Dorothea gave each other a high five.

• ● •

Sylt

One hundred and fifty kilometers to the north, Christine was in Niebüll, getting the Motorail train to Sylt. She came to a stop behind a Mercedes and, after the signal from the parking marshal, turned off the engine, put on the handbrake, and opened the sunroof. The sun shone in onto her face as she pushed back her sunglasses and closed her eyes. One week of vacation, Sylt, the List beach sauna, drinking wine at Wonnemeyer and Gosch, fresh fish, her parents, and—Richard. Despite her excitement she felt a little empty. She hadn't seen Richard for four weeks and longed for him. It's just that it wasn't an unconditional excitement; everything was much too complicated for that.

She had met Richard ten years ago in Berlin. At the time, he was working with her brother Georg for a TV channel, Georg as a sports journalist and Richard as a lawyer. In Christine's memory it was love at first sight, but not without consequences. Both of them were married at the time, and it had been the wrong time to turn their lives upside down. A good five years later, they had come into each other's lives again by chance. By then, Christine was divorced and living in Hamburg. Richard was living in Bremen during the week, where he worked, but was still married. In spite of that they began an affair. At first, it was easy to manage. Christine was still traveling as a rep then and often stayed overnight at Richard's in Bremen during the week. His wife lived in Berlin and led her own life. Christine was surprised at how the woman didn't seem to miss him; there were never visits or phone calls, and the relationship between Richard and Christine was left to develop in peace.

After a year and a half, the first problems began to emerge. At the point when, after the initial excitement of falling in love, a relationship normally develops and most couples begin to make plans for the future, like planning vacations and viewing apartments, they came to a standstill. Christine was surprised at how many of the clichés about lovers turned out to be true, but they did. Lonely weekends, holidays; during all of these Christine was single, while Richard spent them in Berlin. He had tried, hesitantly, to get out of the marriage, but his wife had been rigorously opposed to a divorce. So everything had stayed as it was.

The ease that had initially existed between Christine and Richard was superseded by discussions about crushed hopes or too high expectations. Each of them felt unfairly treated, misunderstood, and sad. After two years they decided to put their feelings on ice and stopped seeing each other for a while.

Christine switched from being a rep to working in the publishing house, thereby ending the chance of them seeing each other in the week. It was a very difficult time for her; Richard was still the first and last thing she thought about every day, and she felt unhappier than she had after her divorce. Dorothea got the apartment next to hers and tried to keep her mind off it. Nothing helped. Neither long weekends by the sea, nor trips to the cinema, nor the constant conversations about the futility and torment of having a relationship with a married man. Dorothea cursed Richard. Christine agreed with her each time, but then dreamed about him at night.

After three months of silence, Richard called. When she heard his voice, everything went right back to the beginning. They met that very evening in a hotel between Hamburg and Bremen, talked the whole night through, and decided to make a real decision. At some point.

That was six months ago. A great deal had changed since then. Yet, at the same time, nothing had. Richard didn't go to Berlin every weekend anymore; he told his wife he was working on a university project in Bremen that took up a lot of his time. Christine started going to see Marleen a lot on the weekend again. At least, that was the official story; Marleen was in on it. Christine always called her from the car on the way back. Whenever Dorothea saw her after one of the weekends and asked after Marleen, Christine felt terrible. But she kept on lying for fear of Dorothea's reaction.

Once, Christine had run into Luise at a rest stop on her way to see Richard. Luise, noticing that Christine looked as guilty as sin, pressed her so much that in the end she told her she was meeting Richard again, not as often, albeit more casually.

Luise looked at her skeptically and then waved it away. "It's nothing to do with me, so I won't mention it. I just hope you know what you're doing."

She hadn't said a word to anyone.

Richard had a conference in Westerland this weekend. His colleague was sick, so Richard had gone alone and already had a double room booked. It was down to chance, or good luck, that the conference was right at the start of Christine's holiday, and that she was on her way to Sylt anyway. Her parents weren't back from their vacation until Sunday, and no one would notice if she didn't sleep in her old room for the first couple of nights.

The train came to a halt in Westerland station. The taillights of the cars in front of Christine's lit up, and the line gradually began to move. The hotel was in Rantum. Just another ten minutes of driving before she got to Richard. Christine put her turn signal on and tried to push her doubts aside.

• ● •

Flensburg

Luise punched the steering wheel angrily with the palm of her hand. "What on earth! For heaven's sake, are they too stupid to think of putting up detour signs? They're all idiots; my God, I'd go insane here!"

She'd been swerving through the area for the last half hour. She had been to visit three bookstores in Flensburg, needed to be in Schleswig in an hour's time, and couldn't find her way back to the highway. Sewer construction works. It seemed the town didn't have enough detour signs: Luise had followed four of them, and after that they had completely stopped. Nothing. There was no highway either. She was clearly in a residential area, there were no signs of any kind, and she had no idea what direction she should be driving in.

Luise searched the street for pedestrians she could ask for directions. She also needed the bathroom desperately, and was hungry, too. She looked at the time; she still had an hour. Then she saw a small shopping center. A supermarket, a bakery; there had to be a restroom somewhere. She looked for a parking space and pulled up.

The restrooms were right by the entrance, and Luise dashed right in without stopping to look around. As she came out, her stomach was rumbling. The baker had a meat and cheese counter and was selling sandwiches. Well, she could take one along with her at least. Once it was her turn, she asked for a cheese roll and a can of cola. "To go, please."

The saleswoman carefully wrapped up the roll and put it in a paper bag along with a napkin.

"That'll be three Euros fifty, *junge Frau*."

Luise laid the money on the table.

"Thanks. Could you tell me how to get to the highway from here, please?"

"Sure, you turn right out of here, then straight on until the gas station, then take a left. From there you'll see the signs. It's really easy to find."

"Great, thank you. Have a nice day."

Luise walked quickly back to the car. She only had forty-five minutes now; it would be tight. In the car she laid the bag on the dashboard and turned the key in the ignition. Before putting the car in reverse, she took the roll from the bag. The napkin fell onto the passenger seat. Luise glanced at it momentarily, then stared. Instantly she turned the ignition off again.

On the napkin was a red company logo. "Number one for years—Meyer Fine Foods, formerly Love Butchers."

Luise grabbed her cell to call the bookstore in Schleswig.

• ● •

Hamburg

Ines rubbed her eyes and yawned. "Come on, I think we've looked at every scrap of paper and photo there is. I'm exhausted."

Gabi laid a pile of tickets and photos back in the box. Dorothea took them straight back out again.

"Gabi! You can't put them back in all organized like that; she'll notice." She rummaged around to make the pile all messy again, while looking at the things they had left out on the table. "I think we did quite well. We've got our first clues about Dani and Lena, and we've got this card, too."

Gabi reached for the postcard: there was a picture of the Emden bay on the front. On the back was some child-like handwriting:

Dear Christine,

It's pretty dull here, it rains every day and my grandma is in a bad mood. But I did get to practice Rumba with my cousin and I can do it now. See you on Thursday, I can't wait.

Lots of love, Marie

Dorf Strasse 2, 2038 Büchen

Gabi waved the card around. "And poor Marie was so homesick that she wrote her home address as the sender's. How sweet."

She thought for a moment then tucked the card away in her bag. "I'll give it to Ruth so she doesn't feel left out of the search. It was her idea after all."

"Fine with me." Dorothea stood up and stretched. "All right, let's clear away the evidence of our investigations, I want to head back to my place. I'll write up the schools Christine went to so we can get a hold of the class lists, and let's just hope there aren't loads of Fraukes. Then I'll give Gabi a call."

"Great. Maybe we can meet up for dinner next week, with Ruth and Luise, and see where we're at."

The three of them looked at each other. By now, even Ines had the kind of facial expression you usually only see on investigators in crime movies.

• ● •

Sylt

Christine and Richard sat silently next to each other in the terrace bar at Wenningstedt Cliff, watching the sun go down. Now and then their hands would touch, or he would caress her back or put his hand on her knee. It was the kind of silence that can only happen when you usually talk about everything.

They hadn't seen each other in four weeks. To Christine it had seemed like an eternity, and she'd had to force herself to suppress her longing for him, to distract herself. And she had managed to: her job at the publishing house and writing the new column for *Femme* took up almost all her time. Thoughts of Richard only came in the evenings, but when they did, they were overwhelming. Every fiber of her being longed for his voice, his hands, his body, his warmth.

Then she would picture Richard with his wife, and wanted to hate him for his inability to make a decision. But she couldn't. She felt torn between the fear of losing him and the burning need to free herself from this double life.

On the way to Sylt, Christine had thought about how it was possible to hear hundreds of stories about the torment of being someone's secret lover, and yet be no smarter for it. Whether it was Glenn Close in *Fatal Attraction* or one of the numerous novel heroines, Christine found them all dire and never wanted to be like them. She had tormented herself with these thoughts right up until the moment when she stood in front of Richard's hotel room door. But once he flung the door open and looked at her, all her thoughts had dissolved.

"Christine, I've been looking forward to seeing you so much."

Richard took her in his arms, and they stood there for minutes on end in an embrace. Christine closed her eyes and had the feeling she was in the right place, at the right time, with the right person.

An hour later they were sitting on the small balcony that led off from his hotel room, smoking and holding hands. Richard leaned over to kiss her again. Then he stubbed out his cigarette and stood up.

"Come on, let's go for a walk along the beach. And on the way back we can go to the cliff for some champagne and celebrate."

Christine looked up at the sky. Everything felt right again.

As they walked along the beach, they told each other about the important and not-so-important things that had happened over the last four weeks. Richard had bought a copy of *Femme* and read Christine's first column.

"I'm so proud of you," he said, stopping for a moment. "Come here and let me kiss you, you star columnist." He had read the story about mothers so often that he almost knew it by heart. "I thought it was really funny. And it made me think about my own mother. Once, when my sister had to go to London on business for three weeks, my mother house-sat for her. My sister had two cats, so someone needed to be there. She lives in this penthouse apartment in Cologne, with a roof terrace, huge windows, everything furnished in black and white, very minimalist. By the time Beate came back, my mother had sewn and hung curtains and put potted plants in front of every window. My sister almost flipped." Richard laughed softly and put his hand under Christine's arm. "So, I'm now a *Femme* reader. No one would have believed that five years ago."

They had arrived at Wenningstedt Cliff, and the beach was bathed in that evening sunlight so typical for Sylt. As Richard and Christine climbed up the steps to the sun terrace, a table right at the front became free. Christine quickened her pace.

"Come on, that table's in the sunshine; let's get it."

She reached it seconds before an older couple who were also steering their way toward the table, and sat down quickly. The older woman shot a poisonous look at Christine and pushed her husband in the other direction.

"Come on, Werner, I didn't come here to have a race."

Christine made an effort to gaze indifferently out to sea and then looked at Richard, who sat down smiling.

"You really forced that woman aside; that was almost a foul."

Christine shrugged her shoulders and tried to look innocent.

"Old volleyball rules, you just have to cut off the opponent's route to the goal. And by the way, there was no bodily contact, so I wouldn't even have gotten a yellow card. I really don't know what you're talking about."

Richard stroked her cheek. "You scare me sometimes. But what a great table." He reached for the drinks menu. "Champagne?"

"Of course. It's the perfect finishing touch."

After the waiter had brought their glasses over, they sat in contented silence for a while and just enjoyed each other's company.

Richard's gaze followed two figures who were making their way along the beach in step, but at a distance from one another. The last rays of sunshine illuminated their blond hair. He looked at Christine. She was watching them, too.

"Lovers?" He spoke softly so as not to spoil the mood.

Christine shook her head. "Two girls, both very young, so friends perhaps."

Richard squinted. Now they had stopped walking and were standing, staring at each other. Christine was right, it was two girls; they were maybe fourteen or fifteen years old. The taller girl said something to the smaller one and stretched out her hand, which the other grabbed. They moved farther away from each other, but still held on tight. Then they started to make peculiar movements. Richard tried to figure out whether they were fighting.

"What's going on? Are they arguing?" He looked at Christine questioningly.

Her gaze was still fixed on the two girls.

"No," she said quietly, "they're not fighting; they're practicing the jive."

Richard was confused. "The jive?"

The two girls were now moving to the same rhythm. They were the only people on the beach. And they could hear music that no one else could.

Christine leaned over and kissed Richard on the cheek.

"Or cha-cha. I can't make out the steps from here. Didn't you ever practice before a dance lesson?"

Richard laughed. "Practice? That's what I went to the lessons for. I would never have met up with a girl beforehand to practice. That just wouldn't have been cool." He looked back over at the two girls. "And if I'd have asked my best friend Christof if he could be the girl, he would probably have beaten me up and declared me mentally ill. Or gay. Our friendship would have come to an end."

"And is it still going now?"

Richard nodded. "Christof lives in Munich, so we only see each other now and then. But we're still good friends. My God, it's been almost thirty-five years."

"When did you last see him?"

Richard thought for a moment. "When was it? Wait, it must have been when he got married, seven, no, eight years ago."

Christine laughed. "Wow, that really is a true friendship. You sound inseparable."

"Why not? You don't have to see each other all the time. We speak on the phone and write. Friendships are different for men than they are for women."

"And how would you know what they're like for women?"

Richard pointed at the two girls, who were now lying alongside each other on the sand.

"Just look at the two of them; it's so typical. It was the same with my sister and in my circle of friends. Girls walk to school together in the mornings, sit next to one another for six hours in class, stand together at recess, then separate when they go home to eat dinner with their families, only to spend half an hour on the phone arranging to meet up an hour later. That just doesn't happen with boys."

"Girls aren't all like that. It's a cliché."

Richard took Christine's hand and kissed her. "I think most of them are. It's in the genes; you always want to be in close contact. Women go to the bathroom together. They share clothes, go shopping together, tell each other all about their love lives, you know, things like that. Sometimes I even envy them for it. So what was it like for you?"

"I go to the bathroom by myself."

Richard laughed. "Well, you're different than other girls."

He put his hand on her knee, and she put hers on top of it. He turned his hand around and intertwined his fingers with hers.

"I'm sure I was the same, at some stage at least. You know, as a young girl you're afraid of the world. Well, I was, anyway. And then another little girl appears, and suddenly everything is easy. I needed friends to be able to start making my way through life."

Richard pressed her fingers tenderly. "It's the same for little boys. You look for fellow sufferers, cowards like yourself, and together you can be strong."

"But that's only the early friendships," Christine continued. "After that everything changes again. At twelve or thirteen I suddenly started to like girls who were completely different than me. I think we look for opposites to try to figure out who we want to be. But it only works for a while before the differences start to show."

Richard looked at Christine attentively. "That's the same with men, too."

"Yes of course, to start with, but men approach friendships differently to women. It's about the friend, his character, his sense of humor, his spontaneity, I don't know. But with women, shared life experience is much more important. If you get to know a friend when you're both single, there are usually problems when she settles down and has less time for you. If two women, neither of whom have children, are friends, and then one becomes a mother, it's just as difficult. If you can't stand the other one's partner, that's a problem, too. Women are much more dependent on external circumstances than men are. Everything has to stay as it is; otherwise it stops working."

Richard looked skeptical. "I think you're being too pessimistic. I hardly know any women who don't have a best friend. I mean, you've got Dorothea, or Marleen."

"It's not that I'm against female friendships," Christine tried to explain. "I think you have good friends or companions for different times and stages in your life. But I must be lacking the gene you were talking about. I don't go the bathroom with Dorothea or Marleen, nor do we tell each other the minute details of our love lives or speak on the phone every day. It's not like that."

A thought flashed across Christine's mind, and she shut her eyes for a moment. Antje's voice on the telephone: "It's me, what are you doing?" Antje in front of the mirror in the bathroom, Christine next to her, using her lipstick; Christine in Antje's leather jacket, Antje all excited, telling her about Olaf. Richard brought her back to the here and now.

"Earth to Christine. What are you thinking about?"

Christine shook the thoughts away. "In my old life I used to have a best friend. At least, that's what I thought. I told you about Antje, didn't I? It just brought some memories back, that's all; let's change the subject. Are the two dancers still there?"

She looked out over the sand. Richard looked at Christine thoughtfully. It made him sad that the thought of Antje still caused her pain. He wished he could help her. "They're gone now. I can't see them anymore."

Christine leaned over to Richard and kissed him. "I thought they were sweet, and hopefully they got the hang of the jive."

She looked out to the sea, then reached for her glass and drank down the last of her champagne.

"Richard, what do you think about a column on dance lessons?"

"As long as I don't have to practice with you, I think it sounds great. I'm such an awful dancer that my lessons were a complete humiliation. I fell over during the polonaise."

Christine laughed and stroked his cheek.

"I know how you feel! Shall we have some more champagne? I'm very happy we're here together, by the way."

Richard kissed her hand, his eyes smiling.

• ● •

"The Dance Lessons"

I saw two girls dancing on the beach on Sylt.

It was a wonderfully warm, romantic evening with a beautiful light, and the perfect stage for great love stories, sunsets, and new beginnings. I felt beautiful, exciting, and young. It was perfect.

And then I saw the two girls dancing down below me on the beach, or rather, I saw them practicing. As the sun went down behind them, they held hands, counted the steps, and looked young and vulnerable. I watched them for a while and then thought about how thirty years is, in fact, a very long time.

Nineteen seventy-four was the year I was supposed to take two big steps in my journey toward being a grown-up. I had my confirmation lessons, and in October, my beginner's dance class began at the Möller Dance School.

My parents were pleased: they saw classical dance training as essential preparation for life, and hoped I would learn manners and how to act like a lady in the process.

A few weeks before, they had caught me smoking for the first time. They were worried I was starting to get out of control. But I really only had one problem. Puberty. Everyone can remember what that's like. Drastically switching between euphoria and depression, always treading that fine line between laughter and tears. And besides that (and this was the real problem) I had fallen in love. The football World Cup was taking place in Germany. My feelings crept up on me slowly and reached their crescendo on the day of the final. It was the seventh of July; Germany played against Holland and won 2:1.

The object of my desire was Johann Cruyff, the Holland captain. He had such sad eyes, even before the defeat, that I thought he was wonderful and wanted to save him. I read in my brother's Kicker *magazine that Johann Cruyff was an occasional smoker, and that's the only reason why I started. My parents would never have understood, so I didn't even try to explain.*

After the game I burst into tears. My parents put it down to puberty. I was crying for Johann.

I plastered my bedroom walls with photos and posters of the Dutch national team, which made my brother have more respect for me but irritated my parents no end. If only it could have been ABBA or Chris Roberts. And then the smoking incident to top it all off.

When the registration form arrived from the Möller Dance School, my parents saw it as a sign. Under other circumstances they might have hesitated, but instead they enrolled me immediately. They hoped that, with Möller's help, I would become normal again.

I didn't mind: most of the girls and boys from my school were going there anyway, and if I couldn't be with Johan Cruyff, then I might as well learn to dance.

My idea of dance events and balls had been shaped by films like Sissi *and* Gone with the Wind. *Beautiful women with big strong men, skirts that circled across the dance floor with a flourish, big orchestras, string sections, velvet and silk, candles and champagne, enchanted faces, loving looks.*

The reality of the Möller Dance School was very different. Plastic chairs piled up next to the wall, neon strip lights on the ceiling, a drinks machine in one corner and a sound system in the other, giggling girls in ironed jeans and pimply boys who were—and this was the worst thing—almost all shorter than me.

Instead of flying across the dance floor in a swishing ball gown in the arms of the heroic Johan Cruyff, I found myself stiffly practicing the basics of the foxtrot with Wolfgang. Wolfgang had been held back at school for two years in a row, and so was older and taller than the other boys. He had a haircut like Mireille Matthieu and wore glasses. He never spoke to me or smiled, only moved his legs below the knees and had no sense of rhythm whatsoever. But he was five centimeters taller than me, so we were paired together. We belonged in that room, with its plastic chairs and neon strip lighting.

There was another girl from my year there, too, Annemarie. Everyone knew an Annemarie. She was medium height, medium blond, average weight, of average intelligence. She wanted to be in on everything, invited all the teenies to her birthday parties, brought tons of sweets with her to school, had the newest editions of Bravo, the best books, the greatest albums. She was always the first one in the ice-cream parlor and would save you a seat, beaming with joy.

She let you win in all the games and would do any favor for you but never forgot to remind you of it. She was your best friend; at least, that's what she decided. At that time I was one of her avowed targets. It didn't matter where I was; Annemarie would be there, too, beaming at me. We called her Sputnik.

Annemarie had signed up for the course, too, of course, and complained after the first session that there were too many girls and not enough boys. She tried to give Wolfgang a high five, but he didn't react, and I didn't understand what she was trying to do, so there was a small scrap on the dance floor. I was unbelievably embarrassed: the others must have thought we were fighting over that dumb sucker.

Mrs. Möller went into the adjoining room, where her husband was teaching the advanced course. I have no idea what she promised them or how she did it, but she came back with four of the advanced male dancers.

All of the girls were relieved: the four boys definitely improved the average. Annemarie leaned over to me conspiratorially and whispered that the second one from the left was staring at me. As I looked over, discreetly, my heart skipped a beat.

He had eyes like Johan Cruyff. And he made the whole room look better. Unfortunately though, he wasn't looking at me.

Mrs. Möller decided that the newcomers would be partnered with the girls who hadn't been paired off in the first round. So Annemarie got "Johan Cruyff Eyes," and I was still stuck with Wolfgang. Annemarie wasted no time in telling me that my hero was called Micha and that he was incredibly sweet. But that I had a nice one, too, so not to worry. Oh how I hated her.

Those were the worst Tuesdays of my life. Wolfgang never progressed beyond the basics of the foxtrot. He suffered from sensitive sinuses and made noises like he was snorkeling while he danced. He told me that he had been prescribed nasal douches, and that was the reason why he missed some of the classes. When he was absent I had to practice with other partners, and to my despair, it was always on those very days that Micha-Johan-Cruyff was absent, too. Everything was going wrong.

The graduation ball in the autumn was a disaster. Wolfgang fell over even as we were walking in and bruised his shoulder. It was a good thing in that I managed to get out of being disgraced during the prize dance, but also meant that I had to sit at my parents' table most of the evening, which really made me feel like a fifth wheel.

But then the evening seemed to take a turn for the better. Out of the blue, Micha-Johan-Cruyff appeared in front of me. Finally! I thought and stood up, beaming with happiness. As we started to dance, I told him I wished the Dutch had won. Confused, he looked at me and said: "Have you got a screw loose or something?"

He kept going until the end of the dance, but avoided looking me in the eyes. After that I realized I could forget about the champagne bar.

As I watched the two girls on the beach thirty years later, I wondered whether you even have to dance with boys in dance school nowadays. It's probably much easier than it was back then. Although Micha-Johan-Cruyff could dance very well. Even if he didn't understand my sensitive female soul. But then, he was young, too.

July, Berlin

The taxi driver found a space directly in front the house. He turned the light on and turned around to Dani. "So, we're here. That'll be eighteen fifty."

Dani handed him a bill. "There's twenty, and could I have a receipt please?"

While the driver wrote it out, she looked up to the windows of her apartment. The lights were on. Her mood sank immediately. Lars must be there. Either that, or burglars. The latter would probably be less annoying; at least they would take off when she came in. Lars wouldn't.

The taxi driver gave her the receipt and climbed out to get her small suitcase and laptop bag from the trunk.

"You're welcome. Have a nice evening."

Dani took out her luggage and went up to the front door. *Don't talk to me about having a nice evening,* she thought. *Maybe you could take the guy in my apartment with you and get rid of him somewhere. Then maybe I'll have a nice evening.*

In the elevator she pressed the button for the fifth floor and leaned her forehead against the cool metal wall. She was the personnel manager of a big Berlin software firm. For the last four days she had been leading interviews in Düsseldorf and trying to develop the company's employee structures. They needed to take on twenty new people, and fifty had been invited to interview, which had made for a very competitive atmosphere. She had spent each evening sitting in the hotel restaurant with the business manager and his assistant, going through the applicants, finishing up with a nightcap in the hotel bar. None of the workdays had ended before midnight.

The elevator came to a standstill with a slight bump. Dani had realized on the flight how exhausted she was; she wanted a bath, a glass of red wine, some late-night entertainment show on TV, and then an early night. Why on earth had she given Lars her house key, and why hadn't she just ignored his text yesterday: "Looking forward to seeing you"? *It's your own fault*, she thought, taking a deep breath and opening the apartment door.

He bounded toward her right away.

"Why didn't you call me? I would have picked you up from the airport. I tried to call you, but your cell was turned off all afternoon."

He took her bag and kissed her. Dani felt her back tense up, and Lars noticed, too. He let her go and looked at her sympathetically.

"I'm sure you're beat; I thought you would be. I made a little bite to eat, come on in. I'm glad you're back. I'll warm the soup up; maybe you want to take a shower first."

"I'm not hungry. I already ate something on the plane." As Dani saw Lars's disappointed face, she felt guilty. "But I'd love a glass of red wine; could you open a bottle? I'll grab a quick shower."

Lars beamed at her, and Dani fled into the bathroom.

Standing under the shower, she turned the temperature up and closed her eyes. They had met six months ago at a computer fair in Munich—at one of the numerous events that always go hand in hand with these fairs. Dani had been standing there in the middle of all the computer people in black suits, all of them important, bigoted, and drunk. Her pumps were rubbing; she was sweating in her close-fitting suit and found the event mind-numbingly dull. Then suddenly, this guy in jeans, jacket, and an open shirt had appeared out of nowhere. No tie, his blond hair was tousled, and he had a dimple when he smiled. "So, pretty lady, would you like to run away with me?"

The chat-up line had been an awful one, but the guy wasn't bad, and Dani, who didn't normally drink alcohol, had already put away two glasses of champagne. An hour later, they were sitting in the bar of Dani's hotel telling each other silly stories. They were both from Berlin, which—in her drunken state—Dani took to be a sign. That was, admittedly, the sum total of everything they had in common. Lars tested computer games for a magazine; he was thirty-two, making him a decade younger than her, and loved action films and boxing. He gazed at Dani, enraptured. She took him up to her room. She had thrown her last lover out of her life eight months ago, and missed the sex. And Lars smelled good and felt even better. Dani drank a fourth glass of champagne and undressed him. He was an unbelievably good lover. The colleagues at the fair stand told her the next morning that she looked amazing, in spite of how hectic the fair had been. Dani had felt satisfied.

She rinsed the shampoo from her hair and turned off the shower. While she toweled herself dry, she looked in the mirror. She was very slim, and went jogging every morning. But in spite of that, her body didn't look thirty years old anymore. Not that it seemed to bother Lars. He worshiped her.

And it was starting to drive her around the bend. She was distancing herself from him more and more, but that only seemed to spur him on. He made plans for a life together, but Dani ignored them all. Even that didn't seem to bother him. On the other hand, he really was an excellent lover. Dani combed her hair and tied it up. Perhaps his attachment to her would start to fade at some point. At least there wasn't the danger that she would fall head over heels in love with him. That was the most important thing.

Although, she did sometimes feel sorry for him when he looked at her with those disappointed eyes and drooping shoulders.

"Well, he can just forget it," said Dani to herself in the mirror. "After all, I didn't make him any promises."

Her reflection leaned forward to contradict her, saying reproachfully: "But you aren't ending it either. You're using him as a lover and to water your plants and do your shopping. You're a bad person."

Dani jumped with a start and stared into the mirror. She must have been working too hard.

When she came back into the living room in her bathrobe, Lars had lit candles and poured the wine. He sat on the sofa, one arm laid against the backrest, and beamed at her. Dani sat down on the seat opposite and heard her inner voice again: "You're a bad person."

Lars took his arm from the backrest and looked at her.

"Is something wrong?"

Dani felt unbelievably tired. She just wanted to sit here, drink wine, and slowly let her head empty itself of thoughts. She didn't want to get drawn into a discussion and end up feeling bad. But Lars was still staring at her, waiting for an answer.

"No." She pulled her feet up onto the chair. "There's nothing wrong. It was just unbelievably demanding and I'm worn out." She raised her glass and toasted him. "I'm sorry...about the food, I mean, but thank you for the wine."

Lars's facial expression relaxed at once. "Now you just rest. I've gotten your mail; do you want me to bring it to you?" He was already standing up.

Dani took a deep breath. "Yes, if you like, thank you."

It would be better to read the mail than sit there in painful silence, she thought, reaching for the stack of letters Lars handed to her.

Right on top there was a letter addressed to her in the name of Füller. She didn't recognize the handwriting. She turned the letter over. Marleen de Vries: the name reminded her of something, but she couldn't think what. She ripped the envelope open and started to read. Then she looked up, sat up straight, and started to laugh.

• ● •

Hamburg

Ruth was standing in front of a mirror in a boutique on the Gänsemarkt and twisting around to see herself from behind.

"It makes me look fat, right? I never normally have such a big ass!"

Gabi stroked the fabric of a suit hanging on the rack nearby and looked over at Ruth. "Maybe it's the color."

Ruth scowled at her in the mirror. "Nonsense, pink suits me. It's the pants; they're cut weirdly."

A saleswoman approached, smiling. She handed Ruth a hanger with another pair of pants.

"This label cuts their sizes very small. Maybe you'd like to try them in another size?"

Ruth took the hanger and looked for the label.

"What size are these? Ten, no, that's too big for me."

The saleswoman seemed vexed. "But you have the eight on now, and they're too small." She tried to salvage the situation. "Although that's not to say you can't carry off figure-hugging styles."

"These aren't figure-hugging, they're bottom-hugging."

Ruth stared in the mirror, by now in a foul mood. The saleswoman fell into an embarrassed silence.

Gabi was struggling to stop herself from laughing. "You look like a sausage: I'm sure it's just the color though, because your butt isn't that fat at all."

Ruth looked at her angrily. "Thank you very much. These pants are cut badly, I always wear an eight, and I'll eat cabbage soup for a month before I go up a size. Or wear skirts with elasticized waists. Besides, I don't like pink that much anyway. Everyone's wearing it nowadays."

She disappeared into the changing room, yanking the curtain shut behind her with much more force than was necessary.

Gabi gave the saleswoman an encouraging smile and gestured toward the changing room.

"She'll be back in three months. I promise. Perhaps you can hold the pants until then?"

"Oh, we can't do it for longer than two, three days…"

"It was a joke."

The saleswoman looked at Gabi uncertainly. Ruth, who had just come out of the cubicle, laid an armful of pants and jackets down on the chair.

"Unfortunately, the pants were cut badly, and I didn't like the rest. Good-bye for now."

She linked arms with Gabi. "Come on, let's look for a café. I need something to drink."

As they left the shop, Gabi stretched her hand out behind her and held up three fingers. The bewildered shop assistant shook her head thoughtfully.

Half an hour later, Gabi and Ruth were sitting in a small café. Ruth stirred sweetener into her espresso and lit a cigarette.

"I have never been a size ten in my whole life. She's crazy."

Gabi unwrapped a cookie from its aluminum foil. "Of course. But Ruth, for heaven's sake, you're so slim and willowy, it doesn't matter in the slightest what the label says."

"It matters to me. I'm getting fat. That's what happens when you're over thirty and in a relationship. It's a statistical fact that women in relationships put on weight quicker than single women do."

Gabi shook her head. "Well, then maybe you should separate from Karsten; then you'd lose weight."

"So you think I've put on weight, too?"

"Ruth, please! No, at least not that I can see. I only said that because you're obsessing about it."

"Maybe I really should separate from Karsten," said Ruth, then looked into Gabi's amazed face. She started to stir her espresso again. "No, I'm serious. The putting on weight is just symbolic. I've had enough. We're like an old married couple. Karsten spends the whole day in the clinic with his X-ray equipment, looking at strangers' insides. But he has no idea of what's inside me."

Gabi unwrapped Ruth's cookie. "And, what is?"

"Oh, I don't know. It's just that life has gotten so boring. Karsten comes home, cooks, eats, sits in front of his computer, then goes to bed. We don't go to parties anymore or meet new people; we don't do anything exciting at all. Every day it's the same old shit. I'm tired of it."

"Ruth, you go on vacation twice a year, you have an apartment on Sylt, a 1500-square-foot apartment in Eppendorf, and he's a really good guy. What more do you want?"

Ruth looked at Gabi, irritated. "Sure, the holidays, great. Two weeks in Tuscany in the summer so Karsten can recharge, and skiing in winter, always with the same group we've been with for the last five years. The apartment on Sylt belongs to him and his brother, and we have to arrange everything with him. And the 'good guy,' as you call him, is always dog-tired."

Gabi wanted to say something in response but stopped herself. There was no point. Ruth looked at her thoughtfully.

"It's fine for you. You can do whatever you want. Your husband works in Frankfurt and you only see him on weekends. You have no idea how much I envy you; Karsten is under my feet every day."

Sometimes Gabi had the burning impulse to give Ruth a good slap. Yet again, she resisted. Instead she said, in her nicest "friend" voice: "It's not easy for me either, especially during the week, when…"

Ruth interrupted her, not even seeming to realize that she had. "A few weeks ago I met a really nice guy. Markus. He's a photographer from Cologne. We both went to the exhibition I wrote about in that article. His pictures were exhibited there—it was really intense."

"Him or the pictures?"

"Both. Anyway, we went for a beer afterwards. He was staying in a hotel, and well…we both got pretty smashed, so I went back with him. Gabi, it was the best night I've had in years."

Gabi took a cigarette from Ruth's pack. She had actually given up three years ago, and now only smoked in exceptional circumstances. She had a feeling she knew what was coming next.

"I didn't think you smoked anymore. Never mind, anyway, I wanted to ask you for a favor, between friends, as it were."

So that was the reason she had wanted them to go shopping together. Gabi had been surprised when Ruth suggested it. They hadn't seen each other outside of work for a while now.

"Markus has just gotten a commission with a Hamburg ad firm. He's starting on Monday and will be there for three weeks. I've told Karsten you're not doing too well at the moment, because you're by yourself during the week, and that we're meeting up regularly again. And that I'll be staying overnight with you sometimes."

"And he believed that nonsense?"

Ruth looked at Gabi reproachfully. "Why are you getting so aggressive? Of course Karsten believes me. You know what a dope he can be sometimes. Come on, Gabi, you're my friend, and I need some fun in my life again. You don't have to worry about me; I'm not in love with Markus. He's just so exciting, and my sex life has gotten so awful. I'm too young to be put out to pasture."

"Ruth, I'm not worried about *you*, I'm worried about Karsten. He doesn't deserve this."

"Karsten won't ever find out. And maybe a little affair will do our relationship good. All you have to do is say the right thing if you run into Karsten and he asks you about it. Come on, Gabi, please, help me out."

Gabi stubbed out her half-smoked cigarette. She felt sick. She had known Ruth for over ten years, had been working with her in the same publishing house all that time, and she had wanted them to be friends from the beginning. Right now though, she had no idea why.

Ruth's voice sounded almost pleading. "Gabi, I know what I'm doing. I'll owe you."

She reached for Gabi's hand, looking excited and ten years younger. Like she used to.

"And you probably won't even run into Karsten, so all you need to do is keep this to yourself, OK?"

She gestured to the waiter and ordered two glasses of champagne. Once it arrived, she passed Gabi a glass, then raised her own.

"And? Say something."

Gabi cleared her throat. "I think it's terrible, but I'm not your conscience, and you're old enough to make your own mistakes."

Ruth smiled contentedly. "Gabi, thank you. Here's to our friendship. This is what friends are for. Cheers, sweetheart."

To Gabi, the champagne tasted flat.

• ● •

Cuxhaven

Marleen put the third bowl of ground meat on the table and, hearing a noise, looked out the open window. They were already there. Three older women, leaning their bicycles carefully against the wall and locking them up.

"Mathilde, aren't you locking yours?'

"No, my son got me this insurance policy, so if my bike gets stolen I get the money to buy myself a new one. And this one is getting old."

"But it won't get stolen here."

"So why are you locking yours then?"

Marleen couldn't hear Anneliese's answer. A moment later the door opened and they were standing in the pub.

"Good morning! Is it just the three of you today?"

They stopped for a moment in front of the cloakroom. Inge hung her coat neatly on a hanger and stuffed her colorful neck scarf into one of the sleeves.

"*Morgen*, Marleen. Gerda has sore feet or tired knees or something like that. She's becoming quite an oddball in her old age, always complaining about something or other."

Mathilde shook her head. "And Gerda is the youngest as well; not even seventy-five yet and she's letting herself go already. She always did whine about the slightest thing. I told her, she just needs her hands to roll the meatballs, not her knees, but she wouldn't listen."

Anneliese took a white apron from her bag and put it on. "Leave her to it, she has her funny moments, there's nothing you can do about it. And we'll manage with the three of us, won't we? Marleen, how many people are you making the soup for?"

"For fifty. You can make a start right away; the meat's on the table, and the coffee's ready. I'll just finish off the table decorations; then I'll join you and lend a hand."

"Take your time, child, we've managed much more than that before."

Inge sat down, buttoned up her flowery apron, and reached into the bowl of meat.

Half an hour later, Marleen sat down next to Mathilde, who was rolling out small meatballs at an astonishing speed while holding forth on the latest neighborhood gossip.

Marleen tried to figure out how to bring the conversation round to Lena. But Mathilde took the decision away from her. She looked briefly at Marleen's hands, then nudged her with her elbows.

"You're not making rissoles, sweetie: use less meat. You young women have no patience. I was at Lena's last week, and she made onion soup with meatballs, and they were huge, too. All so she could get it done quicker, but they don't taste as good."

"Where's Lena living now?"

Inge took one of Marleen's meatballs from the plate, divided it in two, and said in a lecturing tone: "Don't change the subject. Look, they should look like this." Marleen nodded briefly and looked at Mathilde expectantly.

"Lena lives near Kiel now. They bought a house there last year. Jürgen is so good with these things; they redid the whole place. He's really on the ball, my son-in-law."

"Say, Mathilde, do you remember Christine?"

"The brunette who married Bernd Kruse?"

"Yes, that's the one. But they divorced five years ago now."

"No, really? Young people nowadays, they're all splitting up. Do they have kids?"

Anneliese pulled the second meat bowl into the middle of the table. "Claasen's daughter is divorced now, too; her husband was a total drunk. It's awful."

Inge looked up, interested. "The red-haired girl? She was confirmed with our Katja. Just imagine, and she's divorced now?"

Marleen tried again. "Weren't Christine and Lena friends? They used to play handball together, didn't they?"

Mathilde thought for a moment. "That's quite a few years back, but yes, they were friends. Lena took some photos at Christine's wedding; I saw them."

Anneliese wiped her hands clean. "Was her wedding dress nice? I'll get more coffee."

"I think so, yes. It was a long time ago."

Marleen turned back to Mathilde. "Do you know whether they're still in touch?"

"No, something happened there. I'm not sure exactly what; they never said. I think it was something to do with Bernd or Jürgen. I try not to get involved. Why do you ask?"

Marleen stood up and grabbed four glasses and a bottle of advocaat. "I'll tell you in a moment. By the way, I need Lena's address."

• ● •

Hamburg

Christine was sitting on her balcony and staring at the empty notepad in front of her when she heard Dorothea's voice in the hallway.

"Hey, where are you?"

"On the balcony, bring a chair out."

Dorothea was already at the door. She put a bottle of champagne and two glasses on the table, then grabbed herself a chair. Christine looked at the bottle, then at Dorothea.

"Do we have something to celebrate?"

"Not really. I just thought we should drink some champagne together. We haven't done that in months. And I'd like to know why."

Christine looked at her. Dorothea collapsed back into her chair and untwisted the wire on the champagne cork. "Ready, set, and *tschüss*..." she said, her gaze following the cork as it flew in a high arc over the balconies and plopped down onto the street below.

Christine looked at her, shaking her head.

"Someday you'll hit someone, and then you'll get it."

She reached her glass over. As Dorothea poured, Christine tried to decipher her facial expression. Something was up; she seemed annoyed, or at least indignant. Christine wondered what it could be.

"Cheers, Christine, to us." Dorothea looked at Christine, raising her glass and her eyebrows, which gave her a mocking expression. "And to friendship." She drank half of her glass in one gulp and put it down on the table.

Christine out her glass next to it.

"So, what's up?"

"What do you mean, what's up?" Dorothea's voice was louder now, and she was looking at Christine with an almost enraged expression. "You're not seriously asking me what's up? We hardly see each other, we only speak on the phone occasionally, you never have time for me, you don't confide in me anymore, I have to ask your brother to find out how you are, and then you want to know what's up? If I've done something to annoy you, you could have said something. But what I can't stand is this silence. I'm really pissed off."

Christine was amazed. It wasn't like Dorothea to have outbursts like this. She wondered for a moment whether she was joking. But the look on her face made it pretty clear she wasn't.

Christine started to feel uncomfortable. She felt that Dorothea was being unreasonable, but she felt guilty at the same time. She tried to defend herself.

"I'm not ignoring you; it's just that I have so much going on at the moment. I underestimated how much time I'd need for the columns, and it's taking much longer than I thought. And there's so much going on at work that I rarely finish on time nowadays. Last month I was away a lot, and when I was here I didn't have much time. It has nothing to do with you."

"Oh, come on, you can find the time to give me a call now and then. You always managed to before. If I didn't contact you nowadays, we wouldn't ever hear from each other."

Christine took a deep breath. The accusations weren't entirely unjustified; she hadn't been putting much effort into their friendship recently because she was always busy, with work, with *Femme*, with the columns for Ruth, too. And, of course, with Richard.

"And it feels like you're keeping something from me. You only make small talk; you never really share anything with me anymore. That's not how close friends should be with each other."

Dorothea stared at Christine angrily. Ever since she'd heard Richard's voice on Christine's answering machine, she'd felt like she was being deceived. It had been Dorothea and Georg who had invited Christine to that party all those years ago—the one she'd met Richard at. And when their affair started four years ago, it was Dorothea who had encouraged Christine to go with it because she'd noticed that he did her good, that she was beaming with happiness and deeply in love. After the first easy months came the difficult ones. Christine wasn't cut out to be a mistress; the lonely weekends and holidays without Richard were hard on her. So Dorothea had been there for her on the emotional roller coaster. On bad days she uncorked wine bottles, handed out tissues, declared married men to be cowardly idiots, swore vengeance, and told Christine just how much Richard would suffer when she left him to live out the rest of his miserable existence with his horrible wife. On good days she listened patiently to the Richard-is-the-best-thing-that-has-ever-happened-to-me stories and encouraged Christine to stick with it: "Just enjoy it and see what happens."

What happened was a two-week skiing holiday Richard's wife had surprised him with last Christmas. Christine was bewildered when he went ahead with the holiday and the pretence of marital togetherness. Every night he sent longing texts to Christine, while she endured two weeks of veering between rage, jealousy, and devastation. Dorothea, in solidarity, got drunk with her, tried rather unsuccessfully to cheer her up, and cooked for her every night, just to end up freezing almost all of it every time. After a while, she had had enough, and told Christine exactly what she thought. She had ended with the words: "Now start using your brain again finally, and take a good look in the mirror. Look at what you're doing to yourself. Sweetie, you've accomplished so much in your life; why are you letting some asshole make you feel bad about yourself?"

It seemed to do the trick. When Richard got back from his holiday and came by to surprise Christine, she was unsure at first; then his good mood enraged her. He didn't attempt to offer any explanation, and was just pleased to see her. But that wasn't enough anymore. At the end of their argument, she gave him his apartment key back. Richard left, and Christine collapsed into tears and rang Dorothea's doorbell in desperation.

That was six months ago now. After several weeks and various rescue attempts, Dorothea had managed to calm Christine down. After that, she had thrown herself into her work. Dorothea was relieved that chapter was at an end and Christine was back to her old self. Then, suddenly, she heard Richard's voice on the answering machine.

Christine's voice brought her back from her train of thought.

"OK, so, you're annoyed about something, I can see that. But will you please spit it out—instead of beating around the bush we could actually be talking about it."

Dorothea took a sharp intake of breath. "We could talk about it. Great. That's what I thought, too, that we could talk to each other, but clearly I was mistaken. You're not talking, you're keeping a secret from me, and do you realize how stupid I feel?"

Christine looked confused. "I really don't know what you're upset about. What's happened?"

Dorothea finished the last of her champagne in one gulp and slammed it down in the table. She tried hard to stay calm.

"Fine. Then I'll tell you. While you were on your way to Sylt, I brought your mail up for you. At exactly the moment when Richard Jürgensen was blathering away on your answering machine. Super, I thought, his royal highness is trying to get in touch again. But it didn't sound like that.

It didn't sound at all like you weren't in touch anymore. In fact, it sounded like completely the opposite. But you don't have to tell me about it. After all, I'm just your dumb neighbor who gets to clear up all the mess Mr. Jürgensen leaves behind him. It's not like you need to tell me about anything. Thank you, Christine, thank you so much for your trust."

Christine went red and noticed with surprise that Dorothea's eyes had filled with tears. She made herself breathe calmly, reached for the bottle, and poured more champagne. *Just don't say the wrong thing*, she said to herself, *just stay calm.*

She'd often felt guilty in the last few months, even though she had told herself she wasn't lying to Dorothea, just omitting to mention a few things. But she hadn't felt good about it.

"Are you angry because I'm seeing Richard again, or because I didn't tell you about it?" asked Christine cautiously.

"Both. But I think I'm more upset that you don't trust me anymore."

"It has nothing to do with trust, Dorothea. Even I don't know why I started it all up again. We met up at the end of March, and I was weak. It's terrible, especially after the whole Christmas debacle, and I know that, too. I think I was ashamed to tell you that I'd slipped; I was worried about how you would react. I mean, I've been angry enough at myself; you can believe me on that."

Dorothea shook her head. "You have no idea what I'd say. I really don't care who you go to bed with, but I was really worried about you last winter. You seemed to get sadder, thinner, and paler by the day. Through it all I either cursed Richard along with you or encouraged you to go for it, depending on what you needed. And I did that for your sake. Friendship means openness and trust; it means you're there for each other. And for me to find out through some stupid coincidence that my friend is living a double life, well, that borders on betrayal."

Dorothea had talked herself into a rage. Uttering the last sentence, she noticed she was being melodramatic. She took a deep breath and searched for something to say that would soften her tone but not take back the strength of what she felt. Christine was looking at her helplessly. Dorothea stuck her chin out obstinately and said: "Well, it's true."

Her face betrayed a childish expression that took some of the harshness from her words. Dorothea wasn't the type to bear a grudge; she just spoke up about what annoyed her. Christine had been shocked when she launched into her tirade, but now that it was finally out in the open, a feeling of relief had set in. She touched Dorothea's hand gently.

"I'm sorry. You're right, I can't just cry on your shoulder when things are bad and then keep the rest to myself. But on the other hand, I do object to being obligated to share these things. I mean, of course trust is important in friendship, but when I have to constantly prove that by sharing everything right away, I feel under pressure, and I don't like that."

"I tell you almost everything, and I don't do it because I have to but because it makes me feel better. You only talk about private matters when you're prompted."

"That's exactly my point. When you tell me about something, it makes you feel better, relieved. You said it yourself. But it's your decision to talk to me about it. I have to get things straight in my own head before I can talk about them. It's nothing against you. Being open isn't a straight swap, Dorothea, and you have to accept that."

Dorothea thought for a moment. Perhaps this was the problem in lots of friendships.

"I always thought trust was a reciprocal thing. I tell you my stories, and you tell me yours. Otherwise it's one-sided. And…"

Christine interrupted her. "Trust isn't about I'll-show-you-mine-if-you-show-me-yours. Trust means I *can* tell you, but I don't have to. Trust is the ability to be able to share with someone without being forced or expected to."

Dorothea looked at Christine. "And? Can you with me?"

Christine smiled. "Of course I can, Dorothea. Don't be silly." She lit two cigarettes and passed one to her. "Come on, let's smoke a peace pipe. And then I'll tell you about Richard."

• • •

Hamburg

Luise looked at her watch as she climbed the steps to the Italian restaurant. Seven forty-five, she was fifteen minutes early. Ruth had booked the table for eight p.m.; she wanted to discuss the progress of their detective work with Gabi and Ines. Luise smiled as she thought about what she had to share with the others; she was starting to find the search more and more exciting.

She found Gabi at a table by the window. She was lost in thought, playing with her lighter and staring out of the window. She jumped as Luise laid her hand on her shoulder.

"Oh, hello, Luise, sorry, I didn't see you come in."

Luise laughed. "So I see, you looked like you were in another world. Is everything OK?" She sat down, rummaged around in her bag for her cigarettes, and laid them on the table. "I thought I'd be the first to arrive again."

"I came here straight from work. It wasn't worth going home first."

Luise looked at her as she lit her cigarette. "Are you feeling OK? You look pale."

Gabi shook her head quickly. "No, no, everything's fine, I've just got a bit too much work, that's all. And I haven't slept very well for the last few nights. Maybe it's the full moon."

Luise looked at her skeptically. But before she could probe further, the blond waitress came up to the table.

"Good evening, ladies. Would you like to order drinks or a small aperitif perhaps? We have a lovely Prosecco with elderberry syrup."

Luise looked at her. "I'd like a large bottle of water and a glass of your house red."

"Of course." The blond raised her eyebrows for a second, turned around, and went.

Gabi watched her go. "I passed on the aperitif, too, and ordered an apple juice spritzer instead, which didn't go down well. Somehow she always makes me feel a little nervous. One day she'll actually manage to get me to order what she recommends."

"Oh, Gabi, it's ridiculous. In a minute she'll be recommending a load of other things that aren't on the menu and conveniently leaving out the prices. It really gets on my nerves."

"Ruth likes it; she always orders the specials. In all the times that we've eaten here she's never once looked at the menu."

Luise laughed. "Typical Ruth, she has to be given the special treatment; otherwise she gets twitchy."

Gabi didn't bat an eyelash and stayed silent.

"What's up? Are you having issues, you and Ruth?" asked Luise, bemused.

"Well, define 'issues.' Ever since Ruth was made editor of *Kult,* she's been throwing her weight around a bit. She acts like a diva and treats other people as if they're idiots. She expects us all to jump when she says so, and I…"

Seeing Luise's shocked expression, she came to an abrupt stop. The words had just burst out of her; she hadn't even wanted to talk about Ruth. After all, their problem had nothing to do with anyone else. Before she could try to salvage the situation, Ines came in. Luise looked at Gabi briefly.

"Let's talk about it again when we're alone."

Then she turned to Ines, who was unwrapping herself from her hooded jacket and smoothing her hair down with her hands.

"Evening," she said, sinking into the chair next to Luise. "I'm so thirsty; isn't Ruth here yet?"

She looked around. In a shot, the waitress was by their table again.

"Good evening, can I get you a drink, perhaps a small aperitif, I have a wonderful…"

"Yes, a large beer, thank you."

Ines didn't notice the waitress's raised eyebrows, distracted as she was by the other two, who could barely contain their laughter. She looked at them questioningly.

"Did I do something wrong?"

"No," snorted Luise, then pulled herself together.

"Ah, Ruth's here."

Ruth waved at them as she hung her white leather jacket up in the cloakroom. She walked briskly over to their table.

"Hi, sorry I'm late." She leaned over to kiss first Gabi, then Luise on the cheek, then grasped Ines's outstretched hand and shook it. "Ines! It's so great that you're joining us."

She sat down and looked around. Her hair was tousled and her face glowing. She threw Gabi a quick look and winked. Gabi looked back, not reacting, and cleared her throat.

"So, shall we make a start?"

Ruth shook her head lightly, her eyes still fixed on Gabi. Her voice was a little hesitant. "Sure, but I'd like to order first."

The waitress was there in a second. She beamed at Ruth.

"Mrs. Johannis, how lovely to see you. May I offer you a small aperitif? I have a wonderful Prosecco with elderberry syrup; it's really lovely."

Ruth nodded enthusiastically. "That sounds great, I'd love one."

Gabi and Luise grinned. Ruth looked at them. "What's so funny?"

Luise bit her bottom lip before glancing at Gabi, who was fumbling in her purse, and quickly said: "Nothing. Shall we order the pasta for four and just be done with it?"

Ruth paused before agreeing, hesitantly, "If you like."

Ines nodded. The waitress kept her notepad aloft. "Perhaps you'd like an appetizer?"

Gabi shook her head. "Not for me thanks. Ines? Luise? Ruth?" No one answered. "No, that's everything, thank you."

She watched the waitress walk—a little in a huff despite her partial success—back to the bar.

"Can I start? I've managed to find someone." Gabi looked around her at the three curious faces. "I found Frauke. Her surname used to be Müller, but now it's Jensen and she lives near Lübeck. I've already spoken with her on the phone."

"How did you manage to do that so quickly?" asked Ines, amazed. "We didn't even know her surname."

Gabi laughed contentedly. "Sometimes you just get lucky. It was fairly easy. I went out for lunch last week with Christine. There were a few women at the table next to us, talking at the top of their voices about their daughters and which teen heartthrobs they had crushes on. Then Christine says to me that she finds it strange how women seem to forget about what they were like as girls as soon as they become mothers. She said she used to have a Bravo poster of David Cassidy on her bedroom wall, that she used to kiss his mouth every morning before she left for school. And that her friend Frauke Müller used to do the same thing."

Ines gave a loud groan. "Yes, I have a vague memory of that. And then what? I mean, there must be so many Müllers that I'm not sure it helps much."

"It was so easy. I just played dumb and asked when it was. Christine thought for a moment and said it was 1973; she was in seventh grade at Wentorf School at the time. So afterward, I phoned the secretary's office at the school and spoke to a very nice woman there who faxed me the class lists. There was only one Frauke Müller. Her parents' address hasn't changed in all these years. Mrs. Müller could even still remember Christine and gave me Frauke's telephone number."

Luise, who had been holding her breath during the story, breathed out deeply. "Great! And what did she say? What was she like?"

"Really nice." Gabi thought back to the conversation. "At first she was surprised. I mean, she hasn't seen Christine in over twenty years. The last contact they had was a card she sent Christine when she got married. She was invited but couldn't go because she'd just given birth to her third child. She married her childhood sweetheart and has, as I said, three kids. She works half days in her husband's company; he owns a car salesroom. We didn't speak for long. She gave me her address, and I sent her the invitation and questionnaire. And she's coming to the party!"

Ines nudged Ruth, who had been uncharacteristically silent during Gabi's story.

"That's amazing. Ruth, all this was your idea, what do you say to that?"

Ruth looked at Gabi for a long moment, then reached for her purse. "Great work, Gabi. But I already have something, too."

She pulled an envelope out of her bag and took a sheet of paper from it, which she unfolded on the table. Luise leaned over and pulled it toward her.

"That's the questionnaire." She picked it up. "From Marie Erdmann. And it's already filled out. Great!"

Ruth watched her with a contented expression.

"It was easy. Remember you found that postcard in Christine's apartment that Marie had sent her? She's called Annemarie, by the way. Well, she's still at that address; she took over looking after her parents' house and lives there now. She was overjoyed to get the invite, filled in the questionnaire right away, and has already booked time off for the party in November."

By now, Luise was waving the piece of paper excitedly.

"I have to tell you all about my success story. I was in Flensburg for business meetings, had to stop to use the bathroom, and ended up finding this small shopping center. There was a bakery there, and I got myself some lunch. I'd only just got back into the car and started to eat the sandwich when I noticed this on the napkin."

She pulled the neatly folded paper napkin from her bag and showed it to the others. Ines was the first to catch on.

"Number one for years—Meyer Fine Foods, formerly Love Butchers. Love! I don't believe it! Luise, that's amazing!"

Luise looked at the others triumphantly. "I was so excited, I went straight back into the shop and asked the assistant about it. She was very nice but had no idea what had happened to the Love family; the shop has belonged to the Meyers for fifteen years now. But she had a colleague in another branch who had done an apprenticeship with the Loves. So I drove to the other branch to get her details. She's almost seventy now, only works a little, and didn't want to give much away over the phone. So I invited her to have a cup of coffee with me, and then she was really lovely. And then she told me: she knows Linda, too. She talked for ages and really seemed to enjoy talking about old times."

"And? Is Linda Love coming?" asked Gabi impatiently. "That would be amazing."

Luise shrugged her shoulders. "I don't know. Linda worked as a nanny in Canada after she graduated high school. She fell in love while she was out there and stayed. Now she's called Lambert and lives in Vancouver. Hertha—that's the apprentice—gave me her address, and I've already written a letter but haven't had a reply yet. Hopefully I will."

Ruth had been making notes in her day planner. She pushed her glasses back up and nodded contentedly. "So, we're making great progress. I'm sure we'll make the surprise party a success. We've already got three people. Now, who else do we still need to find?"

"Marleen was going to deal with Lena, the basketball player. But I haven't spoken with her yet. She also sent the invitation and questionnaire to Dani, you know, Daniela—Christine's old housemate."

Gabi suddenly remembered something. "I forgot to tell you. Frauke told me on the phone about someone called Gudrun. She used to be friends with Christine, too. Frauke's going give me her contact details."

Luise nodded. "That's right, Gudrun! Ines, do you remember? When we were at your house, Georg mentioned a Gudrun. She had a horse, and she and Christine used to go riding together."

Ines laughed. "Please, horse riding? Christine hates horses. Well, it's all getting exciting anyway. Look, our food is coming."

After the waitress had put the dishes down on their table and given an elaborate description of the pasta, which no one but Ruth paid any attention to, Gabi raised her glass.

"So, my dears, to our continued success. Cheers!"

• ● •

Hamburg

Christine was dreaming. She was sitting with Richard on a sun terrace. The stars were twinkling in the sky, the waves crashing below them. A golden band sparkled on Christine's finger. Richard was smiling at her. She had an uneasy feeling she was forgetting something. She looked at the ring, then at Richard, and wracked her brains in desperation. Suddenly she realized what must have happened. She had married Richard. Her head felt hot, and she awoke with a start, feeling dizzy.

Christine opened her eyes slowly. Her head wasn't just hot; it hurt, too. And where Richard had just been sitting, her wicker chair now stood, piled with her clothes from last night. She had folded her jeans on the ironed crease. Christine groaned. She only did that when she was drunk.

Gradually, the pictures came back. She and Dorothea on the balcony. Two bottles of champagne and a big reconciliation. Then they'd taken a taxi into the city. In the first bar, they'd run into some of Dorothea's colleagues. She couldn't remember their names. Apart from an Alexander. Christine lay back down again. He'd kissed her at some point. There had been a lot of red wine, that she could remember. Then a taxi home, Dorothea had fallen asleep, and Christine hadn't been able to string her words together well enough to tell the driver where they lived. It was so embarrassing. She pulled the duvet over her head. No more booze, no more nights out around the Kiez.

Someone rang her doorbell. They couldn't be serious! She tried to decipher the number on her alarm clock. Eight fifteen in the morning. It rang again, this time for longer. Idiots. At the third ring she got up, sluggishly. All her bones ached. She had somehow managed to fall over getting out of the taxi. Oh God.

Christine picked up the receiver for the entry system and cleared her throat.

"Yes, hello?"

Her voice sounded drunk and hoarse. She tried to act like she had a cold.

A cheerful male voice answered. "Good morning, Frau Schmidt, 'Wine Direct' here, I'm here with your order."

That had to be a joke. Or the rightful punishment. He'd have to just take it all away again; she never wanted to drink alcohol again. God, she felt awful.

"Hello, Frau Schmidt? Please press the entrance buzzer for me."

Christine pressed the button and slumped down into a chair. On the dresser in front of her lay the delivery notice confirmation from the wine store. He was right.

Ten minutes later, five boxes of red wine were in her hallway, the attractive deliveryman had taken his leave with a cheerful "get better soon," and Christine had gone back to bed.

She was too old for these escapades. She pictured two middle-aged women, babbling to each other and with their mascara running, either falling asleep in a taxi or falling over stumbling out of it. Ashamed, she pulled her duvet back over her again and held her hands against her head to stop it from exploding. Just the thought of getting up to grab some aspirin made her feel sick again.

After half an hour, she forced herself to get up. But very slowly. She gingerly made her way into the bathroom and looked at herself in the mirror. She always took her makeup off before going to sleep, even when she was drunk. So it could have been worse. Her gaze fell on her jewelry, lying on the table. She felt overwhelmed by relief. At least she hadn't gotten married. Falling out of a taxi wasn't that bad after all, not in comparison.

She reached for her toothbrush. She had the day off today. She didn't look as bad as she felt, and she hadn't accidentally gotten married: maybe she'd have a good day after all.

• ● •

"The Aging Game"

Last week I went to the hairdresser. My stylist's name is Holli; he's good-looking, charming, gay, and very young. Thirty years old at the most. Holli cuts and washes hair with passion and love, and gives his female customers the feeling they're the hottest chicks in town. He makes them beautiful and confident; both men and women leave his salon with their heads held high and a swing in their step. Including me. That was, until the bliss came to an abrupt end the Wednesday before last.

On that day, Holli bent over to peer at my hairline before washing and gave me a reproachful look. Then he smoothed my part down, gave first my roots then me a strange look, and said in a sympathetic tone: "Christine, honey, this won't do. You were only here six weeks ago and now look at your part. Gray. Really gray. You can forget the highlights now. Either we color for real, or else…"

As he stood behind me, his arms hanging helplessly and a distraught look on his face, I felt guilty. Yes, I'm over forty, I've inherited bad genes, and I've had gray hairs since I was twenty-five; and yes, I'm now so old that—bad genes or not—all my hairs are getting gray, and very quickly at that. I apologized, Holli accepted my apology, and since then he no longer gently highlights but colors forcefully, so forcefully in fact that my scalp has been itchy for the last two weeks.

But that's the only way my stylist can take control of my roots; it's a matter of professional pride after all.

Two days later I had an appointment with my chiropractor. My neck was hurting me, which I put down to stress and my old pillow. My chiropractor, Michi, is in his late thirties, very fit, equally charming, and has a twenty-six-year-old beautiful partner, who sits in reception with her model figure and makes all the female patients feel old. Particularly as most of them walk awkwardly or with a stoop; I mean, otherwise they wouldn't need a chiropractor.

Michi thought it strange that I kept getting tension in my neck, so he sent me to a radiologist. This very young, very attractive doctor bundled me into his X-ray machine. After that forty-minute-long ordeal he beckoned me into the consulting room so he could explain the results.

I sat opposite him with my colored but smooth hair and wrinkles, and discovered that I have arthritis. Apparently it isn't serious, just part of getting older—after all, I wasn't exactly thirty anymore. At a certain point, the consequences of your youth start to show their face. With dignity, I stood up, ignored my backache, and got the address of a physiotherapist.

I broke off my treatment with him after the third session. At the very moment when he explained to me that his goal was to take the tension-related pain away, and that my flexibility wasn't the top priority anymore since I didn't exactly need to go dancing at my age. He was roughly thirty.

As it seems that I'm now of the appropriate age for it, I made an appointment with the most expensive beautician in my neighborhood as a form of consolation. She was very nice but somewhat horrified when she looked at my skin structure with the magnifying mirror. She said that I was clearly looking after my skin—in a tone that implied she thought I was only using water, a washcloth, and soap—but she strongly recommended ampullae treatment for the eye area. Very strongly indeed.

Two hours later I left the salon, one hundred and twenty-five Euros poorer. It turns out that I must have reacted to something in the beauty products though, because my friend Karola, whom I saw that evening, thought I looked like I had a nut allergy. Pimples everywhere.

We spent the whole evening in the Italian restaurant and drank red wine. Karola had no problem with getting old, she said, but just sometimes got annoyed when something new started to ache. The reaction on my face got worse, and my eyes were slowly starting to swell and close. Karola pointed out that it stopped anyone from noticing the wrinkles, and that it hardly showed anyway, only if you got close. And no one would do that. Then we giggled like girls, raised our glasses, and made a toast to the fact we would never be as young as we were in that moment again.

When I woke up the next morning, I had a pounding head-ache, and the pimples had spread to my neck. I could hardly move, and my stomach was in a state. I staggered over to the bathroom mirror and concluded that I didn't look as bad on the outside as I felt inside. I could care less about the pimples anymore, my eye wrinkles were still there even after the expensive ampullae, and my neck wasn't too bad.

What does really annoy me, though, is that I don't seem to be able to handle red wine now that I'm older. Now, that does make me mad.

Karola called at lunchtime. She reckoned the wine was bad; it was often a problem at that bar. Only cheap hooch, she'd heard. And she asked if I wanted to meet for a beer this evening. After all, yeast is supposed to be very good for the skin. Especially at our age.

• • •

Cuxhaven

Marleen looked up from her shopping list as she heard the sound of a car door slamming outside. She looked at the clock. Five p.m. She wasn't due to open the bar until an hour later, but despite that customers often banged away on the door long before, pushing past Marleen with a cheerful, "Come on, we could see you were in here!"

Today she had come in early especially to do the drinks orders and prepare the table decorations for a family party being held there the next day. Her waitstaff didn't start their shifts until a quarter to six. She wasn't in the mood to be looking after customers already.

She looked at the car to see if she recognized it. It was a black BMW cabriolet with a Berlin number plate, and she'd never seen it before. In front of it stood a blond woman, locking it with a remote-controlled key. Her hair was piled high, and she wore black trousers, a light brown suede jacket, and high heels. The woman swung her purse onto her shoulder and walked slowly toward the bar. Marleen sighed and stood up. Women like that with cars like that around here were either real estate agents or selling insurance. And Marleen needed neither a house nor an insurance policy, just an hour of peace.

The cabrio driver pushed down the handle of the locked door as Marleen was still two steps away from it. Marleen mumbled an annoyed, "Yes, just a minute," before turning the key in the lock. As she opened the door she said, in as friendly a tone as she could muster, "I don't open until six."

"Hello, Marleen."

The brown eyes under the blond bangs; the wry, slightly embarrassed smile; the voice. Marleen searched her memory.

"I got your letter."

The penny dropped. "Dani! Heavens, I didn't recognize you! Were you always this stunning?"

She stepped aside to let Dani in and reached for her hand.

"So, hello, first of all, I haven't even greeted you. This sure is a good way of answering a letter! What are you doing here?"

"Well, I had to go to Cuxhaven anyway; it's my mother's birthday tomorrow. My parents still live here. Yesterday when I was packing, it suddenly occurred to me that I could come early and give you the questionnaire myself. Besides, I'm curious and wanted to hear all about the search. All I know is what you told me in the letter."

Marleen led Dani into the bar. "First have a seat and tell me what you'd like to drink."

"Oh, anything, I don't mind. What do you have?"

Marleen went behind the bar and laughed. "I have a bar, so I have everything. What would you like?"

Dani had to laugh, too. "So you do. I'd like a coffee please."

As Marleen started up the coffee machine, Dani looked around her.

"It's lovely here. How long have you had this place? Didn't you used to work in a hotel back then?"

"Back when?" said Marleen, putting some cookies onto a plate.

"When Christine got married."

"Ah, well, that was fifteen years ago now. That's right, I was still in the hotel back then. I bought this place with a friend five years ago. It used to be a country café that only opened on weekends. We renovated it, put in a new kitchen, hired a chef, and then slaved away like mad. But it was worth it; it's all going really well now."

She came over to the table with the coffee and cookies and sat down opposite Dani.

"You and that car of yours, you look every inch the high-flying career woman. When I last saw you, you'd just finished studying and were looking for a job. It must have worked out by the looks of it!"

"Yes, really well in fact. I started in a small software company in Bremen, which was then sold to a big Berlin firm after three years. I followed it to Berlin and got really lucky. I'm now the personnel manager."

Marleen whistled appreciatively. Dani waved it away.

"It sounds much more exciting than it is. It's hard work, but the pay is good, and I enjoy it. But I can't seem to get my private life together. Never mind."

Marleen laughed. "I think Christine said the same thing recently. You still have some things in common, it seems."

Dani looked up curiously. "Yes, come on, tell me. I haven't heard anything from Christine in around, well, eight years or so. We spoke on the phone now and then after her wedding; then she and Bernd sold the house. I got a change of address card from her, but then nothing more. Five years ago she sent a card with her new address in Hamburg, and since then, not a word."

"Well, did you try to get in touch with her?"

Dani smiled, embarrassed, and wiped invisible crumbs from the tablecloth.

"No, not really...no, I didn't contact her. I didn't even know she was divorced. I just imagined her sitting happily on the sofa with Bernd and figured she wouldn't be able to relate to the chaos in my private life. And after a while you get past the stage where you can just pick up the phone."

Marleen raised her eyebrows. "Sitting happily with Bernd on the sofa? You really weren't up to date, were you! So how did you find out about the divorce?"

"It was really strange." Dani shook her head. "It was last year, and I was here for the festival with my sister. Suddenly I saw Bernd in front of me, seemingly overjoyed to see me. When I asked after Christine, he said she was in Hamburg. I didn't really think anything of it. Until he started flirting with me. Saying that he'd always thought I was great, and asking whether I wanted to meet up sometime. I thought I was going crazy. Then suddenly Antje barges between us and starts acting like some hysterical housewife. That's when I realized. But by then I'd unfortunately lost Christine's new address in Hamburg. Since then I've thought about her a lot. That's why I was so happy to get this invitation."

Marleen looked at Dani thoughtfully. "So, let's get you up to speed on everything that's been happening, and then I'd like to take a look at that questionnaire."

While Marleen brought her up to date, Dani's facial expression shifted between horror, amazement, relief, and contentment. Once she'd finished the story, Dani was rubbing her forehead. "God, and I thought she wouldn't be able to relate to my personal life! How dumb am I?"

She leaned over and took an envelope from her purse, which she handed to Marleen.

"The questionnaire. I spent ages brooding over it, and it unleashed loads of thoughts and memories I had suppressed for years. There should be some kind of law that people have to fill out a questionnaire every five years to make them confront the old times. You forget so quickly about the dreams and hopes you once had. And about how many of them you've managed to fulfill. It did me so much good."

Marleen picked up the questionnaire. "Is it OK if I read it? The plan is for Christine's sister, Ines, to put them all together and then give them to Christine at the party."

Dani hesitated for a moment. "I think I'd really like to read the other women's answers. What does friendship mean, what makes a friendship? I don't know if I've ever grasped the importance the different women in my life hold. And how much we take things for granted. Go ahead, read it. But I'd like to see yours, too."

Marleen put her reading glasses on.

Questionnaire

Name, age, and place of residence?
Dani, 43, Berlin
When and where did you meet Christine?
In 1984 at a house viewing. We were both looking for a new place and decided to rent the old house together.
What was your best experience together?
The first New Year's in our house. We'd been renovating for three months and threw a housewarming party on New Year's Eve. It was like sharing student digs with lots of other women; everyone loved it. We danced in the kitchen until 7 a.m. Life was great back then. I felt invincible.
What made your friendship stand out? And what sets Christine apart as a friend?
We each grew up and found our independence while we were living there together. And that made us feel invincible. Christine was always so gutsy; she was so daring in everything she did.

What's your motto in life?

Don't settle, you deserve more.

A friend is…?

Someone I don't need to make an effort with.

What was your first reaction to this invitation?

It's wonderful. It was all so long ago now, and I want the feeling from that time back again. I was very pleased to receive the invite, and have been thinking of old times a lot since then. Some things really were better back then, and often a lot more exciting, too.

• ● •

Hamburg

Christine looked at Gabi, surprised. "What are you doing here? You're supposed to have the day off."

Gabi went over to her desk and pulled her chair out.

"Oh, you know, I just had so much paperwork to do I thought I might as well get it out of the way today."

Christine fixed her with a steadfast gaze. But Gabi looked away and shrugged her shoulders. "And besides, everything is just crazy at home."

Gabi pulled her jacket off and hung it over the back of her chair. Christine looked at her. She suddenly noticed how thin Gabi was. She must have lost at least ten pounds, was very pale, and had dark rings under her eyes. Christine started to feel pangs of guilt; Gabi had been very quiet in recent weeks, and Christine had gotten the feeling her colleague was troubled by something. She had wanted to talk to her about it but kept putting it off. Gabi hadn't said a word either, and before long the moment had just passed by.

Christine liked working with Gabi. They got along well but had always respected each other's privacy. Christine had once said to Dorothea that the nice thing about Gabi was that she had a male attitude toward the working relationship.

"Work is work and champagne is champagne, as my old boss used to say. I work so well with Gabi. We've never bothered with that girlie nonsense of trying to make your colleague into your best friend. She's been to my apartment just two times, after giving me a ride home. I've never been to her place. I don't have anything against colleagues being close friends in principle, but it has to develop naturally. You don't have to be like two peas in a pod just because you're doing the same job."

They did, of course, know a certain amount about each other's lives outside of the office. Christine had told her about the divorce, and Gabi had once come with them for coffee when Ines and Georg had picked her up from work. Christine knew that Gabi lived with Thomas, who had been working in Frankfurt for the last year, and that she had two cats and went jogging every morning.

Any conversations they had that weren't work related normally centered around books and films, or sometimes harmless tidbits of gossip about their colleagues.

Christine watched Gabi as she turned her calculator on and pulled her filing tray toward her.

"Is something wrong?" she asked, as she saw Christine's expression.

"That's what I was just asking myself. You don't look too good. Would you like to talk?"

Gabi looked briefly at the open office door, then back at Christine. "I don't know, well, not here at any rate. What are you doing at lunchtime?"

"We could go and get some food at the café on the Alster."

"Yes, that sounds good. Let's do that."

The telephone on Gabi's desk rang; she nodded at Christine and answered in a practiced tone.

• ● •

Two hours later they were sitting in the café waiting for their food. Gabi was already on her second cigarette, which surprised Christine. Until today she'd only seen her smoke just once, at the Christmas party.

When the waiter brought their cheese and vegetable bakes over, Gabi stubbed her cigarette out and looked at her plate, her face looking strained. She trailed her fork around the edge of the plate, took a small bite of pepper, let her fork fall again, and pushed the plate away. Christine started to eat and waited. Gabi didn't hesitate long before speaking up.

"I'm not hungry at all…"

"Then leave it." Christine kept on eating and wondered whether Gabi was waiting to be questioned or whether she would just come out with it.

"Thomas left me."

Christine looked at Gabi, shocked. "When?"

"Three weeks ago."

"Oh shit."

"You can say that again." Gabi could feel that her eyes were starting to well up, and blew her nose angrily. She didn't want to cry, not now.

Christine pushed her plate aside. "But why? I mean, was it just out of the blue?"

Gabi rubbed her eyes and cleared her throat. "Well, define out of the blue…Thomas was out of work for a year in Hamburg and then got a job in Frankfurt last summer. He's a business management expert and was able to get a position with an insurance company. We agreed that I would stay in Hamburg in the apartment for the duration of his probation period, then take it from there. In January he got a permanent contract. And after that everything changed."

"Him or everything?"

Gabi looked confused. "What do you mean? Oh, I mean him, he's changed. He was working over the weekends, too, and came home every two weeks at the most. But whenever he was here, he always had somewhere else to be: at his parents', the hairdresser, taking the car to the garage, he was always out and about. We hardly saw each other. And when we did, we just argued."

"Didn't you ever go to Frankfurt?"

"Yes, at the beginning, a few times. But I didn't know anyone there. Thomas didn't have much time for me, and he seemed different there. And I don't like Frankfurt much anyway; it's enough having to go there for the book fair."

"But you would have moved there anyway?"

"No, why?"

"You said you were going to think about it after the probation period."

"Well, yes," Gabi answered indignantly, "but maybe Thomas would have found something in Hamburg again. I don't want to move away from here…but it doesn't matter anyway, because he just got stranger and stranger. And then, three weeks ago, he came home unannounced and told me he wanted to separate. He said he found it too hard, the long distance and traveling, and all just to end up arguing with me. He said we didn't have anything in common anymore, and that everyday life wasn't enough."

Gabi's eyes were dry, and she didn't seem that distraught. Christine was slowly starting to suspect she wasn't here to comfort a distraught friend.

"Do you miss him?"

Gabi rubbed her forehead. "Miss him...well, of course, I have to organize everything by myself now. We've got a one-hundred-square-meter apartment that I can't afford by myself, the car is in his name, and so are all our insurance policies. I'm just not in the mood to figure out all this crap. We lived together for twelve years, so everything is all tied up in each other's names. And now he just takes off leaves me with all the chaos."

"And how are you coping?"

"I don't know. I'm bewildered, mad, annoyed. I can't be bothered to starting living life as a single again, and I don't have the energy to explain it all to my family and friends. I'm forty-three now, and I have to start all over. It's so messed up."

Me, me, me, thought Christine, amazed at how differently women dealt with break-ups. She thought back to Luise's tears, to all the nights she herself had spent crying, and wasn't sure how to take Gabi's reaction.

"Is there something I can do to help?"

Gabi raised her shoulders. "Not really. First of all I have to figure out what to do about the apartment. At the moment Thomas feels guilty and is still helping with the rent. But long-term I'm probably going to have to find something else. If you hear of anything, please let me know. Apart from that, can I please just ask you to keep this to yourself? I don't want all the tongues at work wagging about my private life."

"Gabi, a separation like this is nothing to be ashamed of. Heavens, almost all of us have been through it. What did Ruth say?"

"She doesn't know yet. She's much too stressed about things on her own life."

Christine was confused. She had thought the two of them were close, and last week Ruth had mentioned in the office that they met up every week.

"Why haven't you told her? You see each other all the time."

Gabi laughed bitterly. "That's ridiculous. Look, this stays between us: Ruth has a lover who's in Hamburg for a while. At first he was just staying three weeks, but he's still here. I provide Ruth with an alibi so she can see him without Karsten finding out. If I had known she was going to do it so often, I wouldn't have agreed. She's so preoccupied with her own raging hormones she hasn't even noticed what's going on with me."

Christine wondered what planet she'd been living on recently. She had always regarded herself as being sensitive, but she had no idea what was going on right in front of her nose. She shook her head. Gabi took it the wrong way.

"You disagree with what she's doing, too, am I right? And Karsten is such a great guy. I've always envied Ruth for having him. He's a senior physician now, have you met him?"

"Once, just briefly."

Christine didn't want to hear anymore. She'd had enough and looked pointedly at her watch. "Gabi, I don't want to bring our conversation to an abrupt end, but I have to go to the post office. Let's get the check."

Gabi's thoughtful expression was replaced by a disappointed one. "It is that late already? What a shame. Come on, let me pay; I'll stay here for a bit. After all—I do have the day off. Thank you for listening. It really helps to talk."

Christine took her purse and put her hand on Gabi's shoulder briefly.

"Thank you for treating me. I'll see you later in the office then, or tomorrow if not. I hope the rest of your day goes OK."

She smiled and left the café. Outside, she stopped for a moment, closed her eyes, and took a deep breath.

That's women for you, she thought. *So much for the weaker sex.*

• ● •

"Catfight"

I recently spent a day at the sauna with my friend Karola. We go regularly. It's relaxing, makes my skin feel soft, and helps me sleep better. The sauna is very modern and is called S P A, which summons images of beauty and well-being, and also means a day pass can cost ten Euros more than in a normal sauna.

By the time we get to the changing room, we're already feeling relaxed and laid back, and are full of compassion for the other women there. As we get changed and envelop ourselves in the fluffy bathrobes, we know, or at the very latest when we feel the straps of our colorful flip-flops slip between our toes, we know that we are looking out for our bodies and our souls, and that makes us sisters.

That's why there was no question that we would explain to the four women who were there for the first time, in a friendly, almost loving way, how to tackle the lockers and the sprawling layout of the sauna. Thanking us, they introduced themselves and explained that they had been friends for ten years, through thick and thin. Tomorrow the last of the four would celebrate her fortieth birthday, and they were doing the spa day in honor of the occasion. After all, you had to treat yourself now and then.

My friend Karola is always very friendly, particularly at moments like these, and the four sauna beginners assumed from this that they could tag along with us, the old sauna aficionados.

We always start off in the eighty-degree sauna. Karola and I lay down on the higher bench and our new friends followed us, which led to a minor kerfuffle. This was partly due to the fact that Anja only wanted to sit right next to the door, that Uschi couldn't see the sand timer from where she was, that Katja didn't mind either way, and that Dagmar didn't want to stay in there too long anyway because it was too hot.

After five minutes I whispered in a friendly way that you're supposed to keep the noise down in the sauna. After that it was a little quieter, until Dagmar got up, making kind of a show of it, and left the sauna. She slammed the door so loudly that Karola jumped and almost fell off her bench. Katja, Uschi, and Anja stared at the closed door, and Uschi commented softly, but loudly enough for us all to hear, that Dagmar had put on a lot of weight. This was affirmed by the rigorous nodding of three heads.

In between treatments, we usually rest on the wonderful teakwood loungers on the roof terrace. My friend Karola and I hurried ahead but were discovered ten minutes later amid whoops of joy. Katja had treated her friends to a round of apple juices, and each was holding a glass. When Katja saw us, she immediately insisted that we join them for a drink, as her treat. Karola politely refused, but Katja had already gone to get more juice. Anja commented to Dagmar that that was typical for Katja; she always had to pay for everything. After all, she didn't have any children or a husband, so no wonder she just worked and piled up her money. But at some point she would be lonely, and then what good would it be to her?

After ten minutes Karola and I felt the urgent need to make our next trip to the sauna. Katja stayed up on the terrace to keep an eye on the six apple juices; the other three followed us.

Just before we got to the ninety-degree sauna, Uschi ran into a guy she knew and started chatting, so only Dagmar and Anja followed us in. Dagmar started to get dizzy right away. After all, ninety degrees was even hotter, and our chill-out break hadn't been that long. In an effort to distract Dagmar, Anja told her that the man they'd bumped into was Uschi's lover. In an instant, Dagmar forgot about being too hot. She claimed there was no way the chance meeting in the sauna had been a coincidence, and asked about Uschi's husband. Anja said that Uschi's husband was stupid and would never realize, and that Uschi had only married him for his money anyway. After all, he was so ugly, what else could it have been?

My friend Karola had a funny expression on her face and got really hot all of a sudden. So we decided eight minutes were enough for this trip.

After the cold shower, she was feeling better. In the chill-out room—which we had conveniently neglected to introduce our new best friends to—we managed to get an hour's nap.

Later, as we sat in the small bistro drinking lattes, Uschi and Katja came over and asked if we'd seen the others. We shook our heads regretfully, but they sat down with us anyway. Katja tried to make us guess which of them was the oldest. Uschi said right away *that, of course, it was obvious that Anja was the oldest, but that we should guess how old.*

Karola said, carefully, perhaps forty-six or so (which also happens to be her own age).

Uschi turned to Dagmar and said: "You see, I told you, Anja looks really old. She's forty-one but has so many wrinkles, from smoking and the pill, that she looks at least five years older than she is."

She looked at us both triumphantly.

On that day, Karola and I didn't stay as long in the sauna as we normally do. Before we left, we politely said good-bye to our four sauna buddies. They smiled at us and each other and said it was a shame we wanted to leave already, but that maybe we would see each other here again.

We hoped not.

That evening, as I lay on the sofa, relaxed and rejoicing in my delightfully soft skin, my friend Karola called. She asked whether I thought she was fatter than she used to be. Then she pointed out that she didn't have a lover and told me she had married her husband Paul when he was still a poor student. And then she made me promise not to look at her butt when we were next in the sauna.

I believed her, and promised. After all, we're friends.

• ● •

Sylt

Christine was cleaning beer glasses. She waited for her mother to comment, as she always did at moments like this. And today was no exception: carrying a tray of dirty glasses, Charlotte walked into the kitchen and said the very words Christine had been expecting.

"Oh no, you haven't put my good glasses in the dishwasher, have you?"

Christine turned to the side so that her mother could see the dishwasher. "I'm washing them by hand, Mom. Just like I always do."

Reassured, Charlotte cleared the tray. "It's just that they were expensive and I wouldn't be able to replace them."

Christine rolled her eyes. For the last twenty years, these glasses had been washed by hand. For the last twenty years, they had only been used for special occasions, which meant only for guests. Christine's parents loved entertaining lots of guests, who in turn loved to both drink a lot and use lots of glasses. So Christine always ended up with wrinkled fingers after birthday parties.

Outside in the garden, Christine's father was celebrating. Looking every inch the guest of honor, he sat among ten men of the same age who—spurred on by beer—were giving their penny's worth on Bundesliga regulations and the failings of community policy. A few meters away, in the shade, the wives were sitting around a table, talking loudly about Agnes's new grandchild, about fertilizer for the hydrangeas, about Gundula's daughter's impossible new husband, and about the fact that Helma always brought store-bought cakes to the Red Cross bazaar.

As Christine walked over to them with the clean glasses on the tray, she had to simultaneously field questions about her apartment, her ex-husband, and the shade of her lipstick.

"Sit down with us, Christine, won't you? Charlotte, if your daughter does any more washing up, she'll end with hands like prunes."

"Come on, you know Charlotte only had children in the first place so she'd have enough staff for her parties."

Agnes and Renate slapped their thighs in merriment. The mood was already so lively that Christine had difficulty figuring out what they were laughing about. Presumably even they weren't sure anymore and were just in hysterics.

After ten minutes Christine felt exhausted by all the noisy femininity. She longed to slink away and have a cigarette in peace, drink a glass of red wine, and just look out at the sea. She discreetly looked at her watch. It was five thirty; Ines would be here in half an hour. It was her little sister's turn to wash a round of glasses.

Christine stood up and leaned over toward her mother: "I'm just going for a wander down to the marina; is that OK? There's nothing more to do in the kitchen and the oven's on. The meat needs another two hours, and I'll be back by then."

Charlotte patted Christine's hip. "Sure, you go off for a bit. If you're sure you don't want to wait for Ines? She'll be here in a minute."

"No, that'll take at least another half an hour; then she'll have to join in the celebrations, drink some champagne, say hello to everyone, and I don't want to hang on that long. I'll be at the Gosch bar; she can join me in a bit."

Charlotte was already laughing about what Agnes had started to say as Christine went back to the house with her best "I'm just getting glasses quickly" expression. No one noticed her climb over the fence.

Relieved, Christine walked toward the summer dike, lighting a cigarette as she went. She didn't usually smoke out on the street, but Sylt was the exception. She thought back to all the times she and her cousin Sanne had said they were going for a walk, when they were actually going down to the dike to smoke. Afterwards, they would always chew gum to make sure they didn't get busted. That is, until the day when Uncle Paul was up on the roof fixing the aerial and saw the two thirteen-year-old girls smoking down there. He never had been convinced that girls of that age would just go for walks. The trouble they got into afterwards was immense; neither Sanne nor she had smoked much at all in the few years that followed.

Christine smiled to herself at the thought that even now, at over forty years of age, they would still absent themselves from the family Christmas meal with a cheery "we're just going for a walk." Their fathers would shake their heads sadly, while their mothers raised their eyebrows. Afterwards, Sanne and she would still chew gum before coming back.

Christine stubbed her cigarette out in the sand and wrapped it up in a tissue. Before, they had done that to hide the evidence; now it was to help look after the island. So perhaps they had grown up after all, at least in some ways.

The parking lot down by the harbor wasn't as packed now, at the end of August, as it was in high season. The ferry from Denmark had just docked, and there was a cheerful holiday atmosphere, one of the things Christine really loved about Sylt. She ordered a glass of red wine from one of the bars and took it over to a bench with a good view of the sea.

Finally relaxing, Christine exhaled deeply and raised her glass to the sea. The evening sun was glistening over the water, and it felt like a perfect moment. She hadn't been here since her vacation in June. Since her weekend with Richard, to be precise. The official reason was that she had to write the columns on the weekend and found it easier to work at home. But in truth she was scared of the memories of Richard and the feelings they unleashed in her. She had only seen him twice since that weekend. At the beginning of July, she had visited him in Bremen, and after that he had flown out to the US for three weeks for work. They had written each other text messages, full of longing for each other, and spoken briefly on the phone. When he came back, he came over to Christine's for the evening. He seemed dejected but hadn't said why. That evening he had seventeen calls from his wife, Sabine. Richard had explained briefly that she was having problems at work in Berlin and that it was a difficult time for her. Christine hadn't asked questions; they had agreed not to talk about his marriage. Since that night they had only spoken on the phone. And his messages had seemed a little mechanical to her ever since, as if they were lacking real sentiment. He sounded sad, but waved any questions away. Christine suspected that Sabine had discovered her husband's double life and that Richard was panicking. He'd started to go back to Berlin again on the weekends, telling Christine that he had appointments with the bank or that he had to take his car to the garage. She felt full of doubts. She knew he found their situation hard to handle; so did she. But she couldn't bring herself to take the decision out of his hands and end it, and sometimes she loathed herself for that.

"Christine! Christine Schmidt, I don't believe it."

Christine jumped, pulled out of her somber thoughts. She turned around and saw two men walking toward her. She squinted to try to recognize them. One was the director of the publishing house she worked at.

"Hello, Mathias, what a surprise!" She stood up and held out her hand. Mathias gave her a cheerful smile and shook her hand.

"What on earth are you doing here, Christine?"

He certainly wasn't his usual reserved self. Even though he was always friendly at work, Christine couldn't remember him being quite this enthusiastic when they'd run into each other by chance before. *It must be the Sylt sea air,* she thought, a little surprised.

Mathias was still shaking her hand rapturously as he turned around to his companion.

"Sven, let me introduce you. This is the wonderful Christine Schmidt. She used to be one of our reps and now works in the main office. She writes columns for our city magazine and also for *Femme*; she's lovely, clever, and beautiful, the whole package. And she's single. And I have no idea why; it's a real puzzler!"

He giggled foolishly. Christine felt herself go red. Was this a movie or something? Mathias gave Sven, who was looking a little strained, a hefty clap on the shoulders.

"And this, Christine, this is Sven, my best friend from childhood. He builds houses, well, not personally, of course, but he's an architect. He's nice, clever, funny, and only drinks when he's unhappy. And he's unhappy right now, so we have to cheer him up."

Mathias was interrupted by a hefty hiccup and held his hand in front of his mouth. "Oops, I'll go and get a drink of water; it must mean someone's thinking about me! I'll get us some more wine, too; wait here for me."

He winked at them and went to the bar. He seemed a little unsteady on his feet. They watched him go; then Sven turned around to Christine and held his hand out.

"I'm sorry, but we've been drinking since noon. We're not exactly on our best behavior; I hope we're not bothering you."

He had green eyes with long lashes, his blond hair was tousled, he had broad shoulders, and he was a head taller than Christine. There was something a little clumsy about him.

Christine was amused; she choked back a laugh and pointed at the bench.

"No, you're not at all, have a seat. Can you handle any more wine though?"

Sven sighed lightly and rubbed his forehead.

"I'm not sure. I always feel sick so quickly when I drink. I actually switched to water two hours ago, but Mathias is still going at it."

As if at the mention of his name, Mathias was standing back in front of them with a bottle of wine and three glasses.

"So, Sven, I couldn't carry anything else, so if you want something different you'll have to go yourself."

Sven stood up right away, looked at Christine with a wry smile, and said: "OK, I need water for sure, so please excuse me."

Mathias collapsed down onto the bench and watched Sven walk away.

"And? What do you think of him?"

Christine was dumbfounded.

"What do you mean? We've only exchanged a few words. I don't even know him."

Mathias leaned over confidingly to Christine and laid his arm on the back of the bench. "He's a great guy, Sven. We've known each other since the fifth grade and lived together as students. He's a great cook. And he's very clean, you know, around the house. He irons as well."

Christine started to laugh. Mathias, her boss, was sitting here and promoting his best friend to her as a potential partner with the earnestness of a drunken teenager.

"Mathias, are you trying to find a wife for him or something? What is it you're trying to tell me?"

Mathias opened his eyes wide and then shrugged his shoulders.

"Christine, what do you take me for? No, but Sven was left really horribly, by Doris, whom I really couldn't stand; I mean, she left him after twelve years. Seriously, it's really awful, she's really screwing him over; he can't see his daughter, the whole thing's just impossible. For the last year he's just been throwing himself into his work, he doesn't go out anymore, and he's having a really tough time of it. He needs to meet someone. So I said, come on, let's go to Sylt for a guys' weekend. So here we are. And then I see you sitting here on the harbor. I thought to myself, Christine, that could be something. Someone who writes columns like you do must be a pretty decent woman. I just want Sven to realize that not all girls are like Doris."

Christine had collapsed into a fit of giggles and was trying to get a hold of herself. It was actually a very sad story, but all she could picture was Sven ironing while Mathias pointed a video camera at him and talked in his best marketing voice about his various skills and accomplishments. She cleared her throat and wiped the tears from the corners of her eyes.

"Sorry, Mathias, you're a great friend." She exploded with laughter again. "I'm just going to the bathroom."

Mathias nodded with understanding. "Yes, of course, I understand. You girls have to go more often than we do."

Christine fled.

Sven came back with two mugs of coffee. He held one of them out to Mathias.

"Here, I think we should sober up a bit; we're being embarrassing." He looked around. "Or have you scared Christine away already?"

Mathias winked. "You know girls, sometimes they need to powder their noses and all. You know, I think she likes you."

Sven rolled his eyes. "Mathias, please. Stop trying to solve my problems. Maren, Kirsten, and Tanja liked me as well according to you. Just let it go. I'm not in the mood."

"Tatjana."

"What?"

"Tanja was called Tatjana."

Sven laid his head down on the table and sighed. Then he sat back up straight.

"Mathias, please, I…"

"Shh, Christine's coming back."

Christine, who had come bearing a bottle of water and three fresh glasses, stopped in front of the table. "Am I interrupting a man-to-man?"

"No, no," Sven rushed to answer. "Come on, have a seat; we've got enough water now. Would you like a glass of wine? We'll behave ourselves now, I promise."

One hour, three bottles of water, and a bottle of wine later, Mathias was a little more reserved, Sven almost shy, and Christine a little tipsy. An ideal combination. Mathias had read her latest column in *Femme* and was trying to recount it from memory. Christine shook her head at almost all his attempts, so in the end Sven got up and went off to buy the magazine from the bookstore nearby. He read the column aloud, laughed throughout, and said at the end that it was great to see a woman writing about catfights between women. After all, any man who tried to do so would be castrated.

They talked about men and women, about the local herring *Brötchen*, about the Danish royal palace, about Hamburg bars and the HSV handball team. One topic of conversation led to the next; Christine felt lighthearted and cheerful; Sven, young and charming; and Mathias was smiling contentedly. Then Mathias suggested fetching another bottle of wine; after all, the evening was only just beginning. Christine's gaze fell on the large clock in the square; then she started in surprise and jumped up.

"Oh God, it's already eight thirty; I was supposed to be back awhile ago. Boys, I have to go, it was fun hanging out." She laid a hand on each of their shoulders. "Sven, Mathias, maybe I'll see you again soon; enjoy the rest of your night."

She walked off quickly, turning around after a few meters and blowing them a kiss. Sven winked back. Mathias looked at him.

"And just like that, she's gone. Isn't she enchanting? I have her cell number, you know."

Sven shook his head and rummaged around in his jacket pocket.

"You idiot, you never learn. Don't meddle in my love life and we won't get into arguments. Agreed?"

He held out a pack of gum. Mathias waved it away.

"I don't like gum."

"I'm not offering you any. It's the package: write her mobile number down for me. You know, just in case."

Grinning, Mathias scribbled Christine's number down, whistling "On the North Sea Coast" as he did.

• • •

As Christine walked into the hallway, her mother was walking toward her with the empty plates. "I was about to report you as a missing person. Did you fall into the water or something?"

Christine took the plates from her.

"I'm sorry, I ran into some people I knew and totally lost track of time."

"You stink of smoke and booze." Charlotte sniffed at her. "Oh well, you're a big girl now. And? Was he cute?"

"Who?"

"You said 'some people you knew' strangely.' Was it someone handsome?"

"Mom, please."

Charlotte giggled. "I'm allowed to ask, surely! Come on, let's have some champagne with Renate and Agnes; we'll get you nice and tipsy and then interrogate you."

Christine smiled and followed her mother out to the garden.

• • •

Lübeck

Frauke turned around in front of the mirror to look at herself from the side. She sighed. She looked like a sausage in this suit; it was clearly at least one size too small for her. Impatiently, she ripped open the zip, climbed out of the pants, and threw them onto the bed, which was already groaning under a pile of crumpled clothing. She went back to her closet and looked through the clothes that were still hanging up. Everything was old and had been worn a hundred times already. Everything was wrong. And most of it probably didn't fit anyway. Frustrated, Frauke slammed the door shut and looked back into the mirror.

"You're fat, Frauke Jensen, nee Müller, fat, old, and ugly."

She burst into tears and threw herself across her bed into the pile of trousers, skirts, and blouses. At first she cried out of rage, then self-pity, and finally just because she couldn't stop. After half an hour her nose was so blocked she had a coughing fit. And she was freezing cold. Awkwardly, she stood up, grabbed her bathrobe, and pulled it on. She looked into the tangle of clothes for thick socks but could only find an odd pair. It didn't matter anyway. Her hair was disheveled, so she pulled it up with a rubber band, blew her nose, avoided looking in the mirror, and went downstairs to make herself a coffee.

On the kitchen table lay the letter that had started all this misery. And along with it, the photo album.

When the phone call from Gabi had come three weeks ago, Frauke had found the idea of bringing old friendships back to life amusing. She had almost forgotten the call by the time Gabi's letter had arrived yesterday. Over dinner, she had shown it to her husband, Gunnar. Gunnar could still vaguely remember Christine. It was just she, Gunnar, and their youngest, Lisa, at the dinner table that evening: Jule, her eldest, had moved out six months ago, and her son Max was off revising for his school-leaving exams.

After Frauke read the letter and questionnaire out loud, Gunnar had started to laugh.

"Oh, honey, that takes me back. You were both so sweet back then. You know, Lisa, I fell for your mother when I saw her sitting with Christine in an ice-cream parlor. They were sharing one ice cream, not because they were that inseparable but because they were broke. I was already an apprentice and earning a paycheck, so I bought them another one. And do you know what they did?"

Lisa looked at him expectantly. Fifteen-year-olds loved stories like this.

"Mom and her friend refused it?"

Gunnar smiled. "No, as I put the ice-cream bowl down on the table, they looked up for a moment and then leisurely kept on eating the same ice cream. Then, once they'd finished, they pushed their bowl aside, pulled mine toward them, and kept on sharing. No word of thanks."

"Wow, that's really cool, Mom."

Frauke looked at her daughter thoughtfully. Back then, Christine and she had been two years younger than Lisa was now. Thirteen. It was a strange feeling. Gunnar patted her hand.

"Those were the days. We were still young and snappy then. And now, honey, well now we're just snappy."

He laughed out loud at his own joke, stood up, and carried his empty plate into the kitchen. When he came back, he kissed Frauke on the top of her head.

"Where's my gym bag? I have to go in a minute."

Frauke's answer was automatic: "It's where you left it, in the cellar."

Lisa scraped her plate clean noisily. "Have fun at OAP soccer, Dad. I always worry that one of you granddads will break a bone. All it takes is one wrong move and you'll end up fracturing your neck or something."

"Lisa!" her parents reprimanded her in unison. Gunnar went down to the cellar shaking his head.

Lisa looked at her mother with that confidence only teenagers have. "What?"

She trailed her fork around the edge of the plate. Frauke stood up and took the plate away from her.

"My God, you're driving me mad with that scraping sound."

"Why are you so grouchy? By the way, do you have a picture of you and Christine?"

Gunnar came back upstairs with his packed gym bag and pulled his jacket on.

"So, my darlings, I'm off now. When Max comes back later, tell him to put his dirty shoes away; otherwise I'll have an accident. Bye, see you later."

The door slammed shut. Frauke jumped. She was still standing at the kitchen door with Lisa's plate. Everything in the kitchen was a mess, and she still had to put a load of laundry in and balance the company books. But right now she felt too tired. Recently she had felt a dreadful desire to just pack it all in. She couldn't bear to hear it anymore; always "Mom, where's this, where's that, tell Max he should do this or shouldn't do that, call Jule, what's for dinner, where are my keys" and so on and so on.

Lisa's voice brought her back down to earth. "What's wrong? Do you have a picture or not?"

Frauke looked at her daughter, still lost in thought. Perhaps this was a sign, this letter from the past. She must still have the old photos somewhere; after all, she rarely threw things out.

"Yes, I think I have an old album still. Go and have a look in Dad's study, in the white bookcase, at the top. It's a blue photo album. I'm making some tea, do you want one?"

Lisa was already gone. Frauke waited for a moment. Then came the inevitable call:

"Where on the bookcase?"

Frauke nodded. "At the top."

A moment later Lisa came back with a blue album under her arm.

"Got it."

She laid it on the table and opened it. Frauke took it away from her again and clapped it shut.

"Wait for me, I wanted to make some tea first."

Her daughter pouted.

"Well, no one's stopping you from making it. But I don't want one, so I can start looking."

She sat down on the chair and pulled her legs up under her. Frauke sat down next to her daughter and pulled the album toward her. Lisa looked at her.

"I thought you wanted to make tea. And by the way, you've started to sound like Grandma lately."

Frauke took a deep breath. She had noticed it, too: she said a lot of things that made even her cringe. But this child drove her mad sometimes. Lisa tried to grab the album again. Frauke banged her hand on the table.

"Lisa! This album is about my private life. Didn't it occur to you that I might want to take a look by myself first? You could make the tea for once."

"My God, you're in such a mood. And what do you mean, private life? You're my mother. Oh, calm down, I'll go and make the tea."

She stood up, making an exaggerated effort, and shuffled off into the kitchen.

Frauke felt like throwing the album at her. Did she think that women were just mothers and nothing else, that they hadn't had lives before having children? She couldn't believe how impudent her daughter was. And she was annoyed that she was letting herself be provoked. She should just rise above it. *Calm down, Frauke, she's your daughter. Don't get worked up.*

The closed photo album lay on the table in front of her. She brushed her hands over the embossed initials. *FM.* Frauke Müller. She had received the album as a present from her godmother for her confirmation, back in the days when she was still far from becoming a wife and mother. Back then, her main role was as Christine's friend. Until three weeks ago, she hadn't thought of the old times. That was, until Gabi's phone call. Then again this morning, when the official invitation arrived along with the questionnaire. And now she sat here, feeling nervous about showing her daughter the pictures. She felt foolish.

She heard Lisa fill the kettle and put the cups on a tray. A few minutes later she came through the door, balancing the tray with one hand and looking at her mother.

"Don't say a word, I'm holding the tray correctly."

Frauke kept quiet. She really was turning into her mother. She cleared her throat.

"I wasn't going to say anything, just thank you for making the tea."

Lisa put the cups on the table and the milk and sugar next to the teapot.

"No problem, Mom. So come on, let's have a look at the old treasures."

She propped her elbows on the table, resting her chin in her hands. Frauke opened the album carefully. On the first page was her confirmation picture. She looked very young, with a round face: puppy fat.

Lisa waved her hand impatiently. "Keep going, I've already seen that picture; Grandma has a copy in her kitchen. Flick through. Wait, God, who's that?"

The photo was of two thirteen-year-old girls leaning against a tree, facing each other. They were both wearing red pants and yellow T-shirts. They didn't seem to know the photo was being taken, and only had eyes for each other. Lisa laughed.

"Oh, how cheesy. All that color, red with yellow. How awful, who's that? I hope that's not you?"

Frauke brushed her fingers over the photo and smiled.

"I'm afraid it is, my darling, that's me on the left with the curly hair. And on the right, with short black hair, that's Christine."

Lisa didn't seem particularly impressed. "Maybe it's just a bad photo, but you still look like kids. Keep going."

The memories were starting to rush back; Frauke and Christine were in about twenty of the photos. Frauke started daydreaming; she wasn't even listening to her daughter anymore, but immersed in memories from thirty years ago. She answered Lisa's questions on autopilot and without giving them a great deal of thought. Her mind was elsewhere.

Her son Max brought her crashing back to reality. Neither of them had heard him come in, but he was suddenly standing right next to the table: "What's going on here? Taking a trip down memory lane?"

Frauke and Lisa jumped and looked up at him. His mother smiled and then started to answer, but Lisa beat her to it.

"Mom's going to meet up with an old friend, so we're looking at all the old pictures. Seriously, I don't think they'll recognize each other; Mom was a real bombshell back then. She looked completely different. Absolutely stunning. You wouldn't even recognize her."

Frauke felt like she'd just been slapped in the face.

Now, a day later, she was sitting in front of the photo album once again. The kids were at school and Gunnar, at work. She'd told him this morning that she didn't feel well. Gunnar had given her shoulder a squeeze and told her to take the day off: he could manage without her for once. So Frauke had gone back to bed, and then she'd started thinking about Christine's birthday. And about what Lisa had said. Her daughter was right. She had gotten fat, her hair could no longer claim to resemble anything close to a "style," she never wore makeup, just put on some mascara occasionally at the very most, and hadn't bought herself any nice clothes for at least six years.

She was a mother, a wife, a housewife, and an office assistant; she was everything under the sun. Everything except Frauke Müller. And she hadn't even noticed.

Frauke flicked through the album. She found the photo of her and Christine by the tree and stared at it for a long while. It wasn't the connection between them that she saw. It was something completely different that touched her about this picture. Back then, both of them had had this boundless enthusiasm for life. They couldn't wait to grow up; they wanted to become rich, famous, and happy; marry wonderful men; have lots of children, travel around the world, have beautiful houses. They had been so confident they would get what they dreamed of. Back then, they hadn't minded when, but they were sure they would make it, together, no matter what.

Suddenly, she could remember that feeling, the confidence. Frauke Jensen, nee Müller, stretched and clenched her fists.

"Christine Schmidt, I'm telling you—I'll do it after all. I promise."

Questionnaire

Name, age, and place of residence?

Frauke, 44. I live with my family in Lübeck.

When and where did you meet Christine?

We were twelve years old and both head over heels in love with David Cassidy. I stole her *Bravo* magazine and noticed in the school bathroom that she'd already taken out the poster of him. After that I felt really guilty; after all, we were both collecting the same thing. I told her that I really liked him, too, David, I mean. That's how we became friends.

What was your best experience together?

We spent New Year 1974 with my parents and their friends. We were allowed to have eggnog and felt very grown-up. We shared a bed and at 3 a.m. we sang the national anthem. Lying down. Then we talked about what the future would hold for us.

What made your friendship stand out? And what sets Christine apart as a friend?

We both had an unquenchable thirst for life. And courage, too. Christine had such a wonderful imagination and came up with the most amazing scenarios for how our lives would be when we grew up. In the early days I didn't even realize how many dreams I had for the future. And we were always so giggly with each other.

What's your motto in life?

Don't make such a fuss, you can do it.

A friend is…?

Someone who stops you from forgetting who you are. Someone who shares the same memories. Someone who gives you courage when you have too little of it.

What was your first reaction to this invitation?

I had many. First surprise, then fear, and now excitement and anticipation.

September, Hamburg

Christine was awoken by a strange noise. Her throat was sore, she couldn't breathe right, and her head was thumping. With trepidation, she opened her eyes and tried to make out the time on her alarm clock. Eight fifteen a.m. Then she realized what the noise was; her cell phone was ringing. She sat up with a start, which made her feel dizzy, then lay back down again. She felt in desperate need of an aspirin and some fresh air. She must be sick. Today was Monday, and she hadn't even heard her alarm clock. She didn't feel well enough to go to work. Remembering that there was no one here to look after her, blow her nose, or stroke her forehead, Christine felt miserable and at death's door. By now, her cell had stopped ringing. It had probably been Richard, on his way from Berlin to Bremen. Sure, he could call her again now that he was away from his wife. Christine tried to push away the negative thoughts and struggled out of bed. On the way to the bathroom she pulled her robe around her; it was cold, and her entire body ached.

After a shower, she felt a little better, but just the thought of driving to work made her feel dizzy. She made herself a cup of tea, reached for the phone, and called Gabi.

"Morning, it's Christine. Listen, I'm not feeling well, I must have come down with something. Sore throat, head-ache, head cold, the whole lot. I'm staying in bed; can you pass the message on?"

Gabi sounded sympathetic. "You sound dreadful, you poor thing. Do you need anything?"

"I have nose drops and aspirin already, thank you though. I just need to go to bed."

"OK, then do that. I'll call you this evening; feel better soon."

Gabi's sympathy made Christine feel on the brink of tears. Feeling lonely, she reached for her cell in frustration. She looked at the missed calls and saw that the most recent had indeed been from Richard. Returning the call, she heard the ringtone. Then his voice.

"Jürgensen."

Colds tend to go hand in hand with bad moods. *You asshole,* she thought, *my number isn't blocked and you can see perfectly well from the display who's calling.*

"Schmidt, did you call?"

As soon as the words were out of her mouth, she regret-ted her tone. She coughed, which Richard heard, of course. And he was meant to.

"You sound awful. Are you sick?"

"Yes."

"I'm sorry, is there anything I can do?"

His voice sounded warm and intimate, but it still annoyed Christine.

"Well, yes, you could come and take care of me."

"Christine, you know I can't do that; my schedule is packed with appointments. And you've only got a cold.

You're not normally like this. Anyway, I'll be thinking of you."

"How would you know what I'm usually like? We hardly see each other. I'm sick. But of course, I'm not the wonderful Sabine whom you rush to in a second if she has problems. That's different."

"Christine, do you have a fever or something? What's all this about? I call you almost every day, and yes, it's true we can't see each other much at the moment, but I'm sure that will get better. Anyway, I can't talk now, there's a lot of traffic here. Let's talk later; I'm sure you'll have calmed down by then. Get better soon."

"Fine."

Christine pressed the button to hang up, took a deep breath, and shouted at the top of her voice, "You idiot!"

Then she had a coughing fit that brought tears to her eyes.

• • •

Ruth knocked on the office door and walked in. Christine's chair was empty, and Gabi was standing talking on the phone. She only looked up briefly. Ruth watched her. She didn't look good; she was thin and seemed stressed. To make matters worse, she was wearing a gray wool suit that hung off her like a sack. Ruth tried to remember when she had last met up with Gabi outside of work. It had been the evening at the Italian place, with Luise and Ines, which was ages ago now, back in July, and since then they'd only spoken on the phone. She was just starting to feel guilty when Gabi hung up the phone.

"Morning, Ruth, have a seat. Would you like a coffee?"

Ruth felt relieved. "I'd love one, thank you. I actually wanted to see Christine. Is she on a break?"

Gabi put two cups on the table and poured the coffee.

"Christine called in sick this morning. She's come down with a bad cold."

"There's something going around at the moment. Three people are out sick in the *Kult* editorial team, too."

They sat down and drank their coffee. The silence grew and grew. Then Gabi spoke.

"So, is everything wonderful with you?" Her voice sounded a little cool.

Ruth looked uncertain. "Why do you ask? You don't look too good, you know. Has something happened?"

That was so typical of Ruth: answering a question with another question. That had always annoyed Gabi. Recently there seemed to be more and more things that annoyed her about her old friend Ruth. She suddenly felt overcome by a wave of rage.

"I asked first, Ruth. All you seem to care about is your exciting love life. You have no idea what's going on around you. The only thing you care about is making sure your two guys don't run into one another. Are you still telling Karsten you're keeping me company in the week while Thomas is in Frankfurt? Well, if you are you can tell him you need to do it on the weekend now, too, because Thomas is staying in Frankfurt now. He left me. I'm sorry I didn't tell you sooner so that you could have had a weekend alibi, too, but I didn't get the chance."

Ruth went pale. Her friend had gone through a break-up and she hadn't even noticed. She was ashamed, but found the outbreak of rage a little unjust.

"When did this happen?"

"At the end of July, not that you would care."

Ruth ran her fingers through her hair. Gabi stared out of the window. Her posture was tense.

"Gabi, I don't know what I'm supposed to say; this is all such a surprise. I know I'm quite preoccupied with my own things at the moment. That's not an excuse, but it's not easy for me; my relationship with Karsten, which isn't really a relationship anymore, and then my feelings for Markus, who's starting to put the pressure on. I don't even know what I want anymore." Her voice sounded croaky.

Gabi stayed silent, still sitting there stiffly.

"You're angry I didn't notice you were having a hard time, but you could have said something to me, too. Heavens, I'm not a mind reader. You never open up of your own accord; it's like getting blood out of a stone with you."

Gabi turned around sharply and looked at Ruth, shaking her head.

"Ruth, you don't notice anything. We've been friends for years precisely *because* I don't come to you with my problems. You just want friends who tell you how great you are. You're only sympathetic and willing to help if there's something in it for you. If it doesn't take much effort but makes you look like a hero. That's what you thrive on."

Suddenly, Ruth had tears in her eyes. She looked so horrified that Gabi almost felt sorry for her.

"Gabi, I don't understand. I come by to see you and you unleash a tirade of anger at me. What am I supposed to do with this?"

She was crying. Gabi sat down next to her. It was the wrong place and the wrong time for a conversation like this.

She regretted having started it. She had found out yesterday evening that Thomas was seeing someone new, and she felt so full of rage at the world and all women that just the sight of Ruth had been enough for her to blow a fuse. But she shouldn't have let it happen in the office. She handed Ruth a tissue.

"Come on, I'm sorry, our conversation just got a bit out of hand. I didn't mean to lose it on you."

"But you did." Ruth blew her nose.

Gabi waited until Ruth looked up. Her mascara had run all down her cheeks.

"Oh, Ruth, we really should talk about this, but not here in the office, and calmly. I'm really not in a good mood, and you just caught the brunt of it. It's not your fault. I'm sorry."

Ruth wiped the mascara from under her eyes and cleared her throat.

"That's just not fair. You can't just keep things bottled up and then unleash it all on someone all at once like that. You know, we're looking for Christine's old girlfriends because we had that big conversation about the importance of female friendship, and yet we can't even get it right ourselves. I thought we were friends."

"Ruth, we are. But you have to work at it as well. And I know I do, too. Let's meet up soon, OK?"

Ruth threw her tissue into the trashcan and stood up.

"OK, fine. But you should have a good think about whether you've let everything build up recently against me. You could have said something sooner."

"If you ever had time for me, maybe."

"Gabi, that's just an excuse and you know it. Look, I don't want to have another argument, please."

Gabi's telephone rang. She stood hesitantly in front of Ruth.

"I have to get that."

"Of course, we'll see each other soon then." Ruth laid a hand on Gabi's shoulder. "We're OK now, aren't we?"

"Yes, we are. See you later." Gabi picked up the phone.

• ● •

Christine woke up, again disturbed by a noise. It was light in her bedroom in spite of the drawn curtains. She looked at the clock. Two thirty. She thought for a moment, confused, then remembered. She had called in sick at work. And she'd had an argument with Richard. A shitty day all around then.

She heard the noise again. It was the doorbell, probably the mailman. But he usually came in the morning. And he only rang once, then wrote a notification card. It rang again. It could be some insurance guy. Or someone from some religious sect. Her nose was completely blocked. She sat up to blow it. The bell rang again, constantly this time. Christine pictured a huge crowd of people on her doorstep, every one of whom was allowed to ring the bell once. She lay down again and closed her eyes. Her cell started to vibrate on the nightstand. So they had her number, too. She squinted to see the name on the display. Luise. Christine answered, her voice hoarse.

"My God, Christine, are you deaf? I've been on your doorstep for ten minutes ringing the bell—my finger aches."

"I'm sick."

"I know. But open the door."

With difficulty, Christine stood up and went to press the entrance buzzer. She left the door open and went back to bed.

Moments later, Luise was crashing around in the hallway.

"Where are you?"

Christine groaned and pulled the blanket over her head.

"Good grief, it's musty in here." Luise's voice sounded very close now. Christine heard her heels clicking on the wooden floor. Then it got very light in the room, and then very cold.

"You have to let some air in now and then. I'd feel sick, too, if I had the curtains shut when the sun's shining outside. Have you had anything to eat? I guess not. I'll make you something."

Christine played dead. Luise went into the kitchen, and moments later Christine heard running water and the sound of the gas being lit on the stove. Half an hour later, Luise came back into the bedroom and pulled the blanket off Christine.

"OK, I've made some tea and some vegetable soup. Come on, get up; lying around in bed will only make you feel worse. I'm sure you can manage to sit on the sofa and have something to eat."

Christine stood up carefully. She waited for the dizziness to come, but it didn't.

"It's freezing."

Luise smiled contentedly. "That's called fresh air. Come on, it's warmer over there on the sofa. And don't be such a drama queen; you've got the flu, not malaria."

Luise had set the table and put a bunch of flowers in the vase. Next to it lay various packages of medication.

"Thank you Luise. You've really thought of everything."

"Don't mention it; here, your soup's getting cold. Besides, I think I like playing Florence Nightingale."

"How did you know I was out sick?"

"I had two appointments in Hamburg this morning and dropped by the publishing house afterwards to have a coffee with you. Gabi told me you were sick."

"She said she was going to call me again later."

"She and Ruth had an awful fight."

Christine looked up. "What about?"

"I don't know. When I arrived, I ran into Petra from the marketing department. She was in front of your office and said that maybe it wasn't the best time to go in. Apparently Gabi and Ruth had an argument, and Ruth came out with her eyes puffy from crying."

Christine thought back to her lunch with Gabi; she was fairly sure she knew what it was about. Luise poured the tea.

"Of course, I went in anyway. Gabi seemed fine. Do you have any idea of what it could have been about? I thought they were friends."

Christine pushed her empty plate aside.

"That tasted good, Luise. I feel better already."

"You didn't answer my question. Do you know what it's about?"

"Who knows? I think Gabi has a lot of problems at the moment in her private life; maybe she'll tell you herself."

"If you mean her separation from Thomas, then I already know about that. I heard it on the grapevine recently. But that's got nothing to do with Ruth; they've been best friends for years."

Christine had to sneeze before she could answer.

"Who knows what happened? And under the guise of a best friend, there can be all kinds of conflict going on."

Luise thought about Linda Love, Frauke, Dani, and how Christine had no idea about the plans that were in motion. She smiled. Christine looked at her questioningly.

"What's so funny about that?"

Luise answered quickly, "No, nothing. It's just that I know you haven't had much faith in female friendship since Antje betrayed you, and I think it's a shame."

"That's not exactly true. I mean, we're friends aren't we, 'Florence'? And I'm very happy you're here. You have to work at all relationships, nurture them, look after the other person. Girls nowadays are always so quick to declare themselves inseparable and wax lyrical about the sisterhood of women. I think that for every stage of your life you will have people that are important to you. And you have to take care of those friendships. But you don't have to swear eternal loyalty straight away. In the end, people can grow apart as quickly as they come together."

Luise looked at Christine thoughtfully and wondered if they were doing the right thing with the secret search for her old friends.

• • •

"The Dog, the Cobra, and the Wave"

In the last three months I've had seven colds. My friend Karola, whose sister is a medical assistant, said it's probably actually just one very persistent cold. And that it's probably because my immune system is shot, but that can be fixed.

Jutta, a friend of my friend Karola's sister, is an alternative medicine practitioner. She knows a lot about immune systems; even

Karola's sister—as a medical assistant—is sometimes amazed at what Jutta seems able to cure. And with natural remedies at that.

First of all Jutta looked into my eyes, or, more specifically, into my irises, and nodded meaningfully. She gave me four different little vials, the contents of which I had to take in a particular order and at particular times. Which I did. By Friday, I had finished the course. On Saturday, I got another cold. Jutta said that was a good thing: it meant everything was coming out.

Next, she told me about a wonder substance: shiitake. What I'd previously only known as an amusing name for a variety of mushroom was actually a curing method that has been used since the Ming dynasty against colds and to stimulate the circulation. Jutta gave me recipes, and for five whole days I ate only mushroom dishes. On the sixth I woke up with a sore throat. Jutta nodded knowingly. She had already suspected that; after all, my immune system was completely shot.

She sent me to one of her colleagues, Bianca, who had just completed her training as an Ayurvedic massage therapist. She explained the three doshas to me, Vata, Pitta, and Kapha. I didn't fully understand what they meant, but I did grasp that my bioenergies are strengthened by them. Or rather, they would be once I'd had the Purvakarma and Panchkarma therapies. I was a little unsure about the whole thing, but the treatment was actually quite pleasant. Given that I always fall asleep during massages—presumably due to my bad immune system—I didn't really catch much about the sacred oil or about what Bianca was doing with it. The only annoying and slightly revolting thing was that the oil in my hair took three washes to get out.

Afterwards I felt just the same as I had before, only oilier.

Of course, my friend Karola wanted to support my convalescence, and so we signed up—on Jutta's advice, of course—for two new classes. Yoga for Beginners on Mondays and Energy Dance on Thursdays.

The yoga class wasn't bad at all. You wear comfy exercise clothes with warm socks and sit on thick mats. A nice woman showed us the exercises. They all had lovely names: I found the downward dog the most difficult, but was pretty good at the wave and the cobra. The only annoying thing was that I had to keep stopping to go to the bathroom. On Jutta's advice I was drinking two cups of tea every two hours: pansy, lady's mantle and rose, chamomile and St John's Wort, and rose. Exactly in that order. And Karola and I had to leave a little early because she strained her groin during the crocodile. But apart from all that it was really very good.

The class on Thursday was over fairly quickly. Karola and I hadn't correctly informed ourselves about what energy dance really was. So we got a little silly when the teacher, Amrit, tied bells around our ankles and asked us to do the elephant with our ghungroos. This was apparently the way to pay homage to Ganesha, the elephant-headed, luck-bringing god.

Karola circled her arms around and clattered around stamping on the floor to a beat of sixteen. She looked so unlike an elephant that I burst into hysterical laughter, which only seemed to spur her on. Despite her efforts the Indian teacher Amrit, who spoke in Swabian dialect, asked us to leave the room, adding that we clearly weren't ready for Kathak dancing. We were in complete agreement.

Without hesitation, I turned down Karola's suggestion of going to Qi Gong on Wednesdays or Hawaiian Bodywork on Fridays.

Jutta suggested that I get my apartment checked for electromagnetic pollution and that I rearrange my furniture according to feng shui guidelines. She also asked me whether I heard sounds in my ears and about my gut flora, and then kneaded my feet. I listened to everything she was saying, blowing my nose as she spoke. Jutta really was full of ideas.

Over the next few days I took Gingko capsules and olive extract. I massaged my feet in a massage basin with a smelly ointment; I dried rose hips, made nasal cleansing lotions, inhaled spruce, and wore a copper bracelet.

And yet I still had a cold.

To my relief, Jutta finally went on vacation for three weeks and closed her practice while she was away. I threw all my packages and bottles into a plastic bag and took them to a pharmacy to get rid of them.

Over the next two weeks I still had a cold but felt much more relaxed. I started drinking ground coffee again, smoked cigarettes, and my mother came to stay. She brought me three liters of elderberry juice and some chest ointment.

That evening we drank a liter of elderberry toddy, with rum, which makes it work quicker and taste much better. My mother giggled as she put the ointment on my back; I did my front myself. By the time we went to bed at three a.m., my mother was a little tipsy and insisted on making me a compress for my legs.

When I woke up the next morning, the cold was gone.

My friend Karola phoned to tell me that she had caught my cold. She asked if I still had the miracle potions from Jutta. After all, they had really worked for me.

I had a much better idea: I told her to come over and bring a bottle of rum. And if she felt like it, we could even give the energy dance a try. We'd figure it out.

• • •

Kiel

The screech of the whistle silenced the noise from fourteen pairs of feet, encased in tennis shoes and squeaking across the gym floor. Lena let the whistle fall from her lips and walked onto the court.

"Stand still."

The girls, all between eight and ten years of age and clad in workout clothes, stopped in their tracks and stared at their coach. Lena pointed at a blond girl then looked around at the others.

"Look at that. Sissi was completely free the whole time, and yet no one passed to her. Anika, Mila, where are your eyes?"

Anika looked at her innocently. "I didn't even see Sissi; she's so tiny."

Mila was shifting her weight from one leg to the other. She glanced from her coach up where her mother sat watching in the stand.

"Mila, what's up? Are you even listening to me?"

"Yes, but I really need to go to the bathroom. I can't think or run anymore I need to go so bad."

Lena shook her head. "Why didn't you go at halftime?"

"I didn't need to then."

"Oh, go on then, and hurry up."

Mila hurried off and waved at her mother cheerfully, who made an apologetic gesture toward Lena. Lena gave the other girls some further instructions. After a few minutes Mila was back. Lena nodded at her.

"Tuck your shirt in, Mila. Right, now everyone make a bit more of an effort; we still have ten minutes."

She walked back off the court and brought the whistle back to her lips. The sound brought the game back into play.

Half an hour later Lena was helping her charges to get their things together and put their shoes and jackets on. A few of the mothers sat nearby, chatting to each other about the imminent fall break and the next league game over the weekend.

Afterward, Lena walked through the hall and changing rooms one more time. Anika had left her scarf behind, and there were a few hair bands on the gym mats. Lena collected everything together, turned out the light, and locked the gymnasium door behind her.

For the last thirty years she had been surrounded by the familiarity of the gymnasium at least twice a week, always that same smell. Her handball talent had been discovered in a sports lesson at the age of fourteen, by sixteen she was playing for the county youth team, and at eighteen she had gotten her training qualification. Five years ago she had decided to stop playing competitively, or rather, her orthopedist had decided for her. After twenty years of competitive sports, both her knees and shoulder joints were suffering. Lena was happy she could at least still keep going as a coach; without that the withdrawal would have been an awful lot harder for her.

She unlocked her car, which was standing alone on the parking lot in front of the hall, and put her gym bag on the back seat. Just as she was about to start the engine, her cell rang.

"Hello, Coach Maestro, I'm still in the sports center—we've just figured out the game plan for the tournament. Would you be able to pick me up? Then Ulli won't have to drive me."

Jürgen, Lena's husband, was just as sports-obsessed as she was. But his knees were a little more robust, and he was still playing for a team. They called themselves the "Old

Guys." In addition to that, he also trained the boys' team and was involved in the club committee.

Lena looked at the clock. Six thirty. She thought for a moment before answering.

"I told Kathleen she has to be home by seven, and if I know our daughter, I'll bet she doesn't have her key with her. If I come to pick you up first, I won't get back in time, and she'll be standing in front of a locked door."

Jürgen sighed. "That kid drives me crazy, forgetting her key all the time. OK, fine, then Ulli will just have to give me a lift. See you later."

Lena drove off and felt a pang of regret. She would actually have really liked to go by the sports center, have a beer with Jürgen, Ulli, and the others, and to not have to look at the clock for once. But since Kathleen had come into the world, everything had to be organized down to the last detail. Jürgen was at the shipping company all day, and Lena worked half days as an architectural draftsman. Then came schoolwork, doctor's visits, parents' evenings, children's birthdays, and last but not least, their shared love of handball. Jürgen and she organized their schedules down to military precision. On Monday evening he had training; Tuesday was free; on Wednesday Lena trained the girls; on Thursday Jürgen, the boys; Friday was free; and the league games were on the weekends.

Jürgen and Lena had taken Kathleen with them to the gymnasium from a young age; she had grown up amid ball nets and gym bags. It didn't seem to have done her any harm. When she was six, she became an active member and was coached by her mother. She had talent, but despite that she had decided a year ago to give up for a while. She went to a good high school and was very ambitious. She wanted to do her homework in peace and not to have to pack her sports gear twice a week. That's how she had explained it—looking serious—to her parents, who had of course been saddened by their daughter's decision but didn't try to talk her out of it.

As Lena turned into the driveway of their home, Kathleen was just coming around the corner on her bike. Waving at her mother, she climbed off, leaned her bike against the wall of the house, and opened the garage door. Lena drove the car in and turned the engine off. Kathleen was waiting for her in front of the house door.

"It's good you're on time; I forgot my house key."

"I thought so."

Lena pulled the garage door down and walked over. Giving her daughter a quick kiss hello, she opened the front door. Kathleen walked past her mother into the kitchen. As Lena took her shoes off, she could already hear the fridge door opening and the clink of bottles. Then silence.

"Kathleen, use a glass; you know I hate it when everyone just drinks out of the bottle."

Kathleen came into the hallway, the juice bottle in her hand. She grinned. "How did you know I was doing it?"

"I didn't hear you open the cabinet door. And I know there aren't any glasses standing around."

"Impressive," said Kathleen, as she continued to drink out of the bottle. But she put it down when she saw the look on her mother's face. "Oh yeah, before I rode over to Carina's today, I emptied the mailbox. There was a letter for you and I took it by mistake."

Lena laughed. "By mistake? You just couldn't be bothered to come back inside. Show me, what kind of letter?"

Kathleen rummaged around in her bookbag, which was stuffed full with tissues, pencil cases, and books, and finally pulled out a crumpled envelope. She turned it around and read out loud.

"From a Marleen de Vries, or something. Do you know her?"

Lena reached for the envelope and looked at the sender's details.

"Marleen…yes, of course, Grandma helps her out at her pub. How strange. I hope Grandma hasn't misbehaved."

Kathleen giggled. "She must have gotten drunk and sung dirty songs or something."

Lena ripped open the envelope and smoothed out the two sheets of paper. Scrunching her forehead, she skimmed over the words: "…so your mother gave me your address… Christine's birthday…November, would be lovely if you could make it…What's all this about?"

Kathleen looked at her mother questioningly. "Well? Did Grandma get drunk?"

Lena looked up and shook her head.

"No, she says Grandma was a shining example as always and should get an award for making the best meatballs in the world."

Kathleen shrugged her shoulders. "Huh. I always think they're a bit small. Anyway, I have to do my English homework. I'm going upstairs."

"What about dinner?"

"I ate at Carina's; I'm full."

Lena watched her daughter go, then went into the kitchen to get a beer from the fridge, taking it with her into the lounge. She sat down on the sofa, putting her feet up on the coffee table, then raised the bottle to her lips and started to read the letter through again. She looked at the questionnaire.

Christine. Lena thought about when she had last seen her. Kathleen must have been around two years old back then. Christine and Bernd had just moved into their house and had had a housewarming party. Or was it Bernd's birthday? Lena couldn't remember; she only knew it had been a terrible evening. Even today, she could still remember the relief she had felt when she was finally in her car and driving home. The next day she had had a long chat with Jürgen about it. He had advised her to speak with Christine; after all, they had been friends for such a long time, it would be a shame to end things like that. But Lena had refused; she hadn't started it, so why should she be the one to give in?

Her husband had shrugged his shoulders and mumbled something about "girls' nonsense." But after that he hadn't said another word about it.

That was ten years ago now, and it had been the last time she ever went to Christine's place. After that they had run into one another a few times, exchanged brief small talk; it was always uncomfortable. Years later Lena had heard about Christine's divorce through her mother, and Jürgen had suggested she get back in touch. But somehow she had never gotten around to it.

And now this letter. Although, it wasn't from Christine herself. It sounded like she had no idea about the whole thing.

Lena's thoughts were interrupted by Kathleen, who was standing in front of her in her pajamas, wanting to say good night. Lena slipped the letter under the TV magazine lying on the table and stood up.

She would talk to Jürgen about it later.

● ● ●

Hamburg

Christine stood indecisively in front of the flower stall at the market. She bought flowers every weekend, sometimes more, sometimes less, depending on how her week had been. This week had been particularly challenging, so she needed lots of flowers. The florist had already wrapped up two bunches for her, and there were five people waiting behind in the line, so he was gradually getting impatient with Christine's dreamy indecisiveness.

"Why don't you get another bunch of roses; then it'll be fifteen Euros total."

He wrapped up the bouquet, handed it to her, and simultaneously stretched out his other hand. Christine felt rushed but didn't want to start an argument. She pressed the bills into his hand and set off for home. She would maybe have preferred white lilies, but didn't dare go back. Besides, the line was too long now.

She wondered whether she should make the most of the day and go for a coffee. Or a glass of wine at the Italian place; after all, it was already noon. But she had to put the flowers in water. Better to go home first. Although, for those prices, they should be able to hold out for an hour. She stopped at the red light by the pedestrian crossing and looked over to the other side of the road. In front of the Italian restaurant she could see tables and chairs out on the terrace. A glass of wine it was.

"Christine, wait."

As the light turned to green, two young men sat down at one of the free tables. Moments later, the light went red again.

Christine turned around. Ruth was hurrying toward her, breathless.

"I already called out to you twice. I didn't think you could hear me."

Her voice sounded raw. She coughed and pushed her sunglasses up. The light had turned green again and the table was still free. Christine didn't hesitate this time around.

"Come on, quick, there's a free table over there, and I'd like to have a drink." Quickening her pace, she reached the table just a few seconds before two other women who were after the same goal. Christine's flowers were on the table before her rival's grocery bags. The woman threw Christine an angry look, then turned around to her companion.

"Let's go inside; it's too loud out here anyway."

Christine sat down with a smile and waited for Ruth, who was standing aside to let their opponents pass.

"What's gotten into you? Is this the only free table in the neighborhood or something?"

"No, but I'd already decided to go for it before I saw you, and I wasn't about to change my mind." She looked at Ruth, who sank down into the chair, breathing heavily.

"What are you doing here anyway?"

Ruth unbuttoned her jacket, ran her hands through her hair, and straightened her sunglasses. She seemed flustered and a little strained.

"I had an appointment."

"Aha." Christine had learned in a seminar once that giving monosyllabic answers makes the person feel they're perhaps not being taken entirely seriously, but being listened to all the same. She flicked through the menu quickly as she saw the waiter approaching the table.

"I'd like a glass of the house red and a glass of water please. And you, Ruth?"

"The same."

Christine had expected Ruth to want to hear the various wine choices first. It was unlike her to order so quickly. Something was different. Christine thought back to her lunch with Gabi and what she had said about Ruth having a lover. She hadn't seen her for weeks. Ruth had suggested she take a break from writing the columns for *Kult*, and Christine had been very grateful for the suggestion.

"By the way, I really liked your 'Catfight' column in *Femme*. I met up with Ellen Wagner recently, and she's over the moon to be working with you."

"It's fun, and I like having her as a boss, too. But it takes up more time than I thought it would."

"Well, I'm sure you'll figure it out."

Christine didn't get the impression Ruth was really that interested.

"Was the Uschi character based on anyone?"

"Uschi who?"

"The one in the column. The one with the lover, in the sauna."

Christine realized what Ruth was getting at. "Ruth, I surely don't have to tell you that it's all made up! I can't just tell stories about real people."

"Have you spoken to Gabi recently? About me?"

Christine lied, "No, why should I have?"

"Well, sometimes things come up, you might have." Ruth stared at her fingernails. Then she looked up. "OK, I can tell you, too, but please keep it to yourself. I was looking at an apartment here just now, for me. A really wonderful place; I'd love to take it. Right here, over the hairdressers. We'd almost be neighbors! But unfortunately there are a lot of prospective tenants interested. So the estate agent couldn't say either way, and has gone to see the owner now. She's getting back to me later."

Christine waited. Ruth didn't look like she was done. She didn't need any prompting either.

"I met someone over the summer. You know, it happens. I don't know whether you know Karsten; I think you met him once. Well, anyway, things have really gotten into a rut between us. When I met Markus, it really turned things upside down for me. I really did want to make a decision, and I just needed a little more time. But then someone told Karsten. There was a huge scene: as I walked into the hotel with Markus, Karsten was sitting there in the foyer. So, that was the end of us. Karsten asked me to move out; after all, it is his apartment. I just don't know what lowlife told him. It's so unfair."

Christine, who had been holding her breath, exhaled deeply.

"Well, I wouldn't say it's unfair…but at least it's brought things out in the open. How are you handling it?"

Ruth was rubbing her hand over a water mark on the table.

"It annoys me that someone felt the need to stick their oar in. I think it was Gabi, but Karsten won't tell me. And I'm annoyed about having to move. And that Karsten is being so difficult about the whole thing. He can't have cared that much about me after all."

Oh Ruth, thought Christine, *your view of the world is really quite extraordinary.*

Ruth seemed to read Christine's mind. "I know that all sounds pretty cold. But it's not that easy. Karsten and I have been together since we left high school; that's almost fifteen years. In that time we've separated at least four times, and we've always gotten back together again. And to be honest, the last two times I had the feeling we were both just too lazy to look for someone new, let alone live alone. We've just gotten used to one another. Although maybe that just means you're not experiencing any more unpleasant surprises. We haven't talked about our relationship for years; why would we? I go with him to the doctor's ball, and he comes with me to the publishing house Christmas party. Over the years our relationship has become more like a business. He's not exactly devastated either."

"So why did he make a scene in the hotel?"

"Who knows? Perhaps his male pride was injured. Maybe he thought he had to act like the enraged husband, no idea. But it was very effective."

Ruth's cell started to ring, and she pulled it out of her bag.

"Ruth Johannis."

She listened, concentrating, for a moment, then looked at the clock. "I could be there in half an hour. Or would tomorrow morning work, too?" She looked at Christine and gave a thumbs up. "No, no, then I'll come right away. That's great, see you then."

She snapped her cell shut and punched the air jubilantly. "Yes! That was the estate agent. The owner is going on holiday tomorrow and wants to settle the contract today. He liked my application, so the other viewings have been canceled and I can sign right away. I have to go now. Can you pay for me?"

She was already up, pulling her jacket on.

"Oh, Christine, I completely forgot to tell you. When you were out sick earlier in the week, a guy came by the publishing house to see you, Sven I think his name was. He was actually coming to meet Mathias, but he wasn't there. He came over to us in Editorial and asked me for your phone number."

Christine was surprised to feel her heartbeat quicken. "And?"

Ruth looked at her, amazed. "I don't just go around giving your number out, you know, he could be some psychopath. OK, well, I'll call you, bye."

Christine watched Ruth as she ran across the road.

Sven, she thought, *hmmm*.

• • •

Lübeck

Frauke was just pressing the button on the coffee machine when the doorbell rang. She looked at the clock on the kitchen wall. Three o'clock. Gudrun was on time, as always.

She heard Lisa open the door.

"Hi, Mom's in the kitchen. Mom, Gudrun's here. And I'm off to Insa's. Bye."

Gudrun answered, "Don't yell in my ear like that. It's fine just to let me in."

The house door slammed shut, and moments later Gudrun appeared in the kitchen.

"My God, your daughter has a pair of lungs on her, Frauke. Wow! You've been to the hair salon; you look amazing."

They hugged; then Gudrun pushed Frauke away from her for a better look.

"Hey, you look completely different. What's up, have you gotten yourself a lover or something? Or is it some new miracle cream? And if so, what's it called?"

Frauke laughed and freed herself from her grasp. "Sit down; I'll tell you in a minute. By the way, I have an idea."

Frauke and Gudrun had known each other since their school days. Back then, they weren't close friends but were always in the same group. After school they had lost touch for several years; then, after Gunnar took over the car salesroom in Lübeck, they bought a house on the edge of the city and had met their new neighbors at a street party: Gudrun and Hannes. Frauke had been pregnant with Lisa back then, and Gudrun was working as a medical assistant. They hadn't been able to have children: she had come to terms with that, but Hannes hadn't. Three years later he had left her for Bettina, who already had a daughter from her first marriage. They went on to have another three together.

Gudrun had handled it all well on the outside. She hadn't wanted alimony from Hannes, but insisted on having the house. He wrote it over to her; she renovated it completely and then began her new life.

She was now a managerial secretary in the university clinic, had learned English and Spanish, took two big vacations a year, went to a fitness studio, and was enjoying a relaxed, casual relationship with Carlos, a Spanish pediatrician from Kiel. She had just been to his hometown with him for a three-week holiday and looked tanned and happy.

She sat down at the kitchen table and watched Frauke as she took the coffee cups from the cupboard.

"You've lost weight, too."

Frauke turned around to her and smiled. "Is it already noticeable?"

"It sure is. How much have you lost?"

"Ten pounds," said Frauke proudly. "And my hair? You don't think it's too short?"

Her hair, which used to be shoulder length and usually thrown up haphazardly into a ponytail, was now cut just above her jaw line, curled, and highlighted. Gudrun was impressed.

"You look completely different. I'd totally forgotten you had it in you. You look ten years younger. Now please, tell me what brought all this on."

As Frauke told her about the invitation to Christine's birthday, about Lisa's comments, her frustration, and the resolutions she had made afterwards, Gudrun noticed how her friend's eyes were sparkling and how different her voice sounded. She was so amazed at this transformation that she hardly registered whose birthday they were talking about. Frauke stood up and fetched the envelope.

"And this is the questionnaire. I copied it for you before I filled it out. Mine is almost done. If you can do yours before the weekend I can mail them both back together."

Gudrun waved her hand defensively. "Wait, I'm being a bit slow on the uptake here. Who was Christine Schmidt anyway? She wasn't in my class."

Frauke rolled her eyes. "Oh, Gudrun, you can never remember anyone we talk about—it's like you've just suppressed all your schooldays. Anyway, you're invited because I told Gabi that I'm still in touch with you. Christine was in my class; we all did dance class together, then we spent practically a whole summer at the outdoor swimming pool together, with Björn, Alex, and Ingo. You must remember that."

Gudrun looked clueless; clearly none of the names rang a bell with her. Frauke shook her head and picked up the blue photo album, which she started to flick through.

"Here." She tapped her finger at a photo of eight girls and four boys, all in colorful outfits and smiling into the camera. "That's you, that's me, and this is Christine. It was the graduation ball at the Schröder Hotel, for heaven's sake. And you were there."

Gudrun looked at the photo. Suddenly the penny dropped.

"Oh, Christine! Now I know who you mean, I was thinking of someone else. I thought it was the red-haired girl who used to go with Stefan Matthes. I couldn't stand her."

Frauke looked at her impatiently. "She was called Christiane, and she was in the year below us."

Gudrun looked at the photo thoughtfully. "Yes, it's coming back to me now. Of course I knew Christine, but back when you were both friends I didn't know her that well. It was only later, when I was with Torsten. He had a sister, Antje, and she was Christine's best friend. That's right. They were both in our clique, so we saw each other a lot back then. That was a fun time. I took Christine riding with me a few times, but she didn't really get into it. And besides, Antje used to get jealous: given I was already going out with her brother, she didn't want me spending time with her best friend, too."

Frauke looked relieved. "So you're not as senile as I thought after all. Antje was one of the reasons Christine and I didn't see each other so much as time went on. She pushed herself between us and could never stand me."

"And of course you didn't put up a fight." Gudrun looked at her friend, shaking her head. "How can you just let someone push you aside like that?"

"Well, there were other reasons, too; my parents built a new house for us in the next village, and we didn't have the same route to school anymore. The bus connections were bad, and, well, the lovely Antje didn't want anyone stealing her thunder. When you're fifteen you don't really have the self-confidence to stand up to a girl like Antje. She was so pretty and sporty, always wearing designer jeans, and so confident. You knew her, too, so you know what I mean."

"Well, Antje must have been invited to this, too, so we'll have the pleasure of seeing her again."

Frauke nodded. "I'm assuming so. I can't wait. Oh, and there's something else: I wanted to ask if you'd go shopping with me beforehand." She looked both shy and excited at the same time. "I have no idea what to wear."

Gudrun was surprised to see that Frauke had the same expression she'd had in some of the old photos. There was something moving about it.

"Of course. We'll have a real power-shopping day. And by the end of it you'll be a bombshell again."

Questionnaire
Name, age, and place of residence?

Gudrun, 45, Lübeck.

When and where did you meet Christine?

I unfortunately can't remember precisely when it was. We were at school together, then took the same dance lessons, and then I remember meeting her at a party at Torsten's parents' house. He was my boyfriend back then, and Christine was his sister's best friend. Christine came riding with me now and then, but after she fell off the horse four times she'd had enough. So had the horse.

What was your best experience together?

The fit of giggles she had at the graduation ball when her dance partner Wolfgang slid across the floor as they walked in. Even today I wouldn't be able to keep a straight face if I saw him!

What made your friendship stand out? And what sets Christine apart as a friend?

We had a wonderful time together. We weren't taking life seriously yet. And Christine was so dependable and very loyal. But, unfortunately, not that great at horse riding.

What's your motto in life?

Somehow, things always work out.

A friend is…?

A critic, admirer and a soul mate—if it works well.

What was your first reaction to this invitation?

I thought, why not? Let's see what a trip down memory lane will hold for me.

October, Hamburg

The final whistle was drowned out by deafening cheers. The handball fans in the Color Line Arena jumped up from their seats, whistling, singing, and applauding.

"Man, that was close. At the very last minute!"

Sven's voice sounded hoarse. Christine looked at him, her hands sore from clapping. He was whistling with two fingers, jumping from one leg to the other.

"Unbelievable."

Suddenly he leaned over to Christine and kissed her on the mouth. Taken aback, she looked at him. He held her gaze, then kissed her again.

"That was to celebrate the win. Well, not just that, but that, too. Come on, let's go, I need a beer."

Sven reached for his jacket, waited until Christine had pulled hers on, and then fought a path through to the exit for them.

Christine concentrated on looking at his back. She was feeling a little confused. The smell and the atmosphere of the stadium were making her think of old times. She could remember the weight of her sports bag, the feeling of her legs aching, and the elation of winning, the faces of Lena and the other players. She tried to chase the thoughts away; that was all a long time ago now. Instead, she fixed her gaze on Sven's light leather jacket and his tousled blond hair.

Today was the fourth time they had met up. Two weeks ago he had come by the publishing house. Gabi had been on vacation, and Christine was alone in her office. Sven came in, sat down on Gabi's desk, and explained that he'd put Christine's phone number through the wash, after which it was indecipherable. That was so typical of American chewing gum wrappers, he had said; they were useless.

He had gone on to explain his unsuccessful attempt to get her number from the blond ice queen in Christine's office; by the look she gave him she had clearly thought he was some kind of pervert. And Mathias, who was normally very eager to help, wasn't answering his phone. So, as a result he had decided to risk making a fool of himself and invite her out to dinner in person.

They met that very evening. Sven was very good company. They talked about Christine's columns, about his job, about him and Mathias. It was a relaxed evening. Sven was funny, Christine, giggly; they told each other stories about their respective childhoods. All exaggerated, of course, to add to the comedy value.

Later, as she sat in the taxi, Christine thought regretfully about the fact that Sven hadn't been flirting with her. Perhaps he just wanted someone to go out now and again and wasn't—despite Mathias's comments—looking for a new girlfriend after all. She told herself that was a good thing, especially when she heard Richard's voice on her answering machine later. He sounded full of longing to see her. Christine had enough on her plate already when it came to her love life; she didn't need any more complications.

A week later they went to the movies together, had a beer afterwards, and found they had the same opinions about the film. They also discovered they had both played handball, and Sven had said he would get tickets for the HSV.

Two days after that, she was drawing her curtains while on the phone to Sven and managed to rip the curtain pole out of the wall support. The metal pole had cracked her on the head. Christine was telling Sven about the energy dance, rubbing the bump on her head at the same time, and went into a fit of laughter. The next evening Sven came by with his drill, and for the first time ever, Christine canceled her plans with Richard at the last minute.

Sven repaired the curtain pole while Christine cooked pasta. Over dinner they spoke for the first time about their failed marriages and about life as single people. Christine felt an ache in her stomach and put it down to the meat sauce. Sven was still funny, still laid-back, and still noncommittal. That evening, Richard's text messages went unanswered.

And now she was walking behind him and could feel her pulse racing after the kiss. He turned around to her now, and then as they made their way to the exit and walked over to the parking lot together. They stayed silent until they saw his car. He went to the passenger side, opened it for her, and looked at Christine. Standing in front of him, she thought briefly of Richard. Then she saw Sven's face, felt his hand on her back, let him take her in his arms, and shut her eyes.

In the parking lot of the stadium, she thought, *just like the old days.* And her heart started to pound.

• ● •

Hamburg

Gabi stood in front of the hair salon and looked up at the windows on the second floor. It must be here; the lights were on in the apartment. She climbed up the three steps to the entrance door and looked at the names on the buzzer. The third one from the top read *R. Johannis*. Gabi took a deep breath, switched the bunch of flowers into her other hand, and rang the bell. Moments later a voice came out of the loudspeaker.

"Yes, who is it?"

Gabi cleared her throat. "Hi, it's me, Gabi."

The answer was hesitant. "Oh, Gabi…come on up."

The door buzzer went; Gabi pushed it open and walked into the entrance hall.

She hadn't seen Ruth since their argument at work. At first she had thought they were going to make a fresh start. Then Ruth had gone away to Cologne for a week to attend a seminar, and after that Gabi had been away on vacation for two weeks. She had tried to call Ruth but could never get a hold of her. At home she had her answering machine on, and at work Ruth's secretary just kept turning her away.

Gabi had thought long and hard about their fight: she was sorry; she had gotten a few things clear in her mind and wanted to talk to Ruth about them, but she wasn't giving her the chance to.

Eventually, last week, she had spoken to Christine and told her everything. Christine had been flabbergasted that Gabi had no idea about what had been happening. She updated her: shortly after their fight, Ruth's secret affair had come out. Ruth had organized the seminar in Cologne at the last minute to get out of the heat of it. And a week ago she had moved into a new apartment. Gabi was stunned, all the more so after Christine had tentatively asked her if she had been the one who had told Karsten, which was apparently what Ruth suspected.

And now Gabi was standing in front of the apartment door, which was slightly ajar. She rang the bell briefly then walked into the apartment. Ruth was coming toward her, an empty carton in her hand, which she dropped to the floor. She had no makeup on and was wearing old jeans and a checkered man's shirt. She looked at Gabi, her face expressionless.

"To what do I owe the honor?"

Gabi came straight to the point: she was too worked up to be diplomatic.

"It wasn't me that told Karsten. I would never have done that. You accused me last month of never telling you anything. We argued, that's true, but I thought we were on our way to working things out. And now you keep something like this from me."

Her shoulders slumped, Ruth sank down onto a stool in the hallway. She looked up at Gabi.

"You were the only one who knew about Markus. Who else could it have been?"

"Thomas."

Ruth looked blankly at Gabi. "Thomas? Your Thomas? But he's in Frankfurt, what does he have to do with it? Did you tell him?"

Gabi pulled her coat off, pressed the flowers into Ruth's hand, and squatted down on a pile of moving boxes.

"Karsten must have been picking someone up from the airport. He ran into Thomas. And he told him that we'd separated and asked Karsten if you both could look out for me a bit."

"Oh, shit." Ruth suddenly remembered a conversation she'd had with Karsten. She had come home one evening, and he was cooking. As they ate dinner he had asked her—sounding completely normal—how Gabi and Thomas were. Ruth had answered—in an equally normal tone—that everything was fine. Gabi was just feeling very lonely during the week, and Ruth was trying to keep her mind off it all. Karsten had said it was good they had such a close friendship again, and Ruth had agreed with him earnestly.

As she said good-bye to him the next evening, on her way out to meet Markus, he had told her to give Gabi his best. After that, he had followed her in the car and confronted them at the hotel.

Ruth shook her head and rubbed her forehead. "I'm sorry. I thought you said something to him; I knew you always had a soft spot for Karsten. I'm sorry, everything just got so mixed up. I was so bitter, at myself, too. I'm really sorry, Gabi, truly I am, not just for the false accusations but for how I've been acting recently. I always thought I could handle things better than this. I'd forgotten how much change stresses me out." She raised her head and held her hand up in a pledge. "I promise I'll do better in future. I'll start over. I mean, you're doing that at the moment, too; we're both starting a new life, and that's when you need your friends the most." She stood up and spread her arms wide. "Come on, sweetie, let's kiss and make up and then I'll open some champagne."

As they hugged, Gabi looked over Ruth's shoulder and wondered whether she should tell her exactly how she had found out about the conversation between Thomas and Karsten at the airport.

As Ruth released her from her grasp and looked searchingly into her eyes, Gabi suppressed the memory of her evening with Karsten. There were more important things right now.

• ● •

Bremen

Christine was awoken by the final gurgles of the coffee machine. She heard the clattering of cups and the sound of Richard whistling. Groaning softly, she turned on her side and pulled her legs up toward her stomach. Everything hurt: she had a horrid taste in her mouth, her head was banging, she was cold and felt nauseous.

They had seen each other the day before for the first time in a month. On the drive from Hamburg to Bremen, Christine had tried to bring the intense feelings she had felt for Richard over the last three years back to life. His voice, his warmth, the way he looked at her. But all she could think of were the things that tormented her: the secrets, the lonely weekends, his silences, his demanding wife. Christine had been waiting for three years. Waiting for the phone to ring, waiting for him to come to see her, and above all, waiting for a decision. Small things happened, but nothing major. All this waiting was tiring.

She had spoken to Dorothea about it. Dorothea had listened to her for a long time and then asked Christine what she really thought, whether she still believed that this secret affair would one day become a real, honest relationship.

Christine hadn't hesitated long before shaking her head. "I had such strong feelings for him, but this waiting around just corrodes everything." Then she had started to cry.

Two weeks later Sven had been standing in her office.

Richard put the two coffee cups down on the nightstand and sat down on the edge of the bed. He brushed Christine's hair aside and kissed her on the neck.

"Good morning, beautiful. Would you like some coffee?"

Christine pulled the duvet around her and sat up straight against the wall. She reached for the cup and avoided Richard's gaze.

"Thank you, that's sweet of you. What time is it anyway?"

"No idea, probably nine or so. But it's Sunday."

She could feel him looking at her, but tried to keep her gaze fixed on her cup. The smell of the coffee made her feel even more nauseous. Richard put his cup down, lifted the duvet, and lay down next to her. His hand caressed her stomach; his face close to hers, he kissed her shoulder.

"So, Christine, tell me what…"

His phone rang. Richard jumped up immediately. Christine knew who it would be.

"Jürgensen."

She didn't move. Richard took the phone into the next room but left the door open, so she couldn't help but hear what he was saying.

"No, no, I'm awake already, and I'm about to drive into the chambers…Yes. Oh, you'll figure it out, and we can talk about it later, but I really have to go now…yes, I hope you do, too, Sabine. Bye now, bye."

Christine's headache felt worse. Sometimes she wondered whether she should just start screeching like a madwoman in the background during these "check-up" phone calls. Or cough. Or shout out, "Come back to bed, darling." But, unfortunately, she was too discrete for that.

Richard came back, looking embarrassed, but that didn't make her feel any better. Before he could lie down again, Christine stood up.

"I have to go to the bathroom."

"Christine, I…"

"It's fine."

She pushed past him, She needed to be alone for a moment. Closing the bathroom door, she sat down on the edge of the bath. Noticing she was trembling, she stood up and pulled Richard's bathrobe on. It smelled of him. She was fighting tears.

She had felt nervous as she rang his doorbell yesterday evening. To her surprise he had beamed at her and pulled her close. He was pleased to see her and had seemingly forgotten the sad and strained phone calls of the last four weeks. Christine had noticed how awkwardly her body had reacted in his arms, but Richard hadn't seemed to.

They had eaten at the Italian restaurant they often went to, presumably because it was far enough away from the chambers to ensure they wouldn't bump into anyone he knew. Christine hadn't been hungry; she had chewed her meat as if it were cardboard and could barely swallow. But she drank to make up for it in the hope that it would help reduce the tension she felt. Their conversation dragged; Richard was making an effort to tell funny stories about his colleagues, but Christine wanted to talk about something else. When she asked him how he was doing, he waved the question away.

"Come on, I want to enjoy a nice evening with you. Everything is complicated at home; I don't want to talk about that."

He never wanted to. A blond man in a light leather jacket came into the restaurant, and Christine jumped. As he turned around, she saw it was just a stranger.

Richard had noticed her glancing up. He looked at her questioningly and took her hand. Christine felt her heart ache. Why couldn't Sven be Richard or Richard, Sven? Feeling completely confused, she ordered a double grappa. She heard Dorothea's voice: "Why do you feel guilty about going out with Sven when Richard is sharing a bed with his wife?"

She felt her face getting hot. Richard paid, and they went back to his apartment in silence. Christine wanted another glass of wine, so Richard reluctantly opened a bottle. He noticed how drunk she was but didn't say a word. After a while she fell asleep in the chair; then Richard undressed her and carried her to bed. That was all. And now she was crouching on the bath in tears and had no idea what to do.

• • •

Cuxhaven

Marleen answered the phone after the second ring.

"Hello, Marleen, I just wanted to check whether you were already in the pub. I'm on my way to see you," said Christine, sounding relieved.

"I've been here since nine this morning. I have to cook *Grünkohl* stew for forty people for a birthday party here tonight. So you're very welcome to come and peel potatoes with me. When will you be here?"

Christine looked at the clock next to the speedometer. "I'm just passing Osterholz now, so in about half an hour."

"Great, see you soon then."

Marleen hung up, and Christine was reminded once again of how much she appreciated Marleen never asking questions. She was just there for you, and that was that.

Richard had waited half an hour and then come into the bathroom. He sat down next to her on the edge of the bath and took her in his arms.

Christine tried to regain her composure. She failed. Despite her best efforts the tears continued to flow, and Richard had struggled to make sense of snippets of sentences in between the tears like "and next month it will be my birthday again," "I'd like to be able to spontaneously…," and "this damn waiting around." He understood, but couldn't work out what had brought on this outburst.

An hour later Christine had showered and calmed down. She drank another cup of coffee and suddenly had the burning need to be comforted. By Marleen. Richard watched helplessly as she got dressed, and asked if he had messed everything up. Christine shook her head sadly.

"No, at least…not completely. But I don't think this is enough for me anymore; it's not that what we have is awful, but it's certainly not great either. I'm so fed up of having to wait to see you all the time and of having these secrets."

Richard stroked her back. "Me too, believe me. I just can't find a solution to it at the moment."

Christine looked at him sadly. "Exactly. And that's the problem."

He stood at the window as she left the house. She couldn't bring herself to turn around.

Christine honked her horn as she drove onto the parking lot in front of the pub. Marleen waved at her from the kitchen window. Moments later she opened the door and walked out to meet her.

"Now, I hope you're only here because you knew I needed a potato peeler." She hugged Christine and gave her an appraising look. "But it doesn't look like it. Did you get a bit sloshed last night? Your eyes are all red."

"I did a little. But there's something therapeutic about peeling potatoes. I'll tell you as we work."

Marleen laughed. "You'll have to. I don't have time for a leisurely breakfast with you; we have to get to it."

Christine gulped when she saw the mountain of potatoes on the kitchen table.

"Heavens above, you really are making *Grünkohl*. Where are the old ladies that always help you out?"

Marleen handed Christine an apron. "Here, get this on; otherwise you'll ruin your nice clothes. My ladies are off on a bus trip with the Red Cross; they've gone to Schwerin. Mathilde was really excited: her first love came from there, and I think she's hoping to run into him."

"How long ago was her first love?"

Marleen thought for a moment. "She said something about 1949. But she reckoned she would recognize him by his eyes. Anneliese and Gerda are worried she's going to start chatting up all the old men she sees."

Christine laughed. "Mathilde, what a character. I haven't seen her for ages; it's a shame. It must be ten years ago now."

A picture came into her mind of Lena sitting next to her mother, Mathilde, and rolling her eyes as the older woman held forth with a merciless commentary about her daughter's ex-boyfriend. "He might think he's all that now he's got money, but you can't make a silk purse from a sow's ear."

Life was easy the way Mathilde and her friends saw it. Lena had inherited her mother's pragmatism; she just talked problems into submission. And quite rightly so.

Christine reached for the peeler and the first potato.

"Sometimes I miss the old get-togethers. There was something very comforting about Mathilde and Martha. Lena was exactly the same; she never let things get on top of her. She helped me a lot back then. When Bernd came into the picture, everything fell apart somehow."

"Well." Marleen glanced at Christine. "You didn't do much to prevent it."

Christine shrugged her shoulders. "Sometimes you do stupid things and then you can't figure out how to make it good again. I behaved badly back then, I know that now. But I can't just phone and say: 'Hey, I know everything turned out badly and that it was ten years ago now, but let's forget it and go get a beer.' I'm not sure that would go down well."

Marleen tossed her peeled potato into the huge bowl and nodded.

"You're right," she said, thinking about the fact that Lena hadn't answered her letter yet. She would call her this evening. In spite of her initial doubts, the plan was really starting to grow on her.

For a while they sat in silence, just peeling. Then Marleen wiped her hands on her apron and went over to the coffee machine. "We don't have to work in thirst, you know. Would you like a coffee, too?"

Christine nodded and kept peeling. Marleen was much quicker than she so this was her chance to catch up. Even potato peeling could be made into an exciting competitive sport.

Moments later Marleen was back, peeling three potatoes in the time it took Christine to do one. Christine sighed. Marleen looked at her.

"So, come on, tell me. What's happened?"

"You do three to my one."

"What?"

"Potatoes."

"I'm an expert. Don't change the subject. Why are you here and not with Richard?"

Christine took a deep breath and, for the duration of the next forty potatoes, told her about Richard, Sven, and the kiss in the parking lot.

Marleen listened intently, peeling all the while. As Christine talked about the kiss with Sven, she looked up. "And then?"

"What do you mean, and then?"

"What happened after that? Something must have happened after kissing? Come on, don't make me drag it out of you."

Christine stared at a black patch on the potato in her hand.

"Nothing else happened, if you're thinking what I think you are. We drove to a pub, had a beer, and then I told Sven that I really like spending time with him but that my private life is complicated enough at the moment."

Marleen sighed. "Christine. Sometimes you can be really silly. Why didn't you just let it flow? It seems this guy could really be right for you. And you have to go and have scruples about it."

She had let her hands fall and was staring at Christine uncomprehendingly, who continued to peel untiringly.

"I don't have scruples; I'm too old for that. But Sven doesn't kiss as well as Richard does, and I didn't feel like trying out the rest." She looked at Marleen and threw the potato into the water. "In all seriousness, Sven is really funny, but when it comes down to it I just see Richard's face in front of me. It just won't work. I really wish I felt differently, but that's the way it is."

Marleen started peeling again, slowly this time, and thought for a moment. Then she increased her tempo.

"So, is the problem that you could have with Sven what you really want to have with Richard?

Christine wished that removing the layer of sadness weighing on her heart were as simple as peeling potatoes. "Pretty much. And it's becoming more and more clear to me how much I want to have that with Richard and how little chance there is of it ever happening."

They both threw their last potatoes into the pot at the same time. Marleen gathered the peelings together. Then she filled another pot with water.

"Don't start thinking that we're done here. I have the same amount all over again. But first let's have a smoke and a coffee, OK?"

Christine pressed her hands into the small of her back.

"Great. Can't you put pasta in the *Grünkohl* for once? Or rice? These piles of potatoes are horrendous."

She sat down at a table in the bar and pulled her cigarettes from her bag. Marleen put two cups on the table and sank down into the chair.

"I'm really glad you're here; it's so boring doing this by myself." She raised her coffee cup. "Cheers."

"Cheers. And I'm glad I came. You calm me down; I'm feeling much better again."

"That's the potato peeling. But Christine, seriously, you've had far worse times, in spite of this complicated business with Richard. Why don't you try to relax a little? Keep on meeting up with Sven, and just see what happens with you and Richard. You can't make him do anything; he has to figure things out for himself. And if it all goes wrong, you still have me, and Dorothea and Ines; we've saved you from hopeless males before."

At that moment someone rattled at the locked door. Marleen stood up, went on tiptoes, and tried to see who it was.

She laughed. "I don't believe it. Speak of the devil."

Christine turned around. "Who is it?'

"The hopeless male in question: Bernd."

Marleen went to the door and opened it. Christine stayed sitting down with her back to the door. Just what she needed! She hadn't seen Bernd for a long time; he hadn't exactly behaved like a gentleman in the time leading up to and following their divorce. She heard Marleen's muted voice at the door.

"I'm not open yet, what's up?"

"Hi! I just wanted to book our Christmas work party. Hey, isn't that Christine's car parked outside?"

Before Marleen could answer, Bernd had already pushed past her and was standing in the bar. "Well, who do we have here?"

Christine sighed lightly. Bernd was a master of insipid sayings, or at least he was when he felt insecure. Why had she so rarely noticed that while they were married? She turned around to face him.

"My name is Christine Schmidt, and if I seem familiar to you, it's because we were once married."

Bernd, however, was resistant to irony. He sat down on the chair next to her.

"So? Everything fine and dandy? What's new in Christine's world? Marleen, pour me a beer, will you?"

Marleen rolled her eyes. "Well, it'll have to be a quick one; I have to get on with the cooking and I can't be serving guests at the same time."

"Why not? Christine's here, too."

"She's helping me."

Bernd looked skeptical. "Really? Well, if you say so. Anyway, we'd like to hold our Christmas party here on the sixth of December. Thirty people. And we'd like *Grünkohl.*"

"With rice or with pasta?"

Bernd looked at her, baffled. "Why would we want it with pasta? With potatoes, of course."

Marleen looked at her calendar. "Fine, that's OK. Why are there so many of you? Is it partners, too?"

Bernd gave her an innocent look. "A few are bringing partners, but not everyone; I'm coming alone."

Marleen looked at him, just as innocently. "Why? Aren't you with Antje anymore?"

"Oh, on and off, it's nothing serious, just, you know."

Christine was thinking that what her ex-husband really needed was a sharp kick in the balls. She looked at him discreetly while he was talking to Marleen. He had put on weight and it didn't suit him. He looked podgy. The red fleece pullover he had on was at least seven years old; she had bought it for him. The seam was starting to unravel at the bottom. Without stopping to ask, Bernd took a cigarette from Christine's pack. She should have tried to smack his fingers, not just a little slap but a real one. A giggle slowly rose in her throat, but feeling Marleen's well-timed look, she coughed instead.

"Oh, did you catch a cold? You look thin. Suits you though."

Knowing she would lose her composure if she answered, Christine jumped up and hurried to the bathroom without a word. Silently, she imagined her response: "Oh, thank you, you look podgy, but it doesn't suit you." She giggled as she sat on the toilet.

When she came back, Bernd put down his empty glass and looked at her.

"Girls, I have to go. See you soon, stay strong. *Tschüssi.*"

Marleen and Christine watched him go. As the door closed behind him, they looked at each other, then broke out into unstoppable laughter.

"Heavens above." Marleen gasped for air, wiping the tears from her eyes. "And to think he was once the love of your life. And hasn't he gotten fat!"

"Podgy." Christine doubled over, hysterical now. She tried to take deep, steady breaths. "Goodness gracious— as Bernd would say—where did I leave my brain? Was he always like that?"

In doubt, she looked at Marleen, who tilted her head thoughtfully. Then she started to laugh again.

"Yes, I do believe he was. So, the lesson to be learned here is not to take the men in your life so seriously."

She took a deep breath and wiped under her eyes. "Come on, honey, back-to the potatoes; there are more important things in life than filling our heads with complicated love stories. Bernd won't be the last of the hopeless men we have to save you from, I'm sure."

Christine giggled again and reached for the peeler.

Marleen looked at her. "Is this Sven younger than you?"

"I don't think so. I'm not sure. Why?"

"Oh, it's just that Dani has a lover who's ten years younger than she is. It can be difficult."

Christine looked up, confused. "Which Dani? My Dani? How do you know that?"

At that moment the phone rang. Marleen jumped up, biting her lip. *Shit,* she thought, *that was too close for comfort.*

She picked up the phone and took another Christmas party reservation.

• ● •

When Christine opened her apartment door a few hours later in Hamburg, she was glad to be home. Marleen was right; she had survived more difficult times. Everything was better than her old life with "podgy" Bernd and "on-and-off" Antje.

Her answering machine was blinking. Calls from Dorothea, who wanted to know where on earth she was, from Gabi asking her to call her back, and from Sven.

"Hi, Christine, I was just calling to say hello. Call me back if you'd like to. I'm just bumbling around here."

Before the giggles could overtake her, she picked the receiver up and called Richard.

"I just wanted to say sorry. Not for how I've been feeling but for the fact that I didn't talk to you honestly about it. You're too important to me for us to be like that with each other. By the way, Marleen said that the planets are badly aligned for relationships at the moment. It'll be better again by November."

She could hear the smile in Richard's voice. "I understand; it's a difficult situation. How about we forget about last night and I'll come to see you on Tuesday. If you'd like me to, that is. I read today that the planets will be better aligned by the day after tomorrow, and..."

Christine took the phone over to her chair and curled herself up in it.

• ● •

"By the Power of the Moon"

A month ago my friend Karola totaled her husband Paul's car. It happened because she saw a boundary pole too late. Paul was pretty angry and didn't speak to her for several days.

Karola was angry, too, not because of Paul, but because she'd forgotten to consult her annual horoscope. It was all there in black and white. In the week in question, Saturn was retrograde, which meant there was the risk a relationship crisis could come to a head. Besides that she was warned to take care in traffic and in awkward spaces.

I was very impressed, but asked her how long she had been having a relationship crisis; after all, it seemed it was only the totaled car that had brought it about. She explained that only those in third part of the lunar month were affected, and she was in the first, so her relationship crisis was only just beginning.

She looked into it in more detail, and her crisis wasn't supposed to last long; with the advent of the First Quarter Moon phase in two weeks' time, she would have an almost implausibly beneficial constellation with the sun, Mercury, Venus, and Jupiter. Usually,

*people get married and have children under the influence of constel-
lations like that.*

*I pointed out that she had already been married for eighteen
years and that, as Paul is fifty and Karola forty-six, I imagined
their family planning was pretty much decided by now.*

*Karola nodded and said these stars also stand for a recon-
ciliation, so she wasn't worrying herself about Paul's silence—the
Quarter Moon Phase would sort it all out.*

*Besides, the car wasn't a problem either, because Paul's critical
influence from Saturn would be coming to an end next week, following which Saturn would be overtaken by the good luck planet of
Jupiter, which stands for financial success and windfalls.*

*So she wasn't in the least bit worried. Ever since she'd started
having her annual horoscope drawn up for her, she understood
everything much better.*

*I was a little skeptical. According to the horoscope I always
read, I should now be on my seventh marriage, the mother of twelve
children, and a celebrity, none of which have even been close to happening so far.*

*My friend Karola informed me that you have to get your own
individual yearly horoscope made, with your place of birth, time of
birth, and everything. Each year she orders one of these horoscopes
for herself, and for Paul, too, and it almost always turns out to be
true. And, she added, it's already helped her to steer around a lot
of issues.*

*In May, for example, her lunar month was subject to a hard
Saturn transit for four days. In a critical aspect like this she would,
according to the horoscope, immediately overreact to things with
anger and tension. She would argue with everyone, friends would
reject her, and everything would be awful. But because she knew
that in advance, she arranged to take some time off and planned*

a spa weekend with her sister. Admittedly, she ended up giving the owner of the hotel a piece of her mind and argued with her sister, but that was no more than usual. Just imagine what could have happened otherwise, she said.

Or in August, for example, when Mercury was well situated, which means success in exams. My friend Karola triumphantly reminded me of the ADAC automobile safety course we did together. She beat me in every slalom course, and without even breaking a sweat.

And then there was September. On the seventeenth, which was a Saturday, she had the strongest lunar power of the entire year. She set her alarm for six in the morning, slogged away for three hours in the garden, did her taxes, and then, in the afternoon, painted the guest bathroom. And she did it all in the best of moods.

My friend Karola makes sure she only goes to the hairdresser when the moon is in Gemini, and only starts diets when it's in Cancer. Things just work better that way. She also mentioned that you should never have a hip operation when the moon is in Sagittarius. Of course, her hips are perfectly fine.

My friend Karola also says it is particularly important for singles like me to have an official yearly horoscope drawn up. Next year will be a lunar year, so it would be advisable to know on what days the moon and Venus will combine with my ruling planet, Pluto, because those will be the days when I should be keeping my eyes open. That's when he'll come, my dream prince, and Karola said it's very likely indeed. I wouldn't want to make the mistake of staying at home and ironing then.

So a few days ago I ordered myself one of these horoscopes. I didn't want to run the risk of letting my lunar year pass by indifferently and without giving it a good chance, just because I haven't informed myself fully. I read with interest that in February, thanks to Pluto and Venus, I'll get a dream constellation that means I'll be courted by a lion and a bull. Whatever decision I make will be the right one, and based on the astrological calculations involved, November would be the best time for my Lion-Bull and me to start a family—aside from the small matter of my age, of course. By the end of the year I will stand proudly on my victory podium, looking back on an incredibly successful year. Damn right, I thought, for thirty-six Euros I should hope so.

My friend Karola just phoned. The car insurance company told her that Paul didn't have a fully comprehensive policy. So the damage to the car isn't covered. And then a bill from the city authorities came for 168.70 Euros for repairing the signpost. Paul still isn't speaking to Karola, even though yesterday heralded the Quarter Moon phase. Karola is planning to call his mother; presumably she was mistaken about the time of her son's birth, and it would seem that Karola does have a relationship crisis after all. She has to check.

I really hope my mother wasn't mistaken about the time of my birth; that really would be a shame. After all, it's such a lovely horoscope.

• ● •

Hamburg

Ines made a note on a sheet of paper and then pushed it back into its plastic sleeve. She looked at the clock and then over at the door, which opened at that very moment. She saw Luise look around her searchingly; then, seeing Ines, she walked over to the table.

"Ines, hello. I hope you haven't been waiting long."

Ines pointed to her beer glass. "That's my first, and I haven't even started it yet."

"Good." Luise sat down and glanced at the pages in the binder. "Are those our search results? And as Excel sheets, too; wow, you really are organized." She laughed.

Ines brushed her hand over the binder. "You laugh, but how else would you suggest we go about compiling the results? After all, we have all been quite successful."

Luise pulled her jacket off and waved to the waiter. "I can't wait to hear more; I haven't spoken to Ruth, Gabi, or Dorothea for weeks now."

The waiter came over. Luise was just ordering a beer when Dorothea appeared in front of them.

"Evening! I'll have a beer, too. And I'm not the last one to arrive; I thought I would be. Where's Ruth?"

"Here." Ruth appeared, just seconds behind her. "Are you deaf and blind? I've been calling you since the metro. Ten people I didn't even know turned around to me and said hello; it was only you that ran off."

"Oh God, sorry, I was concentrating on how to get here. And besides, I don't pay any attention to people shouting at me in the street anymore; I'm past that age, and in any case it's usually just construction workers." She laughed and looked around at the others. "And even they seem to be getting quieter and quieter."

Ruth asked the waiter what the red wine selection was, had a brief discussion with him about the various choices, and then ordered the most expensive. She sat down next to Ines and picked up the binder. "I see you're prepared. This is great."

Ines nodded. "Yes, I thought I'd get everything typed up to make it easier. I had time last week to get it all in order. I'll wait for your drinks to arrive then give the updates."

Dorothea turned around to the waiter, who was drawing her beer at the bar. "I'm so thirsty, please hurry." She looked at Ruth. "Where's Gabi?"

"She can't make it and sends her best. Her sister's visiting and they're painting the kitchen."

Luise pitched in. "Speaking of Gabi, she told me on the phone that she visited you in your new apartment. Have you settled in well?"

Before Ruth could answer, the waiter brought the drinks over. Once they were all settled again, Dorothea asked: "Where have you both moved to? You had such an incredible apartment in Eppendorf."

Ruth took a long, slow sip of her drink, then put her glass down rather dramatically.

"*We* didn't move; I moved out."

Ines looked at her, shocked, while Dorothea raised her glass without batting an eyelid.

"So, cheers then, welcome to the club." She saw Ines and Luise give her peeved looks. "What? You both live alone, too; it's much easier to look out for your girlfriends that way, and—if you remember correctly—that's exactly what this plan is all about."

"Dorothea!" Ines pulled the sheets of paper out of the binder and shook her head.

"What? I thought I did well in changing the subject there. So, what do we have?"

"OK," said Ines, clearing her throat. "I'll tell you in the order I've organized things here, chronologically according to the time of the friendships. So, first we have Linda Love. As we already know, Luise has written to her. Linda can remember Christine but can't make it to the party. She said she would fill in the questionnaire and send it to me. Then I'll put them all together. By the way, I need your completed questionnaires, too, at the latest in three weeks' time." She looked at the others insistently, then continued: "Frauke was the quickest. She accepted the invite and sent the questionnaire back last week, and not just hers, but one from Gudrun, too; that was the girl with the horse, the one my brother could still remember. So that's three already. Marleen has been on the case, too; she already has Dani coming along and has her questionnaire. And she's also dealing with Lena and called her over the weekend. Apparently Lena was a little hesitant at first but has now said she'll come and promised to fill in the sheet soon. So that's five."

"Six." Ruth opened her purse and took an envelope from it. "This is Marie Erdmann's questionnaire. I showed it to you last time we met up and then took it away with me again by mistake. Here, Ines, I just remembered it. She called me two weeks ago and has already booked a hotel room for when she comes here."

Ines scanned the questionnaire quickly before putting it in the binder.

"That's right, Marie, I'd almost forgotten. The postcard from Emden, right?"

Luise nodded.

"Exactly, the one who did rumba with her cousin on those silly holidays. I think we're doing well here."

Ines counted out loud.

"We've found six women, five of whom are coming. And there are four of us, so that's nine, and Marleen and Gabi, too, that makes eleven. I'm her sister, so discount me for a moment, and that's ten friends. Not bad at all."

Contentedly, Ruth gave Luise a nudge. "Do you still remember our conversation by Alster Lake back in the spring? And how offhand Christine seemed about female friendship? Now she'll be celebrating her birthday with ten girlfriends. Some people just need a little push in the right direction when it comes to their happiness. I think we're going a great job. And I can't wait to see Christine's face."

Ines looked at Ruth, thinking about how badly her sister had been betrayed by her best friend. Perhaps this party really was an opportunity to give her more confidence again, but—on the other hand—perhaps Christine was right, too, and having a best friend wasn't as important as all those glossy women's magazines implied.

Anyway, it was too late to change their plans now; everyone had already been invited.

Ines finished her beer. "So where are we going to have the party anyway? Christine always books a table at the Italian place."

Dorothea shook her head. "No, we'll do it somewhere else; Georg and I will take care of that. We thought everyone could maybe make a contribution, with Georg; you, Ines; and me giving a little more and Christine's parents paying for the rest. That's a good idea, right? Instead of presents." Contentedly, she looked around her, then raised her glass. "Cheers, girls, I think we've done a good job here. The rest will take care of itself. Oh, Ines, show me Marie Erdmann's questionnaire, will you? I still don't know what to write on mine."

She took the sheet from Ines and smoothed it out.

Questionnaire
Name, age, and place of residence?

Marie (Annemarie, in full) Erdmann, 44, Büchen

When and where did you meet Christine?

On the school playground, we were twelve years old and in the sixth year of school. We hit it off right away.

What was your best experience together?

At the graduation ball from our dance lessons when we both wore the same dress. I found that really funny.

It was a great ball. We felt like little Scarlet O'Haras, danced the whole night long, and even drank a little champagne.

What made your friendship stand out? And what sets Christine apart as a friend?

We stuck together through thick and thin, did almost everything together, and were practically Siamese twins. Christine was often too shy so I had to encourage her a lot. But she also made me a little calmer, stopped me from being too hotheaded. Who knows, perhaps I would have run wild otherwise.

What's your motto in life?

Nothing is impossible.

A friend is…?

Someone I know everything about, whom I can tell everything, and who is always there for me.

What was your first reaction to this invitation?

It's great, it's been far too long since we saw each other. I don't know why we haven't done it sooner. Everyone should meet up with their old girlfriends much more often.

● ● ●

Hamburg

Christine was looking for the boxes of her old things. She was sure that they had always been at the top of her wardrobe on the left-hand side. But all she could find was a folder with old insurance documents and a bicycle pump. Finding the pump was just as confusing as not being able to find what she wanted: she had no idea how it had ended up there. Christine vowed to be more organized. While she was up there she wiped the dust away, then climbed back down from the chair. She sat down on the bed, staring at the wardrobe.

The boxes had old photos and letters in them. Five years ago she had fled her old home with Bernd in such a hurry that she'd thrown all her memories and keepsakes haphazardly into boxes. She had meant to sort it all out at some point, but at first she hadn't been in the mood to be reminded of her old life any more than was necessary, and after she'd just forgotten about it it—in the same way that she'd suppressed lots of memories from her old life.

When Marleen had mentioned Dani the day before, Christine was stunned. She had completely forgotten the two of them knew each other from her wedding. She hadn't heard from Dani in over eight years, and now Marleen was casually mentioning Dani's lover. Marleen had looked just as stunned, which had made Christine wonder why, but she quickly brushed it aside. Wanting to hear more about Dani, she pushed for more information.

"There's not much to tell, Christine. A few weeks ago she just turned up here in the pub and asked if I remembered her. She recognized me again right away. She was visiting her parents and had gone on a bike ride with friends. That's all."

"And? Where does she live? What does she do?"

"I don't know, the pub was full to the rafters, and I didn't have time for a proper chat with her."

"You have no idea where she lives, but she told you she has some toy boy lover? Are you kidding me?"

Marleen kept on peeling the potatoes. "She didn't tell me; I just overheard when I was serving her table. Anyway, I thought I'd already told you about running into her; I was sure I had."

They were interrupted by the waitstaff arriving. Marleen seemed relieved.

And now Christine was looking for her old letters and photos of Dani. She must have her parents' address hidden away somewhere; they would know where their daughter was living now. But where were those damn boxes?

• ● •

Berlin

Just as Dani was taking a long soak in the bath, the phone started to ring. She rolled her eyes, which cracked her face mask and left a funny expression. It must be Lars again.

The evening before, they had been at one of his friend's birthday parties. Dani groaned just thinking about it. Jörg was turning thirty, and his girlfriend Svenja was twenty-five. The other four couples all knew each other, but it was the first time Dani had met them. She was the only one in a pantsuit; the other girls—and they were actually girls in the true sense of the word—were wearing barely there skirts, tight-fitting blouses, and colorful tights. Their conversations revolved around the trendiest hangouts, the newest shops, and the relationship dramas of absent couples. Dani felt ancient, which compared to the others, she was. She was also the only one who had to get up early the next morning; all the others were studying or worked freelance, like Lars.

After a while Dani had decided to go home. Lars immediately offered to accompany her, but she refused, waved a quick good-bye to the others, and then took a deep breath of relief as she got in the taxi. She had only just gotten back to the apartment when Lars called to say he wanted to come by; it seemed the party wasn't the same without her. Thinking to herself that she hadn't enjoyed it at all, even *with* him, she told him she just wanted to go straight to sleep. He had sounded hurt and stayed at the party.

And now he was probably calling to apologize, which wasn't even necessary. She had been overjoyed to have her bed all to herself.

Dani propped herself upright in the bath to be able to hear what he was saying on the answering machine. But it wasn't Lars at all. Instead she heard Marleen's voice.

"Hi, Dani, I just wanted to let you know that I almost let the cat out of the bag with Christine. She was at the bar yesterday at lunchtime and I let something slip…"

Dani sank back down into the bath as she listened. As she heard the beeps signaling the end of the message, she smiled. Marleen was worried that Christine was now trying to get Dani's address from her parents. But she wouldn't be able to, because Dani's parents had flown off on a month-long holiday a couple of days before and wouldn't be back until after the party. Christine's friends had beaten her to it.

Dani ran more hot water into the bath and gazed at the lit tea lights at the foot of the bathtub. Her thoughts wandered back twenty years.

Back then, she had just made the biggest mistake of her life by marrying Hannes. She had met him on a skiing holiday. Maybe it was just the intensity of the mountain sun or the high altitude, but once he looked at her there was no holding Dani back. Her sister was appalled: she thought Hannes was a good skier, sure, and he was certainly charming, but apart from that it was a complete mystery to her what Dani saw in him. He was two years older than her, was doing theater studies, and had no money or any real plan of what to do with his life. He told Dani all the things she wanted to hear, read her love poems by Erich Fried, and called her his "beauty." She moved in with him in Bremen and took over paying the rent along with all the bills, waitressing at night and studying by day. Half a year later they were married. Dani was twenty.

Hannes wrote poems, slept late, was very demanding, and found life in Bremen bourgeois. Every day he had new plans and great ideas about how they should live. Dani, tired out from her job and studies, just wanted to sleep, not emigrate. Before long, he found her bourgeois, too. A year later he started an affair with a forty-year-old theater actress, who came to see him in the evenings while Dani was at work, after which he would put clean sheets on the marital bed. To start with Dani was a little puzzled at Hannes's sudden liking for fresh bedding but was too tired to give it any real thought. She only found out why after she slipped in the bar one night and broke her wrist. Hannes didn't answer the phone. When she arrived home from the hospital in a taxi around midnight, with her wrist in cast, the lovers were closely entwined in her bed.

The next morning Dani went to stay with her sister. Her broken heart took much longer to heal than her broken wrist. Then, after eight months of tears, Dani stumbled upon an ad in the newspaper.

Country getaway. Old farmhouse, six rooms, two bathrooms, open-plan kitchen living area, 1000-square-meter garden, in need of renovation, situated between a dike and a meadow, to rent, available immediately.

Just reading the ad comforted Dani. She drove out to view it. The house was old: "in need of renovation" was an understatement, but the location was perfect. Dani couldn't help but think of the idyllic surroundings in the *Gilmore Girls*.

As the realtor led her through the rooms, Dani fell in love. For the first time since that awful night, her heart felt light again. She wanted to live here.

But she wasn't the only one: there was another prospective tenant. Christine. As the three of them stood in the large open-plan kitchen, Dani and Christine looked out of the window down to the dike and said, simultaneously: "It's like paradise." They looked at each other and nodded. Thinking they were viewing the place together, the realtor asked if the rental contract should be made out jointly. Dani was just about to explain when Christine nodded and said:

"Yes, in both our names, please."

The realtor nodded, made an appointment with them for the signing, and drove back to her office. Christine and Dani sat down on the steps outside the front door and introduced themselves to each other for the first time.

Three hours later they stood up, brushed the dust from their jeans, and drove directly to the realtor's office, where they signed the contract.

They only really got to know each other while they were renovating the house. Both took time off work, and they spent days standing on ladders and filling in cavities, ripping up old tapestries, putting new ones up, painting, cleaning...and talking nonstop. There were so many parallels in their lives that they sometimes wondered how it was they hadn't met sooner. They both had two siblings, had been brought up by strict parents, both loved books, liked the same music, and had experienced similar relationships at the same time.

In the very same month that Dani married Hannes, Christine had met Malte. He studied philosophy, read her love poems by Erich Fried, wrote little notes with declarations of love, and believed her love could save him. Christine had moved out of her parents' house and in with him. She worked in a bookstore, but he moped around when she wasn't at home. He phoned her at work, picked her up at the end of the day, and was jealous of the friends—both male and female—that she gradually gave up for him, one by one.

After two years Christine felt suffocated; she had had enough of endlessly having to justify things and suggested to Malte that they separate for a while. He refused, deeply hurt, and after that it just got worse and worse. In the end she had turned to a realtor, who suggested she view this house.

Christine had never lived alone, and when she saw Dani, she immediately knew she wanted a house share. Dani was just as relieved as Christine was.

The first tea light flickered out, bringing Dani out of her thoughts and back to the present. Looking at her wrinkled fingertips, she suddenly realized how cold she was. As she stood under the hot shower, a series of images ran through her head. Christine, sitting opposite her at the kitchen table on Sundays, her hair damp, with one of her three cats in her lap and a book in her hand. Christine, reading her a sentence out loud now and then, which they would then talk about. Christine, lying on her bed in tears after she found out that Malte was living with a fellow student who had moved in just four days after Christine moved out. Christine, lying on a blanket in the garden and watching as Dani and her dance partner Peter practiced rock 'n' roll moves, back when they used to be in a dance club.

In those three years there was nothing in Dani and Christine's lives that they hadn't shared and discussed around that kitchen table. And there was certainly nothing they hadn't found a solution for.

Moisturizing herself, Dani realized she was still using the same brand of lotion Christine had given her as a present back then. She felt a pang of longing to be sitting back at that table with Christine, and to tell her about Lars. Christine would listen, then look out of the window down to the dike for a moment before turning back to her and saying: "Listen, it's simple really, you just need to…"

Dani closed the bottle of lotion and put it back in the cabinet.

Soon, she thought, *very soon.*

● ● ●

Hamburg

Christine closed the second drawer and pulled the third open with a flourish. Gabi looked up.

"What's with all the commotion? Have you lost something?"

Christine rummaged around in her desk. "I can't seem to find anything at the moment, but right now I'm looking for the address stickers. I think I'm going senile; I keep losing things."

"They're behind you, in the cabinet; I put them there. What else have you lost?"

Christine rolled her chair over to the cabinet. "So they are. Thank you. Yesterday evening I was searching for two old boxes for hours and couldn't find them. I have no idea where they've gotten to. They always used to be at the top of my wardrobe."

"You have boxes in your wardrobe?"

"They're small metal ones, with lots of photos and letters in them. Why are you looking at me strangely?"

Christine was puzzled at her shocked expression. Gabi was remembering going into Christine's bedroom with the two boxes, hearing Ines's voice in her memory: "They were at the bottom of the wardrobe." So Gabi had pushed them right to the back.

"What did you need them for?" She felt herself going red. Christine noticed it, too.

"Are you too warm? You can open the window if you like. I'll get us something to drink."

By the time Christine came back, Gabi had regained her composure. She took the glasses from Christine.

"Thanks. So? What did you want them for?"

Christine smiled. "Well, it was really strange. I was at Marleen's on Sunday, a friend of mine who lives in Cuxhaven. I think I've already told you about her."

"The one with the pub, right?" *Now, be careful you don't let anything slip*, thought Gabi.

Christine nodded. "That's the one. Anyway, we spent the whole morning peeling potatoes and laughing about various things." Reminded briefly of podgy old Bernd she couldn't help but laugh again. "And then Marleen suddenly mentioned Dani. She used to be a very good friend of mine; we used to live together. We haven't seen each other for almost ten years, and Marleen saw her in the pub recently."

"And?"

"No *and*. It was just strange. I don't even know where Dani lives now. Marleen didn't get a chance to ask her, but anyway, I thought about her a lot on the drive home. My old photos and letters from her must be in those boxes, along with her parents' address. I was looking for them with the idea of giving her a call."

Gabi breathed out, relieved she had shoved the boxes right to the back of the wardrobe.

Christine played with her glass. "I'd really like to make contact with her again. Never mind, I'm sure the boxes will turn up at some point; after all, it's not like anyone else would have moved them."

Gabi made an effort to keep her facial expression neutral. "I'm sure they will. So why did you lose touch?"

"There were a number of reasons. We were in our early twenties when we moved in together. It was a great time in my life; we didn't know each other before, and only ended up renting the house together by chance. For three whole years it was just so perfect; life felt so easygoing there. We both had complicated relationships behind us, and although we hadn't sworn off men entirely, we weren't interested in getting into anything serious. That is, until I met Bernd, and then I threw caution to the wind. It must have been a bitter disappointment for Dani. I neglected her quite a bit back then. Bernd took precedence, and she felt pushed aside."

"But that's normal. When someone falls in love, particularly at the beginning, the new partner becomes the most important person in their life."

Christine looked at her thoughtfully. "Yes, perhaps, but it shouldn't be at any price. I went about things the wrong way. You can't just drop a friend—and I mean, we lived together, we were practically family—just become some guy comes into the picture."

"But it happens in lots of friendships."

"Yes, Gabi, and that's exactly what annoys me. Everyone goes on about how wonderful and important female friendship is, but then as soon as someone gets a new partner, the girlfriends become an afterthought. It was all my doing back then, and now I'm divorced and don't even know where Dani lives. And to top it all, the reason for my divorce was my supposed best friend. It's crazy. I had lots of friendships that were really important for a while, but at the end of the day I didn't nurture them. Oh well, perhaps a best friend only has a certain shelf life, at least if it's an honest one."

Gabi had been listening with mixed emotions. On the one hand she was bubbling over with excitement at the fact that the plan for the surprise party seemed to be right on the money. Unknown to Christine, the preparations for reconciliations were already underway. But on the other hand, Gabi had suddenly realized that Christine was right.

The ice that best friends stood on was usually quite thin. And it was true that lots of things were brushed under the carpet just to keep things as they were.

At that moment Christine's phone rang, and she picked it up.

Gabi watched Christine and resolved to tell Ruth that she had met up with Karsten. Perhaps it would mean the end of their friendship. But perhaps their best-before date had already run out years ago. She would have to see.

• ● •

Kiel

Lena stared at the questionnaire. So far she had only filled in her name and age. In three weeks' time she would be seeing Christine again for the first time in years. The night before, she had stayed up with Jürgen until one thirty in the morning, talking about old times. About Christine and old times, to be precise. At first it had felt strange, but then all the memories came flooding back, the good and the bad. Jürgen had gotten straight to the point.

"Lena, you have to look at it with a little distance. You were very close friends. You always did a lot for Christine; you helped her renovate her house, you fixed things that were broken, picked her up from places in the middle of the night, and heaven knows what else. But you also told me that she changed you, that she helped you become more laid back and more confident. You benefitted from the friendship, too; otherwise you wouldn't have bothered with it."

Lena shook her head. "But it was never an equal balance. Christine and I used to see each other almost every day, or at least spoke on the phone. You remember how chaotic she was; there was always something broken at her place, or she would lose her keys and need me to go there with my spare, or she would get stranded in her car in the middle of the night because she'd forgotten to fill up the car, and then call me. There was always something."

Jürgen raised his eyebrows. "'But you always went to save her. That gave you a kind of power, too, and I don't mean that in a bad way. Weren't you actually a bit sad when she started seeing Bernd and he took over the emergency calls? I mean, Dani was quite chaotic herself, so she would never have taken away your ability to be the rescuer. But Bernd did."

"Well, maybe a little. But Dani and I liked each other. Bernd couldn't stand me from the word go." She looked at her husband. "And we couldn't stand him either, remember?"

Back then, Christine had phoned Lena and excitedly told her about Bernd, whom she had been seeing for two weeks. She wanted Lena and Jürgen to meet him and had suggested they all meet up in a bar. When Lena and Jürgen arrived, Christine was sitting at the table alone. She said that Bernd would be there any moment, he just had to run a quick errand. He arrived over an hour later, visibly drunk. He sat down next to Christine, who beamed at him, and told never-ending stories about people that no one else knew, about bars in Bremen that were far superior to the ones here, about his ex-girlfriend, and about the fact that he had to repair everything in Christine's house. In Lena's eyes, that was the last straw. She had spent weeks slogging over the renovations, and was angry and appalled when Christine didn't stand up for her. She just sat there, smiling away at Bernd, looking like she had lost her senses.

A few days later Lena had dropped by to see Christine and talk about Bernd. But Christine reacted defensively.

She accused Lena of judging him too quickly and told her to keep her nose out of her private life.

"I was furious at the time. One minute she lets me do everything for her and the next she just kicks me out of her life."

Jürgen tried to calm her down. "Look, you said yourself that she *let* you do everything for her. Take that literally: you wanted to as well. Christine always did what you said back then. You had a very close relationship with her and played such a big role in her life. And then, all of a sudden, Bernd was more important. That annoyed you, which I can understand. She was completely wrapped up in him back then. But remember, the big argument didn't come until four years later."

Lena hadn't forgotten. Initially, she had been very upset that her friendship with Christine had lost importance, but over time they had started to become closer again. By then, Christine was living with Bernd; he had moved into the old house after Dani moved out. Half a year later Christine had seemed to notice there was a life outside her relationship with Bernd, and she started coming to handball training again. Lena and she trained the girls' team together again, and used to go for a beer afterwards. They talked about everything under the sun; everything, that is, except Bernd. Six months later he and Christine got married. Lena and Jürgen came to the wedding, and Lena had photographed the wondrous occasion. Later that night the two women had embraced each other and promised—slurring a little—never to lose touch. Six months later Lena and Jürgen had moved to Kiel.

In the time after that, they still talked on the phone, but their conversations became increasingly superficial and infrequent. One day, Christine turned up on Lena's door-step out of the blue. She didn't look good, and it seemed as though she wanted to tell Lena something but was waiting to be questioned. But Lena didn't want to make the first move; she had gotten used to Christine not being in her life and didn't feel like being an agony aunt. When Christine left, she had looked at Lena sadly and told her she missed her, but Lena had turned around quickly, determined not to give in to her emotions.

For a long time she hadn't heard a word. Then a for-mer handball friend told her that Christine and Bernd had bought a house, and shortly after that the invitation to their house-warming party had arrived. Lena was sur-prised that Christine had moved out of the old house she loved so much; it didn't make any sense. By then, Kathleen was two years old, so they left her with Lena's mother and drove over to Christine and Bernd's place. Greeting them was a little awkward, and there were over twenty guests there, among whom Lena knew very few people. The house was modern, chic, and didn't seem to suit Christine's taste at all.

Christine herself seemed highly strung and was drink-ing too much and too quickly. Bernd did the tour of the house, being sure to name the price and discount he had negotiated for every single piece of furniture.

The way Christine looked at him now was completely different to how she had that night in the bar. Jürgen shook his head and whispered to Lena that something didn't seem right, so she waited for an opportunity to speak with Christine alone. It was difficult: the hostess was running to and fro between her guests in an agitated fashion, followed everywhere by her friend Antje, who had recently divorced and was renting a property near to Christine and Bernd.

Finally, Lena found Christine sitting alone in the kitchen, smoking a cigarette. She sat down next to her and asked how she was. Christine, who was by now quite drunk, looked up at Lena and took a deep breath. Coldly, she asked why she was even interested; it wasn't like she cared a jot about her. Lena should stay where she was, in Kiel, with her husband, child, and house, and not get all sentimental about lost friendships. She also pointed out that Lena had never liked Bernd, so now she must be quite happy. And that Lena had gotten out of it all and left her alone to deal with all the shit. Then Christine burst into tears, upon which Antje had shot into the kitchen like a commando. She grabbed Lena by the arm and told her to leave Christine in peace, saying it would be better if she left right away.

It was the first time in her life that Lena had been thrown out of anywhere, and she didn't hesitate in leaving.

Lena looked at Jürgen. "Just thinking about it makes me feel ill, even now. And especially because we had no idea just how much of a bitch Antje was!"

Jürgen nodded. "And what did Marleen say yesterday on the phone? The affair between Antje and Bernd had already started back then."

"Yes. But Christine had no idea. Which means she probably had an idea that Bernd was having an affair, but would never have thought it was Antje. She came by here that time, and I think she wanted to talk to me about it. But I didn't ask what was wrong and so she didn't say anything. My mistake."

Jürgen stretched, looking at the clock. "Heavens, it's one thirty; we should go to bed. Do you want my advice? Let all the misunderstandings be water under the bridge and think about the time before Bernd came along. Perhaps you two can get back to that. And be honest, you sometimes miss having a close girlfriend in your life, don't you?"

Questionnaire

Name, age, and place of residence?

Lena, 48, Kiel

When and where did you meet Christine?

In 1983 in a gymnasium. She had just moved to Cuxhaven at the time, was looking for a handball team to join, and was standing there with her gym bag in hand. She said: "Hi, I'm the new girl, and I'd like to play with you." I always thought she was very gutsy.

What was your best experience together?

There are so many. She once threw her keys away in a water-filled ditch with some dead old flowers and ended up standing there up to the waist in duckweed looking for them with a pair of diving goggles. I laughed so much that I nearly fell in, too. Or the day when we both got into a fit of giggles at an AGM and got thrown out of the hall. That happened a lot, the fits of giggles I mean.

What made your friendship stand out? And what sets Christine apart as a friend?

We had time for one another. And we helped each other, without hesitation. Christine gave me more confidence in myself; I felt needed. She helped me to become more daring, and more easygoing.

What's your motto in life?

Don't panic

A friend is…?

Someone you look out for, and look forward to seeing

What was your first reaction to this invitation?

My initial reaction was mixed. The last memories of Christine and me were sad ones, but after a lot of thought the good feelings outweighed the bad. I'm now determined to tackle our problems and give our friendship another chance.

• • •

Hamburg

Christine stood up, pulled her jacket on, and looked at Gabi. "I'm just going shopping. I'll be back in half an hour."

Gabi nodded. "Fine, see you soon. I'll go on my lunch once you're back."

Christine left the publishing house and crossed the square in front of the supermarket with a spring in her step. Richard was going to be there around seven that evening. She had pored over cookbooks the evening before and decided to make saltimbocca; it was quick, it looked good, and Richard liked it. She was excited. Silly really, that she still felt her heart pounding after years. But it was nice.

Her cell vibrated in her jacket pocket. Christine stopped, looked at the display and smiled. He must be looking forward to it, too.

"Hi, Richard, I'm just on my way to the store."

His voice sounded strained. "Oh, Christine, I'm really sorry, but I'm not going to be able to make it this evening unfortunately. Please don't be mad."

Christine's heart sank. "Why?"

"Sabine has a seminar in Bremen. She's staying with the others in a hotel but wants to have dinner with me. She said she has something to discuss with me, so I can't get out of it. We'll make up for it soon, I promise."

Christine had slowly kept on walking. To the left of the supermarket was an ice cream parlor; she veered toward it on autopilot. Slowly, she counted to ten: she knew she would be too harsh if she spoke sooner."

"Christine, are you still there?"

"Then I hope you have a wonderful evening with your wife. Bye."

Without waiting for his answer, she ended the call and bit her bottom lip. *Don't cry,* she told herself, *go and have a coffee and then go back to the office.*

She ordered a latté and lit a cigarette. Her hand was shaking. It wasn't a catastrophe, and it wasn't like it was the first time. They were having an affair, no more and no less. When it worked, it was good, but if it didn't, it shouldn't be the end of the world. At least he had caught her before going shopping; last time she had ended up throwing two expensive sea bream fillets in the trash. *Idiot!*

Christine didn't know whom she meant, Richard or herself. Ten minutes ago she had been having a really good day. And now she was letting one single sentence change that. And one man.

She thought about the conversation she had had with Gabi. About Dani and the time when they were living together. If she was still there, she would have driven home tonight, sat down with Dani at the kitchen table, cried a little, and told her about Richard's call. Dani would have been looking out of the kitchen window down to the dike as she told her. As soon as Christine was finished, she would have wrapped a strand of hair around her finger, looked at her, and said: "What an asshole. Honey, you don't need him. Take your mind off it; don't sit around here feeling sorry for yourself. I mean, this is our time. Who are you? The times when we ran around after guys who didn't deserve us are over. Come on, do something, make a date, go out."

Christine stubbed out her cigarette, took her cell from her bag, and looked for Sven's number. As she waited for the ring, she pictured Dani nodding contentedly.

● ● ●

"November"

My editor asked me to write a column about November. It's almost upon us and is supposed to be the worst month of the year.

It's said that in November, everyone is downbeat, it's always raining and constantly foggy, the number of suicides and divorces go through the roof, and there's no daylight and no fun. Now, as a columnist I could give my readers support and comfort, because after reading they'll know that it's the same for me, but that to top it all off I have to write a column about it, too. In spite of the misery, because you just have to get through it. Be a brave girl who can be an example to others. And has to be.

I've been trying to figure out what the worst thing about November is. First of all, I thought of the weather. The worst thing, as far as I'm concerned, is the snow. It starts in November up here in North Germany, but not that's not really enough to put me in a bad mood. I hate the cold, but that's normally worse in December, January, and February. I love thunderstorms; they remind me of summer holidays spent with my grandma on Sylt, and it rains at pretty much any time of the year.

So, weather wise, as far as I'm concerned, there are far worse months than November.

Then there's the topic of suicide and divorce. My friend Karola had an answer for this; she thinks mass suicide only happens in Finland; she read a novel about it. Having given it more thought, it occurred to her that the Finns have a tendency toward it all year round, so November doesn't really play a significant role, at least not statistically speaking. In any case, she didn't think it was the worst month for it.

She has had two big breakups in her life. One was in February, directly after Carnival, when her boyfriend at the time ran off with "Cleopatra," and one in August, after an awful holiday on Amrum, one of the islands off the North Sea coast, where, incidentally, it rained and thundered the whole time.

I found that interesting, because my separation was in February, too, also after Carnival, although admittedly the Cleopatra in my case was a Stone Age woman. (Maybe I should give a column about Carnival some serious thought!)

We came to the conclusive agreement that we had never had a breakup in November, nor did we know anyone that had. My friend Karola was also of the opinion that people were much more likely to wait to get their Christmas presents first; after all, what difference did four weeks make?

Then we came to the issue of the dying daylight and the lack of fun. When it comes to daylight I couldn't help but wonder whether my editor had ever driven through Cuxhaven with a broken head-light on a December evening. Presumably not, because if she had she'd know that it doesn't get much darker than that. There's very little light there indeed, much less than in November.

Now, let's look at the fun aspect. I've thought about this one, too. My siblings and I all have birthdays in the first two weeks of November. Whether that particular baby boom is down to Carnival or stove heating, who knows? So for us, November is full of parties.

I, perhaps, had the least fun, because my birthday was the last one, so all the balloons were wrinkled by then, stored in the room that had been cleared out especially for all the birthday parties, and the streamers were pretty short. But it wasn't exactly devoid of fun either.

My friend Karola wasn't born in November, but she did get married then, so she has lots to celebrate. Besides that, she found out that November is the month when the highest number of dances is held, and she really loves going dancing with her husband Paul.

I really did go to great lengths and effort to be at least a little depressed. I phoned a lot of people. All of them found November depressing but didn't have time to explain exactly why. Leonie had to go to the sauna with her friend, Luise was off to a birthday party, Maren was getting her new car, and Franziska had a great new apartment and was in the middle of moving.

My friend Karola was sympathetic of my efforts to get to grips with the November topic. She said I was making too much work for myself, and that the only reason November has a bad reputation is because it's the only time when people actually have time to be depressed. In October the weather is still too nice, in December everyone is thinking about presents and festive lights, in January they're preoccupied with New Year's resolutions, and in February it's time for Carnival again and winter is almost over. So when, if not November?

This explanation is much too easy for me. I can't and don't want to let it be that simple. I haven't slept well for the last five nights; I'm too upset that I'll be letting my editor down.

As I watch the rain trickle down my windowpanes, turn my heating down a little, and put melancholy music on, I think about the fact that I can't even write a simple column, that I presumably have never done anything well in my whole life, that my editor will look at me helplessly and say: "I expected more from you."

As a tear rolls slowly down my cheek, the telephone rings. I don't have the strength to go and pick it up, and besides, it's pitch black in my apartment because I haven't even bothered to turn on the light.

On the answering machine I hear my friend Karola's voice, saying that between them she and Paul have questioned thirty-two people about the "November Depression." She says I should brace myself, and that none of them has ever had it. They don't think anyone would bother reading this column and so I shouldn't stress myself about it, but just come over to their place: they're making Grünkohl for dinner and fifteen of the people they'd questioned were coming. And everyone is in a really good mood, and in November, no less.

I switch on the light to change out of my gray pullover and into a red one.

Dear Editor, I'm very sorry that I made such a mess of this column. November is just not my month.

● ● ●

Lübeck

Frauke collapsed back into the chair with a groan and stretched out her legs. She shot Gudrun a look of mock distress.

"You've worn me out. I didn't realize what you meant by power shopping. If I'd known I would have ordered online from Quelle."

Gudrun put her three bags down by the table and pulled her jacket off. "Don't make such a big deal. We were only out for three hours."

"But we did twenty stores." Frauke turned around to look for a waiter. "And my mouth's as dry as a bone. I need a coffee right away. Or should we have champagne to celebrate?"

Gudrun laughed. "You really want to make a day of it, don't you? I thought you couldn't handle alcohol in the daytime. We don't want you to have to go to bed afterwards; it's only four."

Frauke waved her hand nonchalantly. "I can't buy a dress like that and then just drink coffee. I want to make this feeling of decadence last a little longer. But I'm not drinking alone. So what do you say?"

Gudrun nodded. She watched Frauke as she ordered two small piccolos of champagne from the waiter, then bent over and arranged her shopping bags, taking a peek into each one.

Gudrun had talked her friend into buying a little black dress. Frauke thought it was too short and tight on her at first, but Gudrun and the saleswoman loved it. She only changed her mind when an older female customer walked past and nodded at her in the mirror.

"Young lady, that dress was made for you. Very feminine, very elegant."

Frauke had blushed and looked at Gudrun with a mixture of embarrassment and pride.

"But I look so different. Do you really think I can carry something like this off?"

The saleswoman pulled the neckline a little lower. "It looks great. If I had your figure I'd only ever wear things that show off my décolletage."

Gudrun was impressed. "You really have only lost weight in the right places; you look great. Show of that figure of yours! I'm really envious of your curves. I can forget wearing something like that with my 30A bust."

Frauke looked at her reflection hesitantly. She felt a little strange, but somehow beautiful, too. And she wanted to feel more confident.

"OK, I'll take it."

After that they had bought shoes and lingerie. Gudrun was adamant that a dress like that needed black underwear. Frauke had giggled shyly when Gudrun showed her a mere whisper of a black bra in the lingerie store. She gasped for breath as she saw the price tag.

"Gudrun, I've never paid so much money for a bra in my life, that's insane!"

"Come on, you can't wear those white mail-order undies with a dress like this. At least try it on."

Frauke had taken two sets and paid with red cheeks.

The champagne arrived. Frauke shared the first piccolo between the two glasses and raised hers.

"Thank you for your help. That was really fun."

"It was. And you look amazing. This invitation really has unleashed something in you; it's like you're a whole new person. Are you excited?"

Frauke wiped a drop of champagne from the table. "Yes. I don't really know why, but I haven't thought about myself as much as I am at the moment in a long while. It's probably silly, but I really want Christine to recognize me immediately. I looked at the old photos. We were laughing in almost all of them. And then I looked at a few photos from the last few years, and do you know how I look on them?"

"How?"

"I only found two pictures I'm really in. Either I turn away at the last moment or my eyes are closed, or you can only see me from the side. There's this picture Max took when Jules moved of me standing in the kitchen and unpacking crockery. And then there's this family photo from two years ago that we did with a professional photographer for the grandmas. And there's me—Mom—in the middle. Dreadful. It's like I don't exist anymore as a person in my own right. I'm always just the mother and wife. And I'm never laughing in the pictures now; I always look stressed. Christine wouldn't recognize me in any of them. I used to be different."

She drank down her champagne, then picked up the second piccolo and topped up their glasses.

"The bubbly's going to my head already." Frauke brushed her hair away from her face, but an unruly curl was sticking out from her head. She giggled softly and looked at Gudrun apologetically. Her eyes were shining. "Mom's tipsy!"

Gudrun quickly pulled her cell phone from her purse and took a photo of Frauke. "There you go," she said, looking at the display. "Now here we have a picture with 'Mom' laughing and her eyes sparkling."

She showed Frauke the picture, then put her phone away. "But there's one thing I don't understand. Why didn't you say you were unhappy with yourself? We could have done something about it sooner. I had no idea."

Frauke started hiccupping and held her hand in front of her mouth. "I didn't even realize. I just felt so tired and… so boring." She pulled her bag back onto her lap and rummaged around in it. "And I don't know why, but I'm finding life exciting again now." She continued to search in her bag.

"What are you looking for?"

Relieved, Frauke pulled a packet of tablets out.

"Heartburn. I get heartburn when I drink champagne, I forgot that in all the excitement." She popped a chew tablet into her mouth. "But I don't care. I've got an incredible dress and some amazing lingerie. And I'm tipsy. Gudrun, this really was a great afternoon!"

She washed the tablet down with a sip of champagne and beamed happily at her friend.

• ● •

Hamburg

Christine opened her eyes for a second, then shut them again immediately. Before she did, she saw a red-painted wall with a pile of clothes in front of it. The bedding was black and white; she could smell fresh coffee and recognized the music that was playing from the night before. Cautiously, she opened her eyes again. She saw her jeans on the floor and her shoes next to them: one upright, one on its side. All the image needed now was an empty bottle of champagne and it would be just like something from a movie, she thought.

She turned her head to the side. There was a half-full bottle of wine on a small table, neatly corked. That was the difference between her and Sarah Jessica Parker. She turned onto her back. At least there was no mirror on the ceiling.

Christine rubbed her eyes. They felt sticky; she hadn't taken her makeup off. If she looked as bad as she felt, it was going to be a bad start to the day.

Someone was whistling in the kitchen, clattering cups. They sounded very chirpy. Christine sat up carefully and leaned her back against the wall. She had a headache, too. She brushed her hands through her hair, which was sticking up in all directions. Another difference between her and Miss Parker.

At that moment the door opened and Sven came into the room balancing two cups of coffee. Christine tried to look relaxed. As if it were completely normal for her to wake up in a strange bed with her makeup smeared and tousled hair, with a few gaps in her memory of what had happened the night before. Sven put the cups next to the corked wine bottle and sat down on the edge of the bed.

"Good morning. Coffee or wine?"

Christine groaned. "No wine, not ever again. What time is it?"

"It's just after eight. What time do you have to be at work?"

Christie rubbed her temple. "At noon. Do you have any aspirin by any chance?"

She watched as he went off to find some and remembered that she had actually taken the morning off to have a late morning with Richard. *Dani,* she thought, *I did it, and it will probably make everything even more complicated, but it doesn't feel as wrong as I thought it would.*

Sven came back with a glass of water and some aspirin. Why did men always look so good—and younger—with their hair messy? Maybe it was down to the absence of smeared mascara and lipstick. She took the pill from him and swallowed it.

"What time did we get in last night? And when do you need to get to work?"

Sven stirred his coffee. "At two. I've already phoned a colleague and said I'll be in later today." He looked at her. Christine feared he was about to ask one of those questions she hated so much in books and films. They usually started with "Was I good?" and ended with "Do you regret it?"

Christine waited. Sven leaned over and kissed her on the forehead. "You look beautiful. So young, and so pure."

Christine thought to herself that she had probably seen too many bad films and read too many bad books. She stroked his cheek. He took her hand and kissed her palm, looking at her thoughtfully, as though he did want to ask her something after all.

They had met up at six the evening before. Christine had, as planned, finished work early. She didn't want to drive home, look at the freshly made bed and set table, and sit around thinking about Richard. So she took the metro to Altona, to the architectural firm that Sven worked in. Just opposite was one of those American-style coffee shops where you could sit at a bar by the window and look out into the street. Gazing in at the lit-up window of the office, she watched Sven walking through the rooms, talking on the phone, speaking with his colleagues. He was wearing jeans, a black pullover, and a jacket. Christine realized how attractive she found him. When she had phoned him at lunchtime he was in a good mood and immediately agreed to have dinner with her. Christine drank a double espresso and thought about Dani and Richard. Just under an hour later Sven crossed the street and came over to the café. He saw Christine sitting at the window, raised his hand, and smiled. It gave her a warm feeling inside.

They went to a restaurant around the corner. Christine ordered saltimbocca. At the very least, she was being consistent. Sven ordered the same. Through the course of the evening he looked at her searchingly quite a few times, and kept asking her how she was. Christine lied, trying to force Richard out of her mind. Sven made it easy though. He was relaxed, funny, and easy to talk to. Around eleven o'clock she realized she hadn't thought about Richard for three hours.

Sven paid the bill and fetched Christine's jacket. As he helped her pull it on, she leaned against him briefly, and he let his hands linger a little longer than necessary on her shoulders.

Christine turned toward him. "Do you want to have another espresso at your place?"

"I'd love to. Should we get a taxi or walk? It's about twenty minutes."

"Let's walk."

They walked alongside each other, Christine's arm in his. Sven pulled her hand into his jacket pocket and looked at her.

"Is everything OK?"

Christine nodded. "Yes, everything's fine."

Silently, they walked back to his apartment. As they stood in front of the front door and Sven looked for his key, an image came into Christine's mind of Richard standing at her door and ringing the bell. She forced herself to picture him sitting in a hotel bar with Sabine, then followed Sven into the hallway.

They didn't drink espresso but had red wine instead. Sven put some music on and sat down next to her. Christine kissed him first.

Now, sitting on the bed, Sven was still looking at her.

"Talk to me," said Christine.

He smiled and brushed his finger softly across her forehead.

"I'm very happy you stayed the night. I want you to know that. And I hope it wasn't just down to the wine."

"No, the wine just quickened the decision, that's all."

"Are you sure? It's just that you were talking in your sleep."

Christine flinched. She suddenly remembered having dreamed about Richard.

• ● •

As Christine opened her apartment door, the door opposite was ripped open.

"Where were you? I was worried. Your cell's turned off; I thought you'd been kidnapped. Oh, did you have a hard night? You look exhausted." Dorothea looked at her curiously.

"Nonsense, I look young and pure. Come in and make some coffee; I'll grab a quick shower and then tell you about it."

"Don't you have to work?"

"I've got the morning off. I've got another two hours."

Christine threw her jacket and bag over a chair and disappeared into the bathroom.

Dorothea turned the espresso machine on and took the sugar bowl and spoons into the dining room. The table was set. Flowers, wine cooler, candles. Dorothea whistled softly, it looked like there had been a major change of plans here.

"Christine? Can we put the china away?"

"What?" The bathroom door opened a little.

"I asked whether the china can get put away? Or are we having a six-course meal?'

Christine stretched her head out of the door. "Oh…yes, it can. I'd completely forgotten about that."

Twenty minutes later they were sitting with their coffee in front of them. Dorothea had left the flowers on the table, and Christine pushed the vase aside a little.

"So, I'm listening. Who was supposed to come to dinner?" Dorothea's eyes were glistening.

Christine wrapped the bathrobe closer around her. "Richard, yesterday evening."

"And where were you last night?"

"At Sven's.'

"What?" Dorothea threw her head back and started to laugh. "I don't believe it. Sven Lehmann? Mathias's friend we met in the wine bar recently? The one you've been to dinner with twice and one handball game with? You spent the night with him? I think I must have missed something."

Christine stirred her coffee. Round and round.

"Three times. I've been to dinner with him three times. And what's so funny about it? I liked him back when I met him in the summer on Sylt. And yesterday things just happened."

"Christine!" Dorothea was looking at her as if she were being moronic. "For the last three years I've been schlepping guy after guy to see you, and you just ignore them all and only have eyes for Richard. Then you run into your colleague and his friend on Sylt. You go out with him a few times, which was allegedly so harmless that it didn't even deserve a mention. And then you go off one day, full of the joys of spring about having an evening with Richard, and end up spending the night with Sven. Are you high? Or did I miss something?"

Christine rested her chin on her hands. "I don't really know. Richard wanted to come yesterday evening, but he canceled when I was just about to get the food for dinner because his wife was in Bremen out of the blue. I was so angry I thought I'd explode if I didn't do something. So I phoned Sven. At first it was just plain revenge, but then I realized how silly that was while I was waiting for him in the coffee shop. I could see him in his office from there, and there was something I really liked about that. About him, I mean. And then we went for dinner, and it was really nice. I drank a lot of wine and suddenly this image of Richard and his wife in a hotel bar came into my mind. It was like the devil got me. Or my hormones are all over the place, who knows. Anyway, we ended up at Sven's and I kissed him. The rest just happened."

Dorothea was listening, magnetized. "And? How was it?"

Christine looked at her thoughtfully. "Wonderful…he surprised me…It was really wonderful, in fact. So wonderful that I feel guilty."

"About Richard?"

"That's the funny thing, no, not about Richard. I think Sven's really falling for me, and I feel as though I just used him."

"Well you did. I mean, that's how it sounds at least."

Christine nodded. "To start with, yes. But then something changed. When I first met him, on Sylt, I already thought that I would really like him if Richard weren't in the picture. Now I'm not sure. And it seems I was talking in my sleep. Sven asked me who Richard is."

Dorothea was horrified. "Oh, shit. What did you say?"

Christine looked at her sadly. "I told him that I would tell him when we had more time to talk, that I had to go. He gave me a funny look; he seemed so hurt."

"Oh, great." Dorothea rolled her eyes up to the ceiling. "You finally have the opportunity to get out of this shitty situation with Richard and you throw it away."

"It wasn't a shitty situation! And what was I supposed to say?"

"Ha, interesting that you're using the past tense. Honey, you could have said anything, that Richard was your first hamster when you were a kid, whatever you wanted. But not the truth."

Christine looked at the clock and stood up. "Everything is so confusing. Anyway, I have to go to work soon, I don't want to, but I have to. Stay and have another coffee."

Dorothea shook her head. "No, thank you, I have to go, too." She stood up and gave Christine a hug. "Chin up, it'll all work itself out. At least you've talked about it. See you later, have a good day."

Christine watched Dorothea go until the door swung shut behind her. Then her glance fell on the roses and candles that were still on the table. She felt torn, and her emotions were riding high. She just didn't know for whom anymore.

• ● •

Questionnaire

Name, age, and place of residence?

Ruth, 34, Hamburg

When and where did you meet Christine?

Four years ago at the publishing house's Christmas party. We were at the same table and ending up making a bet with each other.

What was your best experience together?

Paying my debt after I lost the bet. I had to make roulades, managed to roll up ten of them, and the kitchen looked like a bomb had gone off. But we had a great laugh and a lovely meal together.

What made your friendship stand out? And what sets Christine apart as a friend?

The knowledge that women can work well together. That you can separate your work and private life without making any sacrifices. And that not all women are the same.

What's your motto in life?

I can achieve anything, as long as I want it enough.

A friend is…?

Someone you should look out for.

What was your first reaction to this invitation?

This question doesn't apply to me because I was part of the organizing committee. And it was my idea.

• ● •

Hamburg

Ruth shoved the completed questionnaire into an envelope and put a stamp above Ines's address. She hadn't taken too much time over it; she had wanted to get it over with because the questions unleashed some strange thoughts for her. By contrast, she had spent three evenings now working on her welcome speech. She wanted it to be good. And it would be; Ruth was sure of that.

When she had originally written the questionnaire she had seen herself as a friend. On question four she had thought back to lots of funny stories about times she had shared with her friends. Or at least, in her memory they were funny.

She had thought question five was an easy one to answer back then, too. But sitting in front of it just now, it had made her brain hurt. It was relatively easy to answer the question, at least when it came to her relationship with Christine. They were coworkers, which sounded a little inadequate, but true. Presumably Christine would see it like that, too.

Ruth thought back to the conversation on the banks of the Alster in the spring. The conversation about friendships, when Christine had become more and more defensive. Ruth had been caught up in wedding fever back then. Hanna, her best friend, was getting married a few weeks later. Ruth and Karsten had arranged no end of surprises. They had filled balloons with helium and tied a note to each one: "Hanna and Lars are getting married, please send best wishes to the following address…" Fifty balloons had flown off into the sky. Ruth had put together a wedding book for the newlyweds and had made a speech: the party was a success.

A few weeks ago Ruth had dropped by to see Hanna. As she rang the bell, Lars had opened the door: his wife was at the gynecologist but would be back soon. Hanna was seven months pregnant and had put on twenty pounds so far. She came back an hour later to find Lars sitting in the kitchen with Ruth: he had opened a bottle of red wine and was just telling a funny story about his father-in-law. Ruth, dressed in a short skirt and close-fitting pullover, had roared with laughter and stood up to hug Hanna.

But her friend had kept her distance, her arms stiff and a stern expression on her face.

"Oh, Ruth, it's good you stopped by; I wanted to show you something. Can you come with me?"

Ruth followed her friend into the nursery, where Hanna turned around to her and said the words that had been ringing in her ears ever since:

"Listen up. I don't know exactly why your and Karsten's relationship failed, but I don't want you hanging out with my husband while I'm not here. You were flirting with him at the wedding, too; don't think I didn't notice, but I didn't say anything because I didn't want any stress. Now that we're pregnant we have better things to do than mollycoddle single women. Is that understood?"

Ruth stared at her best friend. She had no idea what the world was coming to. She had known Lars for years, and Hanna was her closest friend. Her attempts to explain that just bounced off of Hanna, who looked at her with an icy expression.

"I don't care how long you've known Lars. He's *my* husband."

When Ruth got back home, she burst into tears of anger and confusion.

Cutting up the strip of four passport photos that she and Hanna had taken in the booth at Cologne train station for two Deutschmarks fifteen years ago, her thoughts turned to Christine.

Hanna hadn't been in touch since then, and Ruth had tried her best to stop thinking about it. And now she had to fill in this questionnaire, and every question made her think of Hanna. How stupid was she not to have noticed how immature Hanna was? As if Lars were her type, with his funny beard and belly.

Ruth stood up to look for her cigarettes. They always used to be in the cabinet in the kitchen. At the kitchen door, Ruth stopped abruptly. She realized that the cabinet was in Karsten's kitchen now, not hers. She went into her study and pulled open the drawers in her new desk, finding them in the fourth. See, she was getting by; what did it matter if things changed?

She fell back into a chair, lit her cigarette, and thought about her old life. Since she had met Markus, everything had been turned upside down. She had a new apartment in a different part of town, her best friend Hanna had turned into a distrusting rival, and Gabi had changed, too; she didn't tell Ruth anything anymore and seemed to have secrets from her. Markus had turned out to be a superficial egomaniac; he never listened to her, he just wanted to have fun and party, and if they weren't in bed she had no idea what to do with him.

Her job bored her; the city magazine always went over the same old topics: hip events, trendy places, beautiful people, the right books, the right music, the right films. And to top it all off, she was organizing a surprise party for old girlfriends. It was all so bitterly ironic it would be almost funny.

Ruth sat up straight. Things weren't that bad. She didn't miss Karsten, strangely, so it seemed she must have been pretending for years now. She was beginning to realize just how little he had been involved in her life in recent years. Her apartment was beautiful, and she felt at home there; from the very start it had given her a feeling of freedom. Admittedly, Markus hadn't been in touch for three weeks now, but Ruth was actually relieved about that.

It had been a long while since she and Hanna had spent much time together anyway: if it hadn't been for the fact they had known each other for so long, they probably wouldn't even still have been friends.

Her whole life was changing.

She lit her second cigarette, then stubbed it out again immediately. She didn't even like smoking really; she just used to buy them because both Hanna and Karsten hated them. So instead, she reached for her address book and looked for Christine's number. She seemed to have things under control despite not having a man in her life and her restrained approach to girlfriends. Ruth needed a distraction. Or some validation, one or the other.

Ruth dialed the number. Christine answered after the third ring.

"Hello, Christine, I just wanted to test out the cliché that single women always spend Friday evenings on the phone."

"Well, if it was true, then my line would have been engaged. I'm not, I'm slaving away at my ironing board."

Ruth whistled. "Wow, how exciting. I hate ironing; either my mother does it, or I take everything to the dry cleaners."

Christine turned the iron off. "My mother lives on Sylt, so she's unlikely to come here just to do my ironing. Did you really want to talk about that or is there something else?"

Ruth answered: "Well, I was just getting a little fed up of my own company, so I wondered if you might like to go for a glass of wine with me; after all, we live just around the corner from each other. So we can afford to be spontaneous."

Christine didn't hesitate long. "To be honest I hate ironing, too. Good, let's meet in fifteen minutes at Franco's."

Franco's was full to the rafters. As Christine walked in, she saw Ruth waving at her from the bar.

"Hi, I couldn't find a table. But this is OK, right?"

Christine waved at the handsome Franco, who threw her a kiss and pointed to the bar, calling out: "All the tables are taken, but one will be free in a moment and you can sit down then. How about a Prosecco on the house until then, ladies, *bene?*"

Christine nodded and sat down next to Ruth on a barstool. "Sounds perfect, Franco." She looked at Ruth. "So, what's up? Tell me."

Ruth tried to look nonchalant. "Nothing in particular. I just wanted to have a glass of wine with you, that's all."

"Well," said Christine skeptically, "I got the feeling that you were a little down on the phone."

Before Ruth could answer, Franco came over.

"So, the table in the corner is just paying; then we can get you seated. I'll bring your Prosecco over to the table."

Within five minutes they were sitting down opposite each other. Ruth immersed herself in the menu for a while, then clapped it abruptly shut. "You know, I think I would like to talk to you about something after all. Something happened a few weeks ago that really threw me for a loop. And the fact it did really annoys me, by the way. I already told you about my friend Hanna, my oldest friend, the one who got married in May?"

Christine nodded and listened as Ruth told her about the scene with Hanna, then about the wedding, Lars, and finally about her leaving.

By the time Ruth finished recounting the story, the helplessness she had felt at the time had come back. She looked up at Christine, who, to her amazement, was laughing softly.

"I'm sorry, Ruth, but as I've always said, women are a funny breed."

"Why? What do you mean? I thought it was awful."

Christine tried to look serious. "It's just that stories like that about women never surprise me much. We spoke about it back in the spring, remember? I think it was even on the very day you were telling me about Hanna and her wedding. I don't really remember what I said at the time, probably not much." She laughed again, this time at herself. "But I can tell you now what I was thinking. All this crap about 'the best friend.' Mine was my maid of honor, and I was hers, too, and godmother to her children as well—because, after all, she was my best friend—and then she goes and starts an affair with my husband. Whereas one of my close girlfriends who didn't like my husband right from the start, I just cut out of my life. You know, it makes me cringe nowadays when women go on to me about their best friends. It's as much of a façade and myth as the words 'we've been happily married for thirty years.'"

Ruth was skeptical. "But it can work out sometimes, too. If Hanna had her hormones under control, it would have been completely different. It's just that she's changed so much."

Christine looked at her thoughtfully. "If you start a relationship with someone, then you have to be able to handle the fact that they will change over time, whether it's a lover or a girlfriend. It would be silly if everything just stayed the same. Love changes; everyone knows that. And if it does, you talk about it, try to save the relationship. But everyone always expects the best friend to stay exactly as she was in the beginning. It's a completely unrealistic expectation. And instead of talking about it, we just go on and on about how essential it is to have a best friend. How often have you seen Hanna in the last five years? And how much does she have to do with your day-to-day life?"

Ruth thought for a moment. "Not that often really. Lars and Karsten weren't particularly keen on one another, and I was always pretty busy."

"How often?"

"Well, around six or seven times, I guess. And we spoke on the phone now and then."

"That's exactly my point. And despite that you just call her your best friend and brush everything else under the carpet. If a woman you only vaguely knew had reacted like Hanna did, you would just have shaken your head and told her to leave you alone. You wouldn't have given it any thought, apart from perhaps pitying her for having so little trust in her darling husband. And by the way, I find her lack of trust in him quite depressing."

Ruth wondered to herself what Hanna had told him after Ruth left without saying good-bye.

"Oh, Christine, I'm just finding life a little too much at the moment. First Karsten, then Hanna, all my old surroundings are just crumbling away. I don't know what to believe in anymore."

Christine looked at Ruth without saying a word. She looked amazing: her blond hair was piled up on top of her head, she was wearing tight jeans and a little black pullover, and was impeccably made-up. Ruth turned around to Franco and pointed to the empty carafe of wine. Moments later, he brought them a full one.

"*Salute*, beautiful lady."

Ruth smiled briefly and then turned back to Christine.

"What are you thinking about?"

"I was just wondering how you really are. I mean, I don't get the impression that you're finding your situation that difficult. After all, you coped really well with the move, the separation, and the new start."

Ruth tucked a strand of hair behind her ear. "I'm not doing too badly. I just find it all so irritating. Hanna's bitchiness got me really worked up; I have no idea how she got those ideas into her head. And my love life isn't exactly great. And my job is really getting to me. I can hardly bear to look at the *Kult* cover anymore. I've made changes in my private life now, and I'd really like to do the same in my career."

"What do you want to do?" asked Christine.

"I don't know. I don't have that many options. I've been at the publishing house for thirteen years now. First as an intern, then in sales, then advertising, and then the city magazine. I've been doing *Kult* for five years now, and I want something different. I've always enjoyed my job, but the magazine isn't enough for me. I need a challenge now and then. You know, I really envied you writing these columns for *Femme*; it's really great."

"Ellen Wagner's pregnant."

"Really? But she already has a daughter."

"Yes, and now she's having another baby. And I don't think she'll be back straight after the birth by any means. Why don't you talk with her? There could be an opportunity for you to get on board."

Ruth beamed at Christine. "At *Femme*? That would be amazing! Thanks, Christine, I'll drop by there tomorrow."

A little later they paid and left the bar. Christine walked Ruth back to her apartment; it was on the way back to her own. As they got to the front door, Ruth said:

"This was nice; I'm feeling much better now. But tell me, you don't steer clear of friendships with women altogether, do you?"

Christine laughed. "No, no more so than I do friendships with men. But I don't differentiate between them anymore. It takes more than just sharing the same gender to be friends. My sense of female solidarity is a little limited by now. But then, I don't like all men either."

They said good-bye. Ruth watched as Christine disappeared around the corner. There were still two weeks to go until Christine's surprise party.

If the questionnaire had unleashed similar emotions with the others as it had with her, Christine wouldn't be the only one the night of the party was going to have a big impact on.

• • •

Questionnaire

Name, age, and place of residence?

Luise, forty-two, Hamburg

When and where did you meet Christine?

We were colleagues before we got to know each other properly outside of work. It happened five years ago when we had a meal together in the restaurant Cox.

What was your best experience together?

A shopping trip to Stilwerk. We spent an unspeakable amount of money that afternoon. We set out to furnish our new lives and, by the end of the day, felt like we'd made it.

What made your friendship stand out? And what sets Christine apart as a friend?

The parallels in our lives. We were both single, had the same job, and suddenly had more money and were pretty scared, too. Christine really helped me get back on my feet again after my separation. She was going through the same thing and could really understand me. She knew what I needed.

What's your motto in life?

What's in the past is in the past. You shouldn't regret what's already happened.

A friend is…?

A strong shoulder, and sometimes a mirror.

What was your first reaction to this invitation?

I hope Christine enjoys the party as much as we enjoyed the organizing!

Hamburg

Ines skimmed over Luise's questionnaire, then put it with the others. She crossed Luise's name off of the list. So far seven had been sent back. She counted the names that weren't yet crossed off. At least everyone had been in touch and she knew who was coming. This evening Dorothea, Georg, and she were going to the restaurant again to discuss the buffet. She didn't have to give them the exact numbers until the day before the party, in two weeks' time.

Ines's initial skepticism had faded away. She was surprised at how honest and heartfelt the answers on the questionnaires had been so far. She had spoken to Frauke and Dani on the phone and could still hear their voices in her ear: Frauke's full of excitement and Dani's with emotion.

After their last meet-up, Luise had told her that she had called an old friend in Berlin for the first time in eight years.

They had chatted for almost an hour and were planning to meet up when Luise next went to visit her father in Berlin.

"All these stories about old times have made me sentimental." By now, Luise was completely won over to the plan. "You forget so many of the people you used to know. Karina helped me a lot back when my parents split up. But since I've been living in Hamburg, I've hardly thought of her, only just recently. And it was only because I wondered who you would have tried to find for me, who has played a part in my life. It's funny, it made me remember people I'd forgotten about. It's contagious, this search."

Ines had been having similar thoughts. "I was thinking about passing around a list to everyone on the night so they can put their names and addresses down. Then the next search team won't have to do so much detective work."

Luise laughed. "But that was the best part. When I think of how overjoyed I was to see that napkin from the butchers in Flensburg. It was like winning the lottery. By the way, has Linda Love sent back her questionnaire yet?"

Ines looked at her, her expression giving nothing away. "I'm not telling you. You'll hear the results of the search in two weeks; it's nice to leave some things as a surprise."

"I can't wait to put the faces to the names. It's going to be great; I'm sure of it."

At that moment, the phone rang. Ines stood up and picked it up.

"Hello, this is Gudrun Peterson from Lübeck. Is this Ines?"

"Yes, hi, you're Gudrun with the horse, right? At least, that's what we call you here."

Gudrun laughed. Her voice was deep and instantly likeable.

"I only borrowed that horse: I did go riding, but I never had my own horse. Anyway, that was ages ago. The reason I'm calling is that I said I could make it to the party and you wrote me that you know a hotel near the restaurant. Could you give me the address?"

"Yes, wait, I've got the details here among all my lists. Thank you for the quick response, by the way. If the Hamburg girls were as on the ball as you are then I'd have everything figured out already."

Gudrun wrote down the address Ines dictated to her and thanked her. "That's wonderful, I'll get a room booked for myself and Frauke right away. Frauke has been excited ever since the invite arrived; this really was a great idea. Tell me, is Antje coming, too?"

Ines laughed, then suddenly realized that Antje had come up in Gudrun's questionnaire, too. She meant the question seriously. Ines cleared her throat.

"Antje…of course, you didn't know. Are you still in touch with her?"

"What didn't I know? Well, contact is a bit of an exaggeration, I know she moved to Cuxhaven or Wilhelmshaven after her divorce, near to Christine. I bumped into her last year at the Christmas market when I was out with my mother. Antje was there with her boyfriend. She introduced him proudly and then fawned over him the whole time; my mother found it so irritating that we didn't talk for long."

"Yes, well, was the boyfriend called Bernd?"

"Yes, that's it! He was a bit chubby and seemed a bit on edge with all the festive hustle and bustle and Antje's clinginess. But then, I don't really know him."

"Well, we do. He's Christine's ex-husband. He and Antje were having an affair behind her back for several years; that's why they got divorced."

Gudrun tried to catch her breath. "Unbelievable! But Antje and Christine were as thick as thieves for years. How on earth did Antje explain herself?"

"She didn't. She told Bernd to end the marriage, which he did, but without giving any real reason. He just told Christine that he wasn't in love with her anymore, that married life was too much for him, something like that. Christine only found out about the affair later, once she'd moved to Hamburg."

"And she never confronted Antje?"

"No, there was no point. Antje was too much of a coward; she just hid behind Bernd, and since then there's been no more contact."

Gudrun paused for a second. Then she said: "I can understand that, but I certainly would have had a few things to say to her; she wouldn't have gotten away with it that easily. That's so awful. But this Bernd really didn't really give the impression that Antje was love of his life."

Ines laughed. "Well, we kind of hoped she wouldn't be, so it seems some wishes do come true."

"But I'm glad you told me. Just imagine if I'd asked Christine about Antje. That would have been really embarrassing."

Ines reassured her. "No, that chapter's done for her, I think. It hurt her a great deal, of course it did, and it's changed her when it comes to close girlfriends. That's why we dreamed this whole thing up. But Antje's dead to her now. I only hope we'll be successful in our attempt to show her that behavior like that is an exception. Then she can finally fill the void her memories of Antje have left her with."

Gudrun took a deep breath. "I think that's the worst thing someone can ever do. It's such a breach of trust, and I'm certain it's an exception. I'll bet she wasn't honest as a friend even before the affair either. Some people are just bad to the core. OK, Ines, I promise you that Frauke and I will do our best to patch up Christine's soul. See you in two weeks. I'm looking forward to it."

• ● •

Hamburg

Christine and Sven had been walking around the Alster in silence for the last half hour. Christine already had a stitch; Sven had set the pace and she didn't dare ask him to take smaller steps. He got quicker and quicker, and she had to make an effort not to pant. But before long she couldn't go on: she stopped and gasped for air. Sven only noticed after a few meters, then stopped and turned around. Christine's face was bright red, and she looked so worn out that he couldn't help but laugh. "What's up? Out of shape?"

Breathing heavily, Christine stared at him. "You...are...so...fast."

"Then say something."

Sven walked back and stopped right in front of her. He looked down at her, shook his head, and pulled her to him. Christine pressed her forehead against his chest as he rested his chin on her head and stared out over the Alster. He asked himself why he could never just fall in love easily, without complications. Every Tom, Dick, and Harry did it, everywhere, every day. Sven released himself from Christine's arms and pushed his hand into her jacket pocket.

"Come on, I'll walk slowly now. Besides, I thought you used to be a top handball player."

"Used to be." Christine took his hand. "With the emphasis on *used to*."

They walked on, slowly this time.

They had made plans to have dinner the previous evening. Sven had wanted to cook, so Christine came to his apartment for the second time. When she arrived, bearing a bottle of red wine, he kissed her briefly on the cheek then went straight back into the kitchen. Turning down all her offers to help, he pointed her toward a seat at the kitchen table and poured her a glass of wine. As he diced the vegetables, he told her about the congress he'd been at for the last three days. He was in a good mood, laughing throughout, and made no references to the night they had spent together. He was just the same as before.

Christine's tension ebbed away as she listened to him, watching him cook. As she drank her wine, she couldn't help but notice how strong his hands looked.

Once the meal was ready and they were sitting opposite each other at the table, Sven raised his glass. "It's great to see you."

"Thank you for the invite. Sven, I just wanted to say, about last week…"

He interrupted her. "After dinner, OK? I just like to chat about lighthearted things while I'm eating. We can figure everything else out over coffee. Please."

Christine nodded and tried, not entirely successfully, to concentrate on the meal.

Their good-bye after the night they spent together had been a little deflated. After Sven told her she had talked about Richard in her sleep, he had looked at her questioningly. Christine had a terrible headache and felt completely confused. Avoiding his gaze, she said softly that, as she had already told him, her private life was rather complicated at the moment. Sven took his hand off her leg and stood up abruptly.

"I'm going to get more coffee," he said, only coming back five minutes later. And without the coffee. Then, he told her about his marriage, about how much he had suffered. Christine had felt like giving herself a slap.

He sat back down on the edge of the bed and looked at her. "I have no idea what's going on in your private life, but I doubt that what we're doing here is going to make it any easier. I could be wrong, but please, Christine, I'm not looking to be used or messed around anymore. I've had enough of all that."

"I don't want to use you, Sven. I will try to explain everything. But please, not now. Give me a few days to sort myself out." She looked at him and laid her finger softly against his mouth. "I had a great evening and a wonderful night. I mean that. I don't regret it, nor was it a mistake. We'll talk next week, OK?"

Sven had done a great job with the cooking. After the sea bream, they had mascarpone crème for dessert. He cleaned everything up afterwards, again refusing her offers to help.

"Go and sit down in the living room. I'll be in soon with the espresso."

Taking her wine glass with her, Christine went and sat down on the black leather sofa, pulling her legs up under her. She'd been impressed by this apartment the first time she saw it. Sven had taste; she liked the furniture, the lamps, the art, the way he'd furnished it all. She tried to make out the titles on the book spines on the shelves; he even read the same books she liked.

If I hadn't fallen in love with Richard... she thought and shook the thought away. Maybe she wasn't even in love with Richard anymore. She asked herself how much hurt and rejection love could actually survive. How much longer she should take his feelings into consideration, how much longer she should keep on hoping he would decide to get a divorce at some point. If that was even a consideration for him. At the end of the day it came down to money. And good old Sabine placed a great deal of importance on her image and role.

And so Christine stayed the lover on the side and was allowed to be with him when it was convenient. She had brushed her needs under the carpet so she didn't pressure him; she wasn't supposed to ask questions, but listen; was supposed to comfort, but not demand comfort for herself. *How stupid are you?* she asked herself. *Even you don't believe anymore that anything would ever change.*

Sven came into the room with the espresso and a bottle of grappa. He put it all down on the table, sat down next to her, and poured.

"Cheers. Now you can tell me all the strange thoughts that have been going around in your head since our night together. But please, be open and honest; I can take it."

Christine looked at him for a long while. He really was a great guy. She drank her grappa down in one shot, put the glass down, and took a deep breath.

"Well, I met Richard in Berlin a long time ago..."

Christine told the story, just as it was. The married man, the divorced but independent lover, the feelings, the torment. She described the jealousy and the loneliness, the impossibility of making plans, and this constant hope for some kind of decision. She told him about the rollercoaster of emotions she went through when incomprehensible things happened, and about the eternal and soul-destroying waiting around.

The longer Christine talked, the less she could understand the magic she had once seen in the whole story. Now, it just sounded seedy.

By the end, Christine was blinking away the tears threatening to spill out. Sven noticed and caressed her. "Go ahead and cry; you must have been suppressing a lot. How long have you been putting up with this? Three years?"

Christine nodded and battled the tears. She didn't want Sven to realize how miserable she had been. He was the first man since Richard she'd felt strongly for. And she didn't want to sit next to him crying. Not about Richard anyway.

Sven poured her another grappa. "I wouldn't have thought you would put up with something like that. You seem so independent."

Christine blew her nose. "I never thought I would either. It all started so slowly. As long as the scales balanced, the good times outweighing the bad, I could cope with it. But after a while there was this big fat kid sitting on one side, and then there was no chance the other could even get off the ground."

Sven laughed softly. "Come here." He pulled her close to him and wrapped his arms around her. "I could tell you you're too good for that, that it would be much simpler to be with me, that you should give Richard his marching orders and send him back to his wife, whatever. But that probably wouldn't help you much. So all we can do is get drunk together, tell each other silly stories, and see what happens. That is, unless you have a better idea?"

Christine looked into his eyes; they were very green. Then she shut hers. And kissed him.

They didn't really get drunk, and ended up making love on the sofa. Afterwards, the tears came again: Christine didn't know if it was her hormones or the sound of a text message on her cell phone. She didn't have to look; it could only be from Richard. Toward one in the morning, she decided to go home, and read the message in the taxi.

Sending my love and kisses, Richard.

She thought about the fact that Sven had probably heard her cell phone, too, and that he was probably thinking it was the reason she had left. She typed a message. *Tonight was wonderful. You're amazing. Let's have breakfast together tomorrow. Kisses, C.*

She made sure she sent it to Sven's number.

He answered right away. *11am at Prüsse, get yourself figured out. Kiss.*

And now they were walking around the Alster. And Sven was hardly saying a word.

Christine stopped abruptly. "Talk to me, please."

Sven looked at her, baffled. "I thought you didn't want to talk. I've been biting my lip the whole time because I was trying not to ask you anything."

"But why? I've been wondering the whole time what I've done wrong."

"Christine." Sven grasped her elbows and pulled her toward him. "You haven't done anything wrong. I'm feeling guilty. I was worried that I took advantage of you being upset to sleep with you, right there and then. And that you're mad at me for it. You were so quiet at breakfast."

"I'm just not that talkative first thing. And I thought you were annoyed that I didn't stay the night and went home. Which, by the way, had nothing to do with that text message."

Sven kissed her on the forehead. "Of course not. I can't expect that something which has been an issue for three years will suddenly resolve itself overnight. Come on, we have to talk about this. We've been walking around the Alster in silence for almost an hour now. So come on, let's make a pledge, repeat after me: I promise I'll do better."

Christine kissed him on the chin. "I promise I'll do better. And, by the way, I wanted it, too, what we did on the couch."

"So, we're on the same page then. I'm sure we'll figure the rest out. And now let's go for a weekend beer at the Alsterperle, my treat."

They joined the line in front of the self-service bar. Christine felt Sven's closeness behind her. She felt unbelievably good around him, in the midst of all these people she didn't need to pretend in front of.

November, Hamburg

Dorothea and Georg left the restaurant, buttoning their coats up. Dorothea pulled her hat from her bag and tugged it down over her head.

"It's so damn cold. I hate November. Why can't your sister's birthday be in May?"

"Because November would still be cold even if it were," answered Georg.

"That's a dumb answer."

"It was a dumb question." Georg looked at Dorothea's hat. Gaudy and colorful with three bobbles. "What a lovely hat. And so practical, too; we'd be able to find you quickly if you were lost in a crowd."

Dorothea stroked her hand over her head. "You're just jealous because hats don't suit you. This hat is sensational."

Georg laughed. "Of course it is. Want to go for a walk? Or do you have to make a move?"

Dorothea looked at her watch. "Fine by me; it's still early, and I don't have to work until this afternoon."

They had just been to Indochine, where the surprise party was due to take place in two days' time. Ines had given them the list of guests, so Dorothea and Georg had ordered the food and discussed the last-minute details with the staff.

Georg had observed Dorothea's excitement with skepticism. He hated surprises of any sort, so an evening like this would be a complete horror for him. In his imagination he pictured a row of pimply youths who had become businessman, civil servants, or teachers, and he couldn't help thinking of the nineties Sparkasse ad: "My House, My Car, My Yacht" where the two businessmen are desperate to outdo each other with the tales of their success. Just terrible.

But fine, his sister was a little more laid back than he was in that respect. He thought back to the party Dorothea and Luise had organized after Christine's divorce. He had tried to talk them out of it, imagining his sister in floods of tears and on the edge of a nervous breakdown after the court hearing. In the kind of mood where the last thing you want to do is celebrate. But when she came into the bar where the others were waiting for her, it had all been fine—although she had been surprised, of course. And he had to admit, it had turned out to be a delightful evening.

Dorothea's voice interrupted his thoughts. "I think it's going to be a really amazing night. And the best thing is that Christine doesn't have the faintest idea about it. I think it's great."

Georg didn't answer. Dorothea nudged him. "You're a real party pooper. You know, I'd be over the moon if someone arranged a surprise party for me. It's so great. Lovely bar, wonderful food, and lots of great, funny people."

"*If* the people are funny. You don't even know everyone that's coming."

"But I know Christine and Luise and Ruth and so on. The others are sure to be fine, too."

Georg looked at her. "Well, you don't know that; Christine hasn't seen some of them for twenty years. They could have mutated into boring, mutton-dressed-as-lamb old bags who don't have a single interesting word to say."

But Dorothea's confidence was indestructible. "That's ridiculous. For starters, they must be nice; otherwise they wouldn't have been friends with your sister; and secondly I can still vaguely remember Dani and Lena from Christine's wedding. And they certainly weren't old bags back then. And thirdly, I've read the questionnaires. So stop it with the doom and gloom. It'll be a nice evening, *basta*."

"OK, fair point," Georg conceded. "I can still remember Frauke and Gudrun, as a matter of fact. I always thought Frauke was great; she had really long hair and was always laughing. I was ten then and a little in love with her. Unrequited love, unfortunately. She completely ignored me."

Dorothea laughed. "Poor little guy. She never even spoke to you?"

"Well, just once. She said: 'Get lost, this is girls' talk.' I mean, she was thirteen, I didn't have a chance."

"She's got three children now, I think."

"And I don't have any," sighed Georg. "Sometimes life is unfair. Well, I'll be interested to see if they all recognize each other. Maybe it'll just turn out to be a completely normal birthday party, the kind where no one descends into an identity crisis, and everyone will just get sentimental about old times, say they love each other and that they never want to lose touch again."

Dorothea nodded. "That, honey, is the plan."

• • •

Hamburg

Christine dropped the wet rags into the bucket, wiping her hands on her jeans as she walked over to the door. The doorbell had already rung three times, and this time for much longer. "I'm coming!"

Christine opened the door and saw Luise, who was hopping impatiently from one leg to the next. "Hey, what brings you here?"

Luise pushed past Christine. "I have to go, desperately. Let me in."

She disappeared into the bathroom at high speed and slammed the door shut behind her. Shaking her head, Christine went into the kitchen and turned the espresso machine on. A few minutes later, Luise came back, visibly relieved. She sat down at the kitchen table and smiled. "You know that feeling, when you suddenly have to go right away? It's such a nightmare. I tried to call you; why is your cell off?"

"I've got a landline, too."

"But I don't have that saved on my cell. You usually have yours turned on. I was starting to worry you weren't here. Then I would have had to hold it until the gas station. God, I had to go so bad."

"Coffee?" asked Christine.

Luise took a cigarette from Christine's pack. "Yes, thanks, and I don't have any smokes either, so I'll have to steal one. So what's happening? We haven't seen each for at least four weeks." She looked around at the kitchen. "Wow, it's really sparkling in here. Are you having a cleaning frenzy? Is your mother coming to visit?"

Christine laughed. "No, I'm not cleaning for my mom. It's just that I can think so clearly when I'm cleaning. And I really needed to. Clean, I mean."

She went over to the espresso machine and pressed the button. Once the cup was full she put it in front of Luise. Then she busied herself, a little elaborately, with making the second cup, leaving Luise talking to her back.

"So, what's new? You know what, that's a dumb question. I'll start over and come straight to the point. I went for a meal with Mathias yesterday, and he told me you've been meeting up with Sven Lehmann, and that he, Sven I mean, has fallen for you big time. According to Mathias. So? Is it true?"

Christine put her cup on the table and sat down. She poured the milk, then spooned some sugar in, then stirred her coffee for a long time and reached slowly for the pack of cigarettes. But Luise held on tightly to the lighter. "Christine? And? Tell me."

Christine looked at her. "At least give me a light if you're smoking my cigarettes."

"Only once you start talking."

"Please." Christine took the lighter from her hand and lit the cigarette. "Mathias is a real gossipy old woman, you know."

"But he wouldn't make something like that up. So?"

"God, Luise, you're just as bad as he is. I told you I had a really fun evening with Mathias and Sven when I was in Sylt. And after that I went to an HSV handball game with Sven and I told you that, too. And we've been out to dinner a few times, too."

Luise looked at Christine searchingly. "I've hardly heard from you, I can't get hold of you, you're cleaning so you can think…you're keeping something from me. But then, it's not like you have to tell me. Why would you? It's only me, Luise."

"Don't be so sensitive, honey. I don't even know myself what's going to come of it, or what it is. I'm just confused at the moment."

Luise leaned toward her. "Then maybe it would help to talk about it. Come on, I'm a good agony aunt. Just like that, problem solved."

Christine kept on stirring her coffee. She looked at Luise, unsure.

"Oh, it's just all so complicated. Sven and I have been meeting up a lot recently, that's true. I think he's really great and feel really good when I'm him."

"What kind of good? Don't make me drag it out of you."

Christine wondered how much she wanted to tell Luise. Although maybe it didn't really matter; back when she used to talk to Dani she had just been thinking out loud. And it had often helped. Perhaps that was part of friendship, being able to think out loud without getting it all straight in your head first. So she just talked. "We've been seeing a lot of each other recently, and two weeks ago I stayed overnight. On one hand it was really great, but a little bit strange, too. I couldn't help thinking about Richard; I can't just shut off my feelings from him overnight. But in spite of that, Sven is unleashing something in me. But I don't know whether it's more the longing for a real relationship than Sven himself. I spoke with Richard on the phone, and then ending up feeling guilty, so I canceled a date with Sven. Only for Richard to tell me a little later that he can't make it to see me on my birthday because his wife is having issues as usual and he's needed back at home. It's enough to drive you insane. Luise, I really don't know what I should do."

She rubbed her eyes, trying to hide the tears that were rising. Luise thought for a while before answering.

"To hell with Richard, you don't deserve this. Do you remember my affair with Alex? These things happen, but they have to be worked out after a certain amount of time. Richard hasn't made a decision so far, so why would he now? You're feeling guilty, but he's the one sleeping next to his wife in bed more often than next to you. Mathias told me a bit about Sven, and I thought to myself, I hope Christine does the right thing. But if you're still hanging on to Richard after all the shit, for some harebrained reason, then you're just kidding yourself. That would mean you've just gotten used to all the waiting and lack of commitment. Then you have a completely different problem."

Christine looked at Luise, her eyes dry. "What?"

"Maybe you're scared of a new relationship, of commitment. If you just keep doing this on-and-off nonsense with Richard then you're not risking anything."

Christine shook her head. She thought about how carefree she felt in Sven's company. And of the sneaking around and alibis with Richard. She was so fed up with it.

"No, I'm not scared of a new relationship. And certainly not of commitment. Maybe I was just still hoping that something would change with Richard at some point."

Luise shook her head. "You can forget it; I'm willing to bet on it. And if that miracle did happen, it could never be really good, not after all the stress of what's happened in the past. Take your time with Sven...does he know about Richard, by the way?"

"I told him. He reacted quite well," Christine replied. She finished her coffee and put the cup resolutely down on the table. Then she looked at Luise, decided. "I think you're right. I've made an idiot of myself for long enough. I'll talk to Richard. Then I'll make a decision, although actually... perhaps I've already made it."

"Really?"

Christine looked at the table, deep in thought. "Well, not already, but just this minute. It's got nothing to do with Sven, but he makes it a lot easier."

Luise pressed Christine's hand. "That's good. And don't rush into a new relationship too quickly. You have us, remember."

"Us who?" asked Christine, surprised.

"Well, all your girl...well, you know, me and Dorothea and Ines and so on. After all, we helped you get through a breakup before."

Luise pressed her fingernails into her palms in annoyance at herself. But Christine hadn't noticed the slip. She stood up to open the window.

"Anyway, let's change the subject. Are you here this weekend?"

Luise tried to keep her facial expression neutral. "On Saturday? On your birthday, you mean? Yes, I'm here. What do you want to do?"

"I've reserved a table at the Italian place for seven o'clock. Just a few people, you and me, Dorothea, Ines, Georg, maybe Mathias, too, and...Sven."

Oh God, we're going to have to let them know, thought Luise, answering loudly: "Great, I'm looking forward to it." She kissed Christine on the cheek. "Thanks for the coffee, and congratulations on your decision. See you on Saturday then; I can't wait."

As Christine watched her go, she wondered at the fact she hadn't commented on her inviting Sven and Mathias. She closed the door. Presumably her birthday wasn't that big a deal; after all, it was just a normal dinner with a few close friends.

The water had gotten cold in the bucket so Christine poured it into the toilet. That was enough cleaning anyway; she had made her decision.

November 10, Berlin-Hamburg

D ani clapped her book shut and laid it on the empty seat next to her. She looked out of the window. November weather, gray and more gray, fog, and drizzle. The train would be arriving at Hamburg main station at two twenty p.m., so she had just under half an hour left of her journey.

She looked in her bag for the package Ines had sent her last week. She pulled a clear plastic sheet out containing a hotel brochure, the details of the restaurant, how to get there, and a list of names. Everything had been marked carefully with different colored pens, and Dani's name was underlined in yellow. Christine's sister really had organized everything to military precision. At five in the evening they were all to meet in the hotel bar for champagne, and after that they would go on to the restaurant together. Dani smiled at the thought that Christine still had no idea what was going on.

She had scanned through the list of names, but some of them didn't ring a bell with her at all. Luise, Gabi, Ruth, they were probably friends from Hamburg she'd only met after moving. But she could remember Lena. Lena, who could do anything and always had time to help. Without her, Christine and Dani would never have been able to renovate the old house in such a short time.

Dani could still picture it now: Lena up on the ladder; Christine pasting the strips of wallpaper, which were falling down on her head as she went; Dani brushing over them afterwards; Lena almost falling from the ladder in laughter. Christine and Lena, on their knees washing away yellow cats' paw prints with turpentine-soaked cloths, all because Dani had left the paint trays lying around and the cats had run through them. Then all three of them at the kitchen table, pizza boxes on their knees, beer bottles in hand, giggling with exhaustion. Looking back now, even the week-long renovation had been a lot of fun.

Somehow, life had been easier back then. The thought reminded her of her grandma, who was always saying the old times were better. She shook her head at herself.

She knew Dorothea and Ines, too, and had spoken to Marleen on the phone yesterday. Christine didn't even know that Marleen was coming; she'd told her there was a party in the pub. By now, Marleen was utterly convinced of the plan. "You know," she had said to Dani, "I don't really think a few old friends will be able to change Christine's cautious approach to female friendship, but in terms of the thrill of the search and a really great party, all this effort has really been worth it."

Dani looked at the clock; another twenty minutes. She was excited, and the journey felt unbearably long. She'd done such a good job of resisting calling Christine so far. Since July, when she'd received the invitation that had unexpectedly triggered all these thoughts.

When she had moved in with Christine back then, the last thing she was looking for was a new relationship. In the three years she spent in the old house, she had a few harmless lovers now and then, nice guys with whom she had a good time but never fell in love with. Her day-to-day life was shared with Christine; in her memory it was perfect, she had really felt alive. And then Bernd came into the picture, and suddenly Christine's door was shut in the evenings. To start with Dani thought it would just be temporary. She thought Bernd was an OK guy but never expected Christine to really fall in love with him. But their relationship got more and more intense. Before long, Christine didn't have time for Dani anymore; they stopped having girls' nights, no Sunday breakfasts, no chatting in the evenings on their beds. Dani retreated into herself; she was hurt, jealous, and wished Bernd would just disappear out of their lives. Their house share lasted another six months, during which there was a wall between them, of guilt on Christine's side and silence on Dani's. Then Dani got a job in Bremen and moved out. Christine seemed relieved; it spared them from having to confront things. Three weeks later Bernd moved in, and Dani never went back to the house again.

Ten minutes to go; the train was already rushing through the Hamburg suburbs. In the last few months, Dani had thought a lot about what had changed in her life since then. What she had concluded was devastating: nothing. At least, not in her private life. Due to her old fear of relationships, she had pushed on with her games. She'd had an almost continuous stream of lovers but would finish with them as soon as she started to develop any real feelings.

Her last two lovers had been younger than she, Lars considerably so. It made her feel like she was thirty again, as if she could still change everything. Just like the old days. "How stupid," murmured Dani, softly so that no one around her could hear. She hadn't felt this lonely back then. And it wasn't because she lived alone now.

She had forgotten how to be enough for herself. Her job wasn't enough for her anymore; she might look like a tough personnel manager on the outside, but in reality she was a complete sissy who needed everyone to tell her what a great girl she was. Dani's self-confidence had gotten lost somewhere along the way.

Since the invitation, her longing for her old life had been reawakened.

Of course, it wouldn't be enough to go back to sharing a house in some isolated location again. She realized she had started romanticizing her memories of the past. Back then, Christine and she had supported, not saved, each other. No more so than Lars or Hanne or Ralf had been able to save her.

The train rolled into the Hamburg main station. Dani stood up and pulled her jacket on. As she retrieved her bag from the luggage compartment, the train came to a halt and Dani heard the station announcer's voice: "Hamburg Central Station. Change here for connections to…"

Maybe I should pay more attention to working out my own connection and not always look for someone who can drive me home by car, thought Dani as she walked down the aisle to the doors. She climbed out and walked along the platform toward the metro.

It felt as though the knot in her stomach had eased.

• ● •

Lübeck-Hamburg

Frauke looked at herself in the wardrobe mirror as she draped her new scarf around her just like Gudrun had shown her to. Her gaze fell on Gunnar, who was sitting on the steps and watching her. She smiled at him.

"And? How do I look?"

Instead of answering he asked: "Why are you guys leaving so early anyway? You're not meeting the others until five. What are you going to do the whole day?"

He was in a bad mood, just like he had been for days now. Frauke had no intention of being drawn into an argument.

"We want to have a look around the harbor and have a coffee somewhere. If I'm going to be in Hamburg, I want to make the most of it."

Gunnar's expression didn't change. "You're acting as if I've locked you up in the house for the last fifteen years. As if we never go anywhere."

Frauke turned around. "Oh, Gunnar, I didn't say that. What's all this about? Heavens, I'm just going away for the day for once, and I'll be back by tomorrow at lunch, or the afternoon at the latest. So what's wrong?"

She was getting drawn in after all. Frauke shook her head indignantly, turned back to the mirror, and painted her lips with her new lipstick, pressing them together firmly. She thought the color looked beautiful. Gunnar cleared his throat, and she tried again.

"And, how do I look now?"

"Strange." Gunnar stood up and went into the kitchen. Frauke watched him go. As she contemplated whether or not to go after him, the doorbell rang. Frauke opened the front door and let Gudrun in.

"Good morning, beautiful. I think I'm a little early, aren't I?"

Frauke looked at the clock. "A little, but I'm almost ready, so we can make a move in a minute."

"OK," answered Gudrun, "I'll just say good morning to Gunnar and go to the bathroom. Where is your darling other half?"

"In the kitchen." Before Frauke had the chance to mention his bad mood, Gudrun was already in the kitchen. Frauke followed her.

Gunnar was sitting at the table, the newspaper open in front of him, the coffee pot next to it. He nodded at Gudrun but didn't get up, just kept on reading.

Gudrun looked at him, baffled. "What's up with you? Did you get out of bed on the wrong side or something?"

Gunnar gave an embarrassed smile and stood up awkwardly. "Sorry, I'm not feeling great. Maybe I'm getting the flu."

Frauke looked at him, amazed. Gudrun laughed. "The flu? You don't get the flu just because you have to spend the weekend without your better half; that's not how viruses are spread. Well, I hope you have a good morning; tell us to have a good time, too. And now I have to go to the bathroom." She gave him a comforting pat on the shoulder and disappeared.

Frauke sank down on the chair and stared at Gunnar. First he tried to avoid her gaze; then he sighed resignedly. "I'm sorry, but you're so different and you're always thinking about the old days and you're going shopping with Gudrun and cutting your hair off and…"

He looked at her uncertainly. Frauke stood up, stood in front of him, and pulled his head to her chest. "You dope," she said, kissing him on the head. "It's nothing against you. I have my cell with me, so call if you need me."

"You'll be in touch anyway though, won't you?"

Gudrun was back in time to hear the last sentence. "Gunnar, it's not like we're not going to Bali for three weeks. I'll deliver Frauke back here in one piece tomorrow afternoon. So, shall we make a move?"

Frauke nodded. "Yes. OK then, darling, see you tomorrow."

Gunnar walked them out. "Make sure you behave."

He watched them go with a pained expression.

Frauke and Gudrun stayed silent until they were on the motorway. Then Gudrun glanced at Frauke, who was grinning at the glove compartment.

"What are you thinking?"

Frauke looked first at Gudrun, then at the road. "I'm happy. About this afternoon, tonight, about my new haircut, about my dress, that I've realized some things about myself, and—you're going to laugh, but about coming back tomorrow, too. Somehow everything feels brand new."

Gudrun smiled at her. "This invitation really was a kiss of life to you, wasn't it?"

"Yes." Frauke nodded contentedly. "And it was about time."

• ● •

Kiel-Hamburg

Lena fastened her seat belt and waved to her daughter, who was standing next to her mother-in-law by the front door. Kathleen put her hands either side of her mouth and shouted:

"Have fun and bring me something!"

Jürgen beeped twice and drove slowly out of the driveway. As Lena turned around, they had already disappeared into the house. She looked at her husband. "No one could say Kathleen has separation anxiety."

Jürgen laughed. "She can watch TV until she passes out, eat chips to her heart's content, Grandma will read her fortune and tell her about her golden future, and then she'll spend hours on the phone with her girlfriends without you there to interrupt her. What's there for her to be upset about?"

He tried to find a channel on the radio. "Who's been playing around with the tuning? I always have it on NDR 2; can't people just leave the radio where it is?"

"I went shopping with your mother. She wanted to listen to something lively, not that foreign rubbish, as she called it. We listened to Hansi Hinterseer, Udo Jürgens, and Nana Mouskouri, all the golden oldies; it was wonderful."

"Aha." Jürgen laughed. "She doesn't dare do it when she's with me. I told her music like that makes me dizzy, and that it's dangerous when I'm driving."

He turned up the volume. Herbert Grönemeyer was singing "Airplanes in My Stomach." Jürgen whistled along softly.

"This takes you back, doesn't it?"

Lena nodded. "Dani used to sing along to it while she was scraping the wallpaper off. It's a really sad song though. But she didn't mind. Completely the opposite, in fact; it always got her going."

"And you? Are you still feeling sad about Christine? Do you really think it's the right decision for me to be coming with you?"

Lena laid her hand on Jürgen's knee. "That was two questions. Firstly: no, I'm not feeling sad anymore. After all, I've spoken to Marleen and Ines already, so now I'm just curious as to how things will be with Christine. I'm looking forward to seeing Dani and Ines again, but above all to seeing Christine. I'm relaxed though. And secondly, I do think it's the right thing that you're coming. You always liked her. If you'd had your way, perhaps we would still be friends now. I've been thinking, and perhaps I really was too stubborn and bitter after the night at her housewarming party. After all, it takes two to end a friendship."

Jürgen pressed her hand. "Well, you were pretty angry at the time. Perhaps you were both just more sensitive then. Women always take criticism from their friends much more personally than men do. It always seems like the end of the world to them."

"Is that what the woman in you thinks?" asked Lena mockingly.

"Hey, I've got a mother, four aunts, three sisters, a wife, and a daughter. Don't try telling me I don't understand women. You've all made me this way."

Lena laughed. "That's true. But you do it very well, sweetheart. Well, I'm curious about what it will be like. In any case, I'm sure it'll be an exciting evening; we've got a lovely hotel and we're going away by ourselves for a change. So it's all worth it, right?"

Jürgen nodded. "Of course it is. And I'll be paying close attention to whether two women who were once the best of friends will only take a matter of seconds to get over the nonsense they caused years ago in their youthful ignorance. You really were silly."

Hopefully, thought Lena, *hopefully it will be that easy.*

• • •

Hamburg

Carefully, Marie hung her new dress on a hanger in the hotel wardrobe. She didn't want to show up at that chic restaurant looking all wrinkled. She'd already been there at lunchtime to check it out. It truly was very stylish—trendy, as her niece would say. The waiter had come up to her immediately.

Marie had told him she was part of the group for the surprise party that evening. He was very friendly and showed her the room, which was already prepared. She drew his attention to the missing candles and gave him a few more suggestions for the table decoration. He seemed grateful for her input.

Marie was sometimes amazed at how little people seemed to think for themselves. She had been a teacher for almost twenty years. In her job you had to take on a great deal of responsibility, and she had gained a lot of experience in organization and, above all, how to motivate people. It made her nervous when things were done sloppily. Marie was surprised that neither Ines nor Ruth was at the restaurant already. The waiter had said some nonsense about six o'clock, but Marie knew the plan was to meet at five in the hotel bar. She wondered whether the two of them were at least in the restaurant by now. Personally, she would have stayed until everything was to her satisfaction. But she had offered Ruth her help, and she had turned it down.

Taking her cosmetic bag from her suitcase, she went into the bathroom to put the various tubes and bottles in the cabinet, everything in a particular order, of course. She moved everything around until she was content. Just as she always did. The way it had to be. Then she washed and moisturized her hands. As she put her ring back on her finger, she realized that Mischa hadn't called yet. She looked at the clock; it was already two thirty. He'd said he was going to the weekend market that morning, and then to the mechanics. Why was it taking so long? Marie walked briskly across the room and picked up her phone from the windowsill. She selected Mischa's number on the speed dial, then heard her husband's voice as he picked up.

"Oh, Annemarie, I was just about to call you; I've literally just come through the door."

"What have you been doing this whole time? I phoned the landline twice and your cell was off."

The lie just tripped off her tongue. Mischa always had his cell turned off because he was paranoid about radiation, and at home he hardly ever heard the phone; it was in Marie's office. His voice sounded immediately remorseful. "I'm sorry. I went for a coffee with Mrs. Hoffmann; we bumped into each other at the market."

Marie had met Mrs. Hoffmann once; she was a redhead—from the bottle—and a colleague of Mischa's. If you could call a teacher at a vocational school a colleague, that is. Marie felt herself getting angry.

"Why are you going for coffee? I thought you were going to take the car to the garage! Fine then, I'm not going in the car with you anymore."

Mischa tried to calm her down. "I took the car in earlier. It'll be ready on Monday afternoon. So, did you get there OK? Have you already met the others?"

Marie rolled her eyes. "Of course I got here OK; it's not like it's the first time I've been to Hamburg. And if you'd been listening to me you'd know we're not meeting until five. I honestly don't know why I bother telling you anything."

"Marie, please, let's not argue. Have a good time this evening."

"I'm not arguing. What are you doing now?"

"I have to correct some class tests, and then I might go for a beer with Stefan later."

"Well, don't drink too much if you do. Remember we're going to the theater tomorrow evening, so you don't want to be tired for that. See you then."

She hung up without waiting for his answer. Marie looked out of the window, which had a view of the harbor. She had no idea how her husband would ever survive without her. Sometimes she felt like she had had enough of her marriage; that's what happens when you're still married to the guy you met in dance class thirty years ago. Mischa had been so talented back then. Admittedly he would never have started studying to become a vocational school teacher after his training if it hadn't been for her. As if Annemarie Erdmann could live with a car mechanic. But he'd been smart enough to realize that, too. Although, as a vocational teacher, Mischa wasn't technically a proper academic. But she had been willing to compromise.

Marie thought back to their dance lessons. Back then Christine was head over heels for Mischa; everyone had noticed. Just imagine the expression on her face when she heard that Marie and Mischa celebrated their silver wedding anniversary two years ago. And in Schröder's Hotel no less, the same venue as the graduation ball. It had been a great party, with around a hundred guests. Mischa had whined about the cost, of course, but she didn't care. If Marie Erdmann did something, she did it right. And she had proved that to everyone yet again.

Marie checked to see if she had all the photos with her. Christine would want to see them for sure. She flicked through them slowly. Her parents' renovated house, the holiday home in Föhr, Marie playing tennis, her school, some photos from the last school trip with her in the middle, beaming away, and the good-looking math teacher next to her. Marie smiled. It was worth teaching sports, too; her figure was still like it had been back then. She'd only put in an old photo of Mischa. Christine didn't have to know that his optician's prescription now stated five diopters, that he couldn't see anything without glasses and hardly had any hair left. But back then he had been a really handsome guy.

Marie put the photos back in her purse and decided to go for a coffee. Once again, it seemed she had everything under control.

• • •

The Countdown

Hamburg

Marleen knocked on the hotel room door.

"Coming."

Dani opened the door and hugged Marleen. "Oh, I'm so glad you're staying here, too."

Marleen was wearing a red dress, and her dark locks were piled high. She was carrying a black jacket and had a small purse with her. Dani looked her up and down.

"Wow, you look great. Although, I have to say the kitchen uniform suited you, too."

Marleen took a bow. "Thank you. You've got to make an effort. You know, when the cook comes to the big city." She looked around the room. "This is a really nice hotel; I can even see the harbor from my bed. I normally stay at Christine's, but I told her that I have a birthday party to cater at the pub today. For forty-four people; unfortunately she didn't get the pun."

Dani laughed. "I never thought we'd all be able to keep it a secret for so long." She looked for her lipstick in her purse and stood in front of the mirror to finish her makeup. Her blond hair was falling loosely down over her back, and she had a brown pantsuit on that matched the color of her eyes. She turned around to Marleen.

"OK, I'm ready. Let's get the party started."

"Good, you look great by the way. Come on, let's go."

• ● •

Luise walked into the hotel bar and looked around for the others. In a corner two small tables had been pushed together: two women were sitting next to each other, one of whom was looking at Luise questioningly. With long strides, she walked over to them.

"Code word 'Christine'?" she asked.

Both laughed and stood up. The taller one had short dark hair, was slim, and wore black pants and a green velvet jacket. Her handshake was firm and her voice, deep.

"Hi, I'm Gudrun."

Luise nodded her hand. "Gudrun with the horse. Lovely to meet you, I'm Luise. So that means this must be Frauke?"

Frauke was impressed by Luise's model figure, her black locks and close-fitting black and white dress. Discreetly, she pulled her neckline up a little, feeling plump. She gave Luise her hand. Her voice sounded a little faint.

"Yes, that's right, I'm Frauke. Hello."

Luise looked her over. "That's a wonderful dress you've got on. I'm always a little jealous when I see women with such beautiful cleavage."

Frauke went red. She smiled at Gudrun.

At that moment they heard loud laughter coming from the entrance. Ines, Ruth, and Gabi came in together and veered over toward the table. Ines, casual as always in black jeans and a black jacket, introduced herself first; then Ruth, dressed in a pink outfit with a mass of colorful jewelry; and then Gabi in a blue suit with a white T-shirt. Ruth beckoned the waiter right away and ordered two bottles of champagne with eight glasses. They sat down and started to talk excitedly.

Once Dani and Marleen arrived, Ruth interrupted the chatter and raised her glass. "So, I'd like to say something; are we all here?"

"Not yet." The voice that came from the door belonged to a tall woman with a dark pageboy haircut and a loud voice. She was wearing a cream-colored dress, a black silk scarf, and lots of gold jewelry.

"Good evening, everyone. It's not even five yet though."

Ines stood up. "Marie?"

"Who else?" Marie shook Ines's hand and gave the others a brief nod. Luise was sitting next to Frauke, so noticed when she briefly groaned. Luise looked at her questioningly. Frauke leaned over to her.

"That's Annemarie Erdmann, right?" she whispered.

Luise nodded. Gudrun had overheard and was coughing into her hands so as not to laugh out loud. Luise looked at them both. Frauke bit her lip and tried to keep a straight face.

"She was the biggest bitch from our dance school days. Who found her? And why did she even come? She wasn't even friends with Christine."

She couldn't hold the giggles back any longer, and before long Gudrun's shoulders were twitching, too. Luise, confused, tried to catch Ines's gaze. But at that moment a couple came over to the table, both very tall; she had short blond hair and he was very dark. Both were wearing jeans and blazers. Before Ines could stand up, Dani cried out: "Lena! How wonderful. And Jürgen, hello, how are you both?"

Their answers were lost in the orchestra of voices. Ruth had another three glasses brought over and poured the champagne. Once everyone was seated, she tried again, raising her glass and clearing her throat loudly.

"So, I'd like to say something." Ten pairs of eyes looked at her expectantly.

"My name is Ruth and this was my idea. I'm really pleased we found everyone we were looking for. So, first of all, welcome."

"Thank you for the invitation," called everyone at once, knocking on the table loudly, so that Ruth had to call for order again.

"While we were sitting by the Alster back in April—and by we, I mean Gabi, Luise, and I—talking with Christine about the subject of female friendship, the idea came to us of organizing this party. To start with it was just an idea, but then we started the search in earnest. It got more and more exciting, and by the end even the last skeptics were convinced. Isn't that true, Luise and Marleen?"

Both nodded and laughed.

"And now we've got almost everyone together, and the best thing is that Christine still doesn't have the faintest clue of what we have in store for her. She'll be picked up by Dorothea in an hour and still thinks she's walking around the corner to her favorite Italian restaurant to have a meal with her brother, sister, and three or four friends. We'll be waiting for them in Indochine. I also wanted to..."

Ruth was interrupted by Luise, who had suddenly jumped up. "Oh, shit, Ruth, I forgot something. Christine invited Mathias and Sven as well. I completely forgot about them, and they'll be on their way to the Italian place. Have you got Mathias's cell number?"

"Why Mathias? And who's Sven?" asked Ruth, confused.

"It doesn't matter, but we'll have to call them right away. Have you got the number?"

Ruth fished her cell phone from her bag and looked through her contacts. The murmur of voices set in again. Ines leaned over to Marleen.

"Who's Sven? The guy from Sylt? The one Christine went out to dinner with a few times?"

"That's the one," Marleen whispered back. "Hmmm... then it seems a few more things must have happened since then."

Ines grinned. "Good for her!"

Ruth had stepped aside to make the phone call in peace. She held a hand to her ear and spoke so loudly that everyone else heard.

"No, we canceled the table…in Indochine…yes, exactly… No, of course she doesn't know about it; it's a surprise…You can head out now; we're leaving in a moment, too…Luise just thought of it…No, all the others know…What?…Are you crazy? No, Dorothea is picking her up right now; everything's organized. OK, see you soon."

She came back to the table and put the phone back in her bag.

"Heavens, Luise, you could have remembered that earlier. And why did she even invite them? Is something going on with this Sven guy?"

Luise tried to sound noncommittal. "No idea, they all spent an evening together on Sylt back in the summer, so maybe that's why." She looked at her watch. "It's almost six o'clock. We should start to make a move."

"Good, I'll pay for the champagne quickly; then we can set off. My treat."

Ruth stood up, pulled her jacket on, and went to the bar. Ines looked around; all the others were talking all at once. She knocked on the table.

"Ladies…and gentleman, time to go. You've got the whole evening in front of you to catch up."

Ten minutes later, all the witnesses of Christine's old life were on their way.

The Party, Hamburg

Christine stood there for a long while, stunned. Eventually, Dorothea gave her a nudge forward into the room.

"Come on, Christine, say good evening."

As if in slow motion, her gaze swept over the faces. Everything looked quite normal at the first table: Luise, Ines, and Georg. At the second table was Marleen, next to someone who looked like Dani. But it couldn't be. Then more familiar faces, Mathias, and Sven, a happy sight. The third table: Ruth and Gabi, then two faces who seemed familiar, one of whom looked like the mother of an old friend of hers, Gudrun. Next to her was—although it couldn't really be, surely—Frauke, but a grown-up version. As she looked at the fourth table, her knees started to tremble: Lena and Jürgen. Both of them. And they were smiling. Christine pushed her arm through Dorothea's.

"I feel dizzy. What's going on here? Am I dreaming?"

And suddenly, they all got up and came over to her. As Dorothea pressed a glass of champagne into her hand, Christine stood there, still in the middle of the room, undecided as to what she should do first. But the decision wasn't hers to make; everyone started to hug and kiss her.

Ines and Ruth directed the waiters to serve, and soft jazz played in the background. After a while, everyone went back to their seats, and the conversations and laughter at the tables started back up. Marie ran from table to table with a digital camera, telling the guests to look lively.

Christine sat down next to Frauke and looked at her for a long while.

"You haven't changed in the slightest, Frauke. I'd have recognized you anywhere. Tell me everything, what you're doing, how you are."

Frauke updated her on everything, laughing and nudging Christine in the side at the exciting bits, just like the old days.

Gudrun, who looked like her mother had at the same age, laughed loudly at one of Gabi's jokes, and then turned back to Christine.

"Look," she said, pulling a photo from her bag. "Can you still remember this?"

The photo showed Gudrun and Christine sitting behind one another on an ancient pony. Christine looked just as unhappy as the gray horse did.

"The horse was called Käthe," explained Gudrun, "and we were pretending to be Butch Cassidy's sisters."

Christine could remember it well. "Well, you were pretty convincing, but then the old nag went and bit me."

"Horses don't bite." Gabi looked at the picture. "God, you were both so young."

"Twelve," answered Christine. "And Käthe did bite."

Jürgen came over and took Christine's arm, leading her to their table. "So, come and have a sip of wine with us for a bit." Lena fetched a glass for Christine and put it in front of her, while Jürgen poured. They toasted one another. Christine looked at them both, one after the other.

"I really feel I should say something about what happened between us back then."

Lena shook her head. "What for? That's all over and done with. Silly things like that always are, so let's stop wasting time. By the way, we've bought you a ticket for a handball game next week, HSV against Kiel. It's here in Hamburg on Wednesday. Can you make it?"

"Of course, I'd love to."

"Great," said Jürgen, smiling. "Then we'll pick you up. We'll get to the stadium an hour early so we can fit in a hotdog first."

Just like the old days, thought Christine, as someone tapped her on the shoulder.

Next she sat down with Dani for a while, opposite Sven and Mathias. Mathias told the story of their meeting on Sylt, exaggerating hideously about the amount of alcohol they had consumed and smirking about his storytelling. He was also flirting outrageously with Dani. Christine felt Sven's foot nudge hers under the table. She looked at him and had a warm feeling; he was smiling at her and looked as if he were in love.

Recognizing Dani's perfume, Christine leaned over to her and said, under her breath: "Still Boss Woman?"

Dani nodded. "That's right; you bought it for me once, and I've worn it ever since." She looked across the table. "Do we have any water left?"

Sven stood up. "I'll get some more. Mathias, will you come with me?"

"You've got two hands."

"Mathias. Please!"

"Fine, OK."

Dani watched them go. "Well, they're discreet, aren't they! Come on, is there something going on between you and Sven? He seems head over heels for you."

Christine watched Sven as he stood at the bar waiting for water. "I'm not sure yet what will come of it. But it feels good."

Dani pressed her hand. "Just go with it. I'm really happy I'm here. I never was that good with my private life until I discussed things with you."

Christine laughed. "Your private life always a bit chaotic. Whether you talked to me about it or not."

Dani looked serious. "But it's getting more so now. Hey, is Mathias involved with anyone?"

Christine kissed Dani on the cheek and stood up. "You man-eater. I think he's single at the moment. Enjoy!"

Dani laughed and raised her glass. "Thanks."

Frauke joined Christine at the bar. She started telling her about her children and her job at Gunnar's garage.

"...and then my daughter said to my son that I used to be a real bombshell, and that no one would recognize me now. It was a real wake-up call to me."

Christine gazed at her. "But, seriously now: you've hardly changed. You look amazing, by no means a frumpy mother."

Frauke smiled shyly. "You have no idea how good it is to hear that. But it was hard work."

Marie's camera was pointing at them. "Give me a smile, ladies, thank you." Then she disappeared. Frauke watched her go.

"She's so ridiculous."

Christine shrugged. "Well, perhaps you have to be in that job. I find it more ridiculous that Ruth or Gabi or whoever hired someone to take photos. It must have cost a fortune, and it's not like it's my eightieth birthday."

Frauke looked at Christine, amazed.

"Hired? You don't mean you don't know who that is?"

Now it was Christine's turn to be confused. "No, I mean, I did wonder why she hugged me, but I've got no idea."

Frauke burst out into loud laughter, which sounded exactly like it had in the classroom thirty years ago. With tears in her eyes, she crumpled over, stammering her words and laughing hysterically. The people around them watched in amusement as Christine doubled over, too. Then Frauke whispered something in her ear, making Christine laugh so much that she lost her balance.

As they saw Ruth coming over to them, they stood back up. Frauke wiped her made-up eyes carefully and gasped for air.

"Heavens, what must I look like? Have I smudged my makeup?"

Ruth looked at them both questioningly. Christine was about to say something, opened her mouth, then looked into her uncomprehending gaze and snorted with laughter again.

"Christine didn't recognize our dear Annemarie Erdmann," wheezed Frauke, before starting to giggle again.

Christine, who was trying to stop the onset of another fit of laughter, said apologetically: "Well, we were never friends, but it's nice to see her again all the same."

Both of them doubled up with laughter again. Ruth, on the other hand, didn't have the slightest clue what was so funny.

By now the buffet had been laid out, and one of the waiters was speaking quietly to Ines. She nodded and beckoned to Ruth.

Christine, who had calmed down by now, was watching. She passed Frauke a tissue and asked Ruth: "What's happening now?"

Ruth took a champagne glass from the bar and linked arms with Christine. "Now, sweetie, we're having the speeches. Sit down at the table, take giggly old Frauke with you, and listen up."

She pushed Christine in the direction of the table Marleen and Dani were sat at. Frauke followed her. "Oh God," she whispered, "we always used to go into hysterics during speeches. I think I'd better sit next to Gudrun; if I even look at you it'll get me going again."

She pressed Christine's hand and went to the next table. Christine watched her go; then Marleen pulled her down to her seat.

"Come on, birthday girl, sit down. Is your glass topped up?"

Christine held her empty glass out. "No, but I think I'm going to need some wine if there are speeches. That's awful, what on earth are they doing?"

Marleen poured the glass full and looked at Christine sympathetically.

"Come on, you have to grin and bear it. How are you anyway? Did we do good?"

Christine let her gaze wander around the room. Everyone had come here for her; it made her feel proud. She gave Marleen a quick hug.

"It's unbelievable. I have no idea how you guys pulled it off, but I'm very happy you did."

At the same moment Ruth clinked a spoon against her glass. The room quieted down a little, and all faces turned toward her, standing in the middle of the room with a few sheets of paper. She looked around until the last of the chatter had died down.

"Before we open the buffet, I'd just like to say a few words. Don't worry, it won't be a long speech; I know you're all hungry. So, dear Christine, dear friends, dear guests, most of you already know how this evening came about, but for the others, and especially for Christine, just a short explanation: Christine, do you remember when I told you about my friend's wedding, back in April when you, me, Gabi, and Luise were sitting by the Alster? Well, you seemed a little dismissive back then. We got the feeling you didn't have much trust in the concept of having a best friend for years and years, and we wanted to show you that it can work. That's how the idea was born. Ines, Marleen, and Dorothea helped us in the search for your long-lost friends, and I'd like to thank them now. I was actually planning to read out a poem about friendship, but then I realized I had something even better. Christine, do you remember this?"

Ruth unfolded one of the pages in her hand and waved it in Christine's direction, who looked at her uncertainly and shook her head.

"No idea. What is it?"

Ruth smoothed out the sheet of paper and walked over to Christine's table.

"Oh God, is that the rough draft of my article? Where did you get that from?"

"It fell out of your folder in my office when you brought the 'Linda Love' column to me. Can I read it out to the others?"

Christine laughed. "Oh, Ruth, it's not like I can really say no. I'm not even sure what I wrote anymore. It was just for me. But fine, I only have myself to blame, and it doesn't matter now."

As Ruth walked back into the middle of the room, she kept on speaking:

"On that day in April, I asked Christine to write a column with the title 'My Best Friend.' Thanks to Luise the title was changed to 'My First Friend,' something I wasn't as happy with. Christine told me that she tried to do both, but she preferred the 'first friend' one, so 'Linda Love' was the one we printed. But she left this draft behind by mistake and I kept it. And now, listen to the thoughts that Christine had about 'my best friend.'"

"My Best Friend"

My editor wants me to write a column about my best friend, and now I'm sitting here at a loss. Because—and I know this might sound ridiculous—I don't actually have a best friend. It's even more ridiculous, in fact, because I now have to research by calling women I know, my sister, my cousins, my neighbors, my colleagues, and all because I'm supposed to write about what it's like to have a best friend, something I don't have. I hate research like this; it takes up too much time and it's no fun whatsoever.

I don't suppose men ever get asked about their best friends: primarily because we assume that they're either lone wolves or travel in a pack. (Why do the gay penguins from the Bremerhaven Zoo suddenly spring to mind?)

Women, on the other hand, clearly can't get through life without a best friend; they need symbiosis. Preferably through a husband and a best girlfriend. Both of whom need to like each other. But not too much. Anyway, I'm veering off the topic. Why don't I have a best friend? Could it be because I'd rather be a lone wolf or travel in a pack?

I do have a very nice pack, by the way. I have one wolf for the sauna, one for work, one for holidays, one to get drunk with, one to cook with. Everyone's there, just not a best one.

My friend Karola would probably say we're too old for best friends. We used to have them, years ago. But they made fun of our Barbie dolls, got good grades in math without letting us copy, got honorary certificates at the Federal Youth Games rather than our measly participant's one, had less pimples, bigger breasts, stole our boyfriends, and got their driver's licenses before we did. Those are the kind of things that drive you apart. And all that happens before you've even truly grown up. Once you are, the problems really kick off: if your best friend marries the wrong man, gets too big a house, or if her children are too fat. Because she's only doing it to annoy the best friend. That's what they're like. Just mean.

Writing this, I've just remembered that all my friends had bigger breasts than I did, which wasn't difficult to achieve, to be honest. And we did our driving tests at the same time. And only one girl ever got the honor certificate, and she was pretty dumb anyway and never my friend. I didn't have pimples, and my boyfriend, who was rather dumb himself, was stolen away from me by the honor girl. Looking back now, she was welcome to him.

So what does all this tell us? Nothing. That we should have several best friends. But we do. So maybe the myth about the best friend will finally give up the ghost.

Dear Editor, dear Ruth, as you can see I've messed this up: all I can think of is nonsense. So I have decided to write about Linda Love after all. Such a lovely girl. The one I never heard from again. Even though she was my best friend.

As the guests laughed, Ruth folded the sheet of paper back up. She walked over to Christine, who was sitting there a little stiffly. She only looked up once Ruth was standing right in front of her.

"Thank you, my friend." To Ruth's relief, she was smiling. "But come on, I did a really good job of 'Linda Love.'"

"Of course you did, Christine."

Ruth turned around to the others.

"There are copies of the 'Linda Love' column we're talking about on the bar, for those who haven't yet read it. And before we all hit the buffet, I'd like to wish this pack and all its wolves a wonderful evening and *Guten Appetit.*"

After the food, coffee and grappa were served. It was warm in the room, so Gabi stood up from her seat and went out toward the roof terrace. Someone had already propped the door open. She walked out and took a deep breath. She went over to the railing, from where she could look down over the lights of the harbor. Out here, the laughing and hum of voices was muffled.

"I don't think we could have done a better job of that, do you?"

Gabi jumped as she heard Ruth's satisfied voice.

"Ruth! You scared me; I didn't hear you come out."

"Sorry, you seemed lost in thought. I saw you come out here. Is everything OK?"

Gabi nodded. "Yes, of course. It's turned out to be a great night. And they're all over the moon to see each other again. It couldn't be better. Your speech was wonderful. It all was."

"Well, apart from the mess-up with Marie Erdmann."

"What do you mean?"

Ruth pulled her shawl more closely around her. "Well, it seems I was a little overzealous and didn't listen closely during my conversation with her. They weren't even friends. Christine thought she'd been hired to take photos here. Frauke just told me that she's the Annemarie from the dance lessons, you know, the one Christine mentioned in one of her *Kult* columns. It's pretty awful."

Gabi laughed. "Oh, shit! Is that why Frauke and Christine were in hysterics earlier? Did Marie notice?"

"Marie held the camera on them and said to Dani that she was amazed at how childish women of that age could be. Which just made Dani giggle like a hyena."

They both stared over at the harbor lights in silence. Then they both started to talk at once.

"Tell me, Gabi…"

"Ruth, I wanted to…"

They laughed, embarrassed. Ruth looked at Gabi.

"Can I go first?"

"Please."

Ruth hesitated for a moment. "I've been thinking about myself a lot over the last few months. And, because of our search, about what I'm like as a friend. I don't think I've exactly covered myself with glory in the last few years."

Gabi opened her mouth to speak, but Ruth held up her hand to stop her. "No, wait, I'm not done yet. So, to be brief,

I know I'm egotistical and too ambitious. And I also know I haven't been there for you. And that I've taken advantage of you, and others, sometimes. I've known for a few weeks now that you've been meeting up with Karsten now and then; he told me himself. I was angry to start with, then I waited for you to tell me yourself, and then I realized I never give you the opportunity. By which time I realized I don't actually mind anyway. I mean, I don't have feelings for Karsten anymore, and I haven't for a long time. I just didn't want anyone else to have him. But that's ridiculous, and I know it. So, to cut a long story short, I was being a real idiot...I can't really explain what's wrong with me; I'd really like to be a good person...Now you say something."

Gabi was amazed. "Well, yes, you were quite a handful for a while there. And it's true that I've been meeting Karsten. Nothing major has happened, but we've talked a lot and been out to dinner a few times. I've always liked him, and I told you that, but I don't know whether something will come of it. And by the way, you're not such a bad person."

They looked at each other. Ruth started to laugh.

"Oh, Gabi, here we are organizing the mother of all reunions, and we're acting like fools ourselves. Come on, let's go and have a drink to friendship."

They linked arms and walked back into the restaurant.

By now, the seating plan had well and truly broken down. Some were standing at the bar, and others were in small groups. Christine made her way over to Marleen, who had just been brought a glass of champagne by the waiter.

"Christine, would you like a glass, too? We haven't had a moment to have a toast together." She beckoned to the waiter, who offered the tray with the glasses for a second time. Christine nodded and took one.

"Thank you. And for everything else, too. It's wonderful that you're here."

They took a sip; then Marleen leaned over to her.

"Now tell me, what's going on with you and Sven?"

Christine tried not to give anything away with her facial expression. "Why?"

"I saw him kiss you outside earlier. And anyway, even a blind person can see there's something going on there. When did you decide?"

Christine looked over at the table where Sven, Mathias, and Dani were sitting. Mathias was talking in an animated fashion while Dani hung on to his every word. Sven was listening and laughing. He had dimples. Christine felt a warm feeling in her stomach.

Marleen was watching her.

"You're in love." It was a statement, not a question. Christine pulled her gaze away from Sven and looked back at Marleen.

"I think I am, yes. I only made the decision a few days ago, when I was cleaning. First of all, to end things with Richard, so I phoned him that evening. But he's in Berlin this weekend and staying there until Wednesday, because Sabine has so many problems and needs him. I'd finally had enough of it. I told him I can't do it anymore and that we have to stop seeing each other. Richard just thought I was angry because he couldn't come to my birthday. I don't think he really understood what I was saying. I told him that I've met someone, but he said that was just blackmail. It was a horrible conversation."

Marleen stroked her back comfortingly. "It's better that way. I don't think there was ever any hope with him; you would have stayed the secret lover forever. So, how do you feel now?"

Christine thought for a moment. "Good. My feelings for Richard had already started to die; I realized that when I was on the phone to him. I was living too little, just hoping and waiting. It shouldn't be like that. But I don't know what will happen with Sven either; I need a bit of time. We'll see."

Marleen didn't have a chance to answer, for at the same moment Marie steered her way over to their table with two glasses of champagne and collapsed into the chair opposite Christine. Sounding disappointed, she looked at Christine's glass and said:

"Oh, you already have a glass. Never mind, I just wanted to make a toast with you. To friendship, my love, and to seeing each other again."

She raised her glass and beamed at Christine, who started to feel guilty.

"Yes, Marie, it's lovely that you came. Cheers."

Marie put her glass down and looked at Marleen searchingly.

"And you're friends, too? Lovely. I have something to show you, Christine. You know, it's good when you don't get rid of things. Look, do you remember?"

Rummaging in her bag she produced an envelope and handed it over to Christine proudly. She opened it. It contained a strip of film with passport photos on it. Of two girls, who had crammed themselves onto a small revolving stool in a photo booth. Christine recognized Marie, who was looking at the camera and smiling. Her shoulder was blocking part of Christine's face, who was looking past the camera with a serious look on her face. Christine remembered that Marie had insisted they get them done; she had collected these photos of herself and her girlfriends. Everyone used to do them back then. They cost two Deutschmarks and then hung on the fridge with magnets for years.

Marleen looked at the photos. "Wonderful. I used to have some like that, too, of my friend Heike and me...but I have no idea where they got to."

Christine gave Marie the photos back. She felt sorry for her for some reason. She seemed so strained. Christine smiled at her. "It's a long time ago now, but it was a great time. Can I have two of these?"

Marie nodded and took some small scissors from her bag. She cut the strip through the middle, handed Christine two of the photos, and then looked at hers again. "I brought them with me for you. I was happy I still had them. You know, friendships that last a lifetime are the best things in life. We really should meet up more often. I'll organize something."

Christine was saved from having to answer, as Ines walked into the center of the room and called attention to herself with a loud "Could you all be quiet for a moment?" Once it was still, she pulled a couple of sheets of paper from her jacket pocket.

"Thank you, everyone. Before we get so tipsy that even the simplest of things are difficult to understand, I'd like to read out a few sentences to you. Christine, sweetheart, Ruth came up with a questionnaire that all the girls had to fill out. I'll read one of them out to you, and the others I've put together in a folder for you so you can look at it later. So:

"*Name, Age, and Town: Marleen, 48, Cuxhaven*

"*When and where did you meet Christine?: My ex-husband is Christine's ex-husband's best friend. Before Christine got married she had to meet us to get the official seal of approval. And she did a great job; it was the beginning of an important friendship.*

"*Your best experience with her?: There are many 'best' ones, and I hope there will be many more.*

"*What sets your friendship apart? And what is Christine like as a friend?: The certainty that there is no situation in life when you are completely alone. That you have shared moments and experiences that you can look back on together. Christine has never hidden her true feelings, neither in her sadness nor her joy.*

"*Your motto for life?: 'I hurry to laugh about things so that I will not be forced to cry' (Beaumarchais).*

"*A friend is...?: 'Friendship is not just a precious gift, but also an ongoing responsibility' (Ernst Zacharias). And a responsibility one should take seriously.*

"*What was your reaction to this invitation?: I was able to take part in organizing it and saw this as a responsibility, one which I fulfilled well.*"

Ines folded the sheet of paper and looked at her sister. Christine wiped her hands under her eyes. She leaned over to Marleen and kissed her on the cheek. Then she stood up and went over to Ines, wrapped her arm around her sister's waist, and looked at the guests.

"I think I should say something now, too, although I really don't know where to start. I'm completely surprised, moved, and lost for words. Ruth said earlier that I was dismissive when we were talking about female friendship, but that's not true. Without some of you, my new start a few years ago would have been much more stressful. I was and am happy that you're in my life. Marleen wrote that friend-ship is a lasting responsibility. It's possible I haven't always made a good job of it in my life. Dani, Frauke, Lena, I'll make an effort from now on, I promise you. So, before my emotions overwhelm me and I start to cry, I would like to thank Ruth, Gabi, Luise, and you, my darling sister, for this party. And now maybe someone can put the music back on; otherwise I really will be in tears."

Ines hugged Christine and waved her hand to interrupt the hum of voices and applause.

"Just a moment, I'm not done yet. I have one more let-ter I'd like to read out. Admittedly, it's written to Christine, but unfortunately I'm going to have to break the secrecy of the letter—too many people have been waiting for this answer."

She took a pink-colored letter from an envelope, which she unfolded and held up. It was written in an awkward, childlike handwriting, and the edges had little pictures stuck onto them. It was clearly written by a child who was just learning to write.

Ines cleared her throat:

"Dear Christine,

"I can write really well now, that's why you're getting this let-ter. I'm fine, and Klaus is, too, and all the others. The sun's shin-ing here, and we've already gotten to numbers over thirty at school. Tatjana sits next to me, but she's stupid. Mom's looking for your address, and then I'm sending this in the mail. I cut my knee roller-blading, but it doesn't hurt anymore.

"Lots of love,

"Your friend,

"Linda."

Ines raised her hand as people started to chat and laugh again.

"That's one letter. And then there's another, which Christine can read out."

Christine blinked, took the envelope from Ines, and pulled another sheet of paper out. She scanned through it, took a deep breath, smiled, and started to read, her voice hoarse:

"Dear Christine,

"When the letter from Hamburg arrived, inviting me to your birthday, I was very moved and got all sentimental. Immediately, I pictured us sitting on the steps in front of the butcher's shop: we always had Band-Aids on our knees, do you remember? And, for some reason, it was always summer.

"I took myself off to my attic and spent forever looking through my old boxes until I found this letter. I did write to you, back then, around three months after the move. But we lost your new address. I wanted to keep the letter; after all, I'd spent the whole afternoon writing it, drawing lines, writing in pencil first, then erasing the marks and sticking all the pictures down carefully. That was a lot of work for a seven-year-old! And then we couldn't find the address. But I think I always knew you would get this letter someday; that's why I kept it for thirty-seven years. And now you finally have. Isn't that great? We should all have the confidence of a seven-year-old more often.

"I hope you have a wonderful birthday, full of wonderful memories and confidence. In April I'll be coming to Germany for two weeks with my husband and my youngest son. Maybe we could arrange to meet? I'd really love it if we could.

"Until then perhaps,

"With lots of love from your old friend,

"Linda Love."

Christine wasn't the only one with tears in her eyes.

Epilogue: April, Hamburg

Christine stood by the open balcony door in her bath-robe, a mug of coffee in her hand. Today was the kind of day when you noticed the winter was past. The birds were singing, the sky was blue, and spring was in the air. Christine took a deep breath and sat down at the table. She pulled the letter from Gudrun toward her and read through it for a second time.

Gudrun had given her notice in at the hospital, as had her boyfriend Carlos, the pediatrician from Kiel. They had been living in Spain since February. A few days before the move, Gudrun and Christine had met up in Hamburg for a bite to eat. "You know," Gudrun said, "when I was sitting in front of that questionnaire back in October, thinking about the old days, I realized that I was only continuing with the things I'd once started for reasons I couldn't even remem-ber. But it wasn't what I wanted anymore. Carlos and I had a semi-committed relationship, only seeing each other on weekends, and he was unhappy in his clinic, just as I was in mine. After the party I told him about what Linda Love wrote to you—about the confidence a seven-year-old has, about this belief that you can do anything you want to. So then Carlos looked for a job in Spain, for an apartment for us both, and now we're doing something new, something we both really want. I'm so unbelievably excited. You'll have to come and visit once we're settled. Why don't you come over with Frauke? Remember, we all wanted to work on fulfilling our 'responsibility' to each other in the future."

Gudrun had written her a long letter. They were renting a house near the sea, Carlos was working in a small practice; Gudrun, in a hotel. Every single word seemed to burst with enthusiasm. The letter ended with these words:

So, as you can see, this decision was the best one I've ever made in my life. Frauke wants to come visit in May, so maybe you can arrange it together; we have enough room and it's wonderful here. I hope you're doing well; write soon and let me know how the others are too. Your party was like a wake-up call to me. They were all wonderful women, and I think of them often.

See you soon,
Your Gudrun

Christine found her writing pad and started her reply.

Dear Gudrun,

That all sounds amazing. Frauke already told me some of the details after she spoke with you on the phone. When I went to the opening of her shop a month ago we talked about wanting to come over and visit you at the end of May for a few days.

The opening was wonderful; it's a shame you missed it. Frauke looked great, and her decision to open a boutique for children's clothing was right on the money. She has great taste, both in terms of the clothes and the way she's designed the place. It was full to the rafters; Gunnar said there were about seventy people there. He was bursting with pride, pouring champagne and showing everyone around. It was so sweet. And Frauke looked as if she'd been doing it her whole life, such a natural!

I went with Ruth and Gabi, and then dropped them off at the airport afterward; they were off to Mallorca for two weeks to concentrate on their writing. Gabi's now writing columns for Femme; *they're really funny. And Ruth's been the editor of the magazine since February, so they're working together again now.*

I'm seeing Dani a lot more again now, which has to do with the birthday party, of course, but not just that. Did you notice that my boss at the time, Mathias, was flirting with my old housemate throughout the evening? I thought it was just the party mood, nothing serious. Well, in any case, it seems Mathias went to Berlin to see her the very next weekend. Dani only knew the evening before and went into a panic because she still had some "loose ends" to tie up. (Which were called Lars, by the way.) But she managed to sort it out in time. She always did work well under pressure! Mathias is on cloud nine and so is Dani; he's really good for her.

I went to Borkum for Easter with Lena, Jürgen, and her daughter Kathleen. There was a tournament for former handball players. I played with Lena in a team again for the first time in over ten years, and it was great. We won 15:9; it was just like the old days when we were still young and ambitious. I'm sure we didn't look as sporty from the outside as we felt on the inside, but it was still great fun.

Marie Erdmann sent me a Christmas card. Did you know her husband left her a woman he works with? Marie is outraged, some red-haired tart apparently, and she wants her to drop dead.

Linda Love is coming to Hamburg the day after tomorrow. She's in Germany with her family, and we've made plans to go for a meal at Indochine—it makes sense; I had such a great night there before. At first she suggested we both wear patent leather red shoes so we'd recognize each other. But then we agreed to put a box of Band-

Aids on the table, because we always used to mess up our knees roll-erblading. I'm really looking forward to it.

There's quite a lot going on with me at the moment, too. In January I got a call from a publisher. He's called Dr. Frank Fuchs and is from a paperback publishing house. His wife read my columns and really liked them. He suggested that I publish a collected volume of them. It's going to be called "My Friend Karola" and will be published next autumn. I'm spending every evening on it. Just imagine, a real book, I'm really excited! It's a lot of work, but fun, too.

I'll have to dedicate it to Sven, because the poor guy has to listen to what I've written every evening, and I have the feeling he's starting to hate Karola.

Apart from that he's really fantastic; he carries my groceries in, makes me coffee, opens bottles of wine, and does what he in short calls "author support."

He suggested that I give notice on my apartment and move in with him. At the moment we're commuting back and forth. I've promised to think about it. First of all I want to deal with a few of my "responsibilities"; I'm worried that otherwise our re-invigorated friendships will sink into oblivion again and that would be a shame.

Gudrun, I hope everything continues to go really well for you. We'll see each other in May, and I can't wait!

Until then, all my love,

Your Christine

Christine folded the letter up and tucked it into an envelope. As she wrote Gudrun's address, she heard steps in the hallway, and a few moments later, the sound of a key in the front door.

The End

Acknowledgments

I would like to thank Kristina Arnold, Claudia Danners, Marietta Frick, Anne Haupt, Monika Köhler, Laura and Melanie Köttner, Gabriele Mertl, Christine Rulph, and Michaela Ullrich. You all already know why. And my editor, Silvia Schmid, who also knows.

Dora Heldt

About the Author

Dora Heldt, born in 1961 on the North Sea island of Sylt, trained as a bookseller. Since 1992, she has been working as a sales representative for a publisher and lives in Hamburg. Her novel *Vacation with Dad* became one of the best-selling titles of the year 2008 and was on the best-seller list for sixty-one weeks.

About the Translator

Jamie Lee Searle is a translator from German into English, translating literary fiction, short stories, and articles for publishing houses and organizations throughout Europe and the US. She lives in London and in addition to translating also teaches German language and translation at Queen Mary, University of London. In late 2009 she co-founded the publishing collective And Other Stories, which seeks to promote and publish international literature in translation in the UK.